OUT OF THE Pocket

OUT OF THE Pocket

Bill Konigsberg

DUTTON BOOKS

DUTTON BOOKS
A member of Penguin Group (USA) Inc.

Published by the Penguin Group
Penguin Group (USA) Inc., 375 Hudson Street, New York, New York 10014, U.S.A. • Penguin Group (Canada), 90 Eglinton Avenue East, Suite 700, Toronto, Ontario, Canada M4P 2Y3 (a division of Pearson Penguin Canada Inc.) • Penguin Books Ltd, 80 Strand, London WC2R 0RL, England
Penguin Ireland, 25 St Stephen's Green, Dublin 2, Ireland (a division of Penguin Books Ltd)
Penguin Group (Australia), 250 Camberwell Road, Camberwell, Victoria 3124, Australia (a division of Pearson Australia Group Pty Ltd) • Penguin Books India Pvt Ltd, 11 Community Centre, Panchsheel Park, New Delhi–110 017, India • Penguin Group (NZ), 67 Apollo Drive, Rosedale, North Shore 0632, New Zealand (a division of Pearson New Zealand Ltd) • Penguin Books (South Africa) (Pty) Ltd, 24 Sturdee Avenue, Rosebank, Johannesburg 2196, South Africa
Penguin Books Ltd, Registered Offices: 80 Strand, London WC2R 0RL, England

CIP Data is available.

Published in the United States by Dutton Books,
a member of Penguin Group (USA) Inc.
345 Hudson Street, New York, New York 10014
www.penguin.com/youngreaders

Designed by Liz Frances

Printed in the USA First Edition

ISBN 978-0-525-47996-3 10 9 8 7 6 5 4 3 2 1

Acknowledgments

To a great mentor and friend, the real Jim Blasingame, who asked for nothing more than a part in the movie. For Chuck Cahoy, always there with exaggerated praise: thanks for being my life. Patrick Moore was there at the beginning and helped me form the plot. Larry Glidewell offered extremely kind critiques when I needed them. Sarah Shumway, my awesome editor, and Caryn Wiseman, my terrific agent, shared and improved my vision. My nephew Sam, the bravest guy I've ever known, reminded me that Bobby Framingham does exist. His wonderful mother, Karen, strongly suggested I stop killing off parents in my stories. Thanks to my terrific family. My mother, Shelley, the most effusive and unconditional supporter I'll ever have, shared this process with me. My father, Bob, whose sense of humor I (sadly) acquired, offered irreverent ditties for Bobby Framingham—The Musical. Thanks to everyone at the creative writing program at Arizona State University, especially Ron Carlson, who tried to mold me into the writer I hope someday to be.

For Chuck Cahoy

OUT OF THE Pocket

I was in the closet with Tamara Muncie.

It was dark and cramped and a hanger was poking me in the back.

"So," Tamara said. I could hardly see her, but I could hear her voice, her slightly asthmatic breathing. Her face was inches from my chest. "What do we do now?"

I chuckled, because it was all so ridiculous. Outside I could hear the laughter and shrieking from the party, what sounded like the bassline of a Gnarls Barkley song I liked.

When one of the cheerleaders said we should bring back "seven minutes in heaven," a game we played in, like, seventh grade, Martin Somers, one of my teammates, said, "That's so gay."

I'm here to tell you. It's the opposite of gay.

It was a stupid game, and if one of the guys on the team had suggested it, he would have been called lots of names. But since a cheerleader wanted to, what do you know? Suddenly all the guys were into it.

And as much as I didn't want to, I had to play. There were certain things you had to do as a team.

When I laughed, Tamara did too, and I immediately felt more comfortable. She was as nervous as I was, just for different reasons.

"I really can't, you know . . ." I said.

"No," she quickly answered. "I know. Carrie and all. I totally get it."

I exhaled. Saved by the Carrie. Again.

"Thanks," I said, and I gently put my arm on her shoulder to show her I was not repulsed by her or anything.

"Carrie is really lucky," Tamara said. My eyes had adjusted a bit and I could see her eyes and the triangle of her mouth as she spoke. "I mean, there are a lot of girls who wouldn't care that you're taken. I mean, a *lot* of girls."

"Hmm," I replied, taking my hand off her shoulder and crossing my arms over my chest.

Things got quiet, and on the other side of the door I heard my best friend Austin Rivera's voice crystal clear. He was laughing and saying, "Yo, dude, you gotta believe, you gotta believe." I tried to put the words in some sort of context, and it pissed me off that here I was, in a closet, not out there with my team, joking around. I hated not being in on the joke. But that's life.

"It's just . . ." Tamara said, in that way people talk on television when they want to share a secret but want the other person to think they really don't want to. "No . . ."

I could see her silhouette as she dramatically looked down and away from me. A fleece collar nuzzled my ear and I resisted the urge to tear the coat or whatever it was off its hanger.

"What?" I said.

"I shouldn't," she said, and I thought, *That's true, you probably shouldn't.*

"It's okay," I said.

Tamara looked up at me and I could see the whites of her eyes. She exhaled. "It's just, I haven't been kissed in a really long time. I mean, I know you can't, but I just wish . . . never mind."

Probably some people in my position would have been real asses about this, and would have run out and told all their friends, and made fun of Tamara forever. Instead, I reached out and stroked her shoulder.

"How about this?" I said, and I tentatively leaned down to kiss her lightly on the cheek. As my lips zoned in on the soft skin of her cheek and I began to feel the heat of her body next to mine, she ever so slightly turned her lips toward mine.

I flinched, and instead of her cheek, I planted a quick dry one on the corner of her chin.

It was weird.

As I pulled away, I blushed and averted my eyes, because something had happened. A moment earlier, I had all the power. And now I just got this feeling that Tamara knew.

I was one hundred percent sure that my lips had given her all the knowledge she needed, and I couldn't look in her eyes. *She knew.*

We exited the closet together, to catcalls.

"Did you do anything I wouldn't do?" asked Austin, a major ladies' man, when I sat back down next to him and the next person spun the bottle.

"I think so," I said.

The head-shaving thing was my fault.

Later at the party, the football posse was in Rahim Bell's room, hanging out, when Rahim asked what we were going to do for team unity this year.

It was a Durango Bulldogs tradition. Before the school year, the seniors on the team came up with something and everyone had to do it.

Last year, the seniors wore maroon armbands. Seriously. That's what they came up with. It wasn't a really good group of seniors last year. On the first day of school, there they were, six guys wearing armbands. It was way weak.

"How about tattoos?" asked Rickey Mendez, our running back.

"Uh, no," said Martin Somers, one of our best receivers. "No ink. Nothing permanent."

"True dat," said Austin, turning to me. "What you got, Bobby?"

"I don't know," I said, sitting up. I had been reclining on Rahim's bed. "Shave our heads?"

The room got very quiet, and I realized I had just suggested something drastic that was now going to happen. And I was going to have to start it.

I could feel the enthusiasm pour across the room like a wave, starting with Geoff Bolleran and Kyle Colby.

"Yeah!" yelled Bolleran. "Shaved heads!"

"That's freakin' awesome," said Colby. "Shaved! Shaved! Shaved! . . ."

Colby started the chant, and suddenly the whole room was doing it.

Rahim leaped to his feet, put his fist in the air, and yelled, "Whose house is it?"

That was this call-and-response thing we did before games to psych ourselves up. The seniors called and the underclassmen answered.

But since underclassmen were mostly not invited to this party, we all answered.

"Our house!" we yelled. A couple kids in the hallway stopped and watched.

"Are you ready to conquer?" Rahim yelled.

"Hell yeah!" we screamed back.

"Lock and load!" Rahim shouted, pretending to aim a rifle.

"Open fire!"

He pounded the bed, his eyes darting to each of us. "Are you ready to kill?"

A new voice responded from the doorway of Rahim's room. "Hell yeah!"

We all looked over and there was Rocky.

"Rock-ee!" yelled Austin. "Now that's what I'm talkin' about!"

"We got ourselves an underclassman," said Rahim. "Are you ready to fight?" he yelled, aiming his pretend rifle at Rocky.

"Hell yeah!" screamed Rocky, pounding his chest.

Rocky's real name was Phan. He was a kicker, a sophomore, and too tall and skinny to look like a football player. He got his nickname because of how he walked, with his chest puffed out and his arms really wide.

It looked stupid, but that was how he walked. He was more a poet and writer type, but he wanted to be on the team and he had worked really hard. He was actually a pretty good kicker, and even though we gave him tons of grief, he was one of us.

"Shoot to kill!" Rahim bellowed.

"Kill at will!" Rocky yelled back, and Rahim and Austin jumped in the air and bumped chests. Dennis, a little drunk, did his usual and took off his clothes. Seriously, I'd never been to a party where Dennis didn't wind up in his boxer shorts.

Taken out of context, I guess, the team antics seemed a little scary. But that was the point. We wanted to be scary out on the field.

While Dennis streaked around the house, scaring underclassmen girls, Rocky hung with us, but not before we made him do twenty push-ups.

It had happened to us, too. Now it was our turn to tell the underclassmen what to, do and it felt awesome.

While Rocky huffed and puffed, I jumped off the bed, took a deep breath, and said, "C'mon. Where are the razors?"

Rahim stood next to the sink with an electric razor in one hand and a towel in the other. In front of the sink was a chair, and Rahim draped the towel over its back.

"Take a seat," Rahim said. People were lining up in the hallway to get a look at the quarterback who was about to be bald.

"Okay," I said. "But I want everyone's word. We're all doing this, right?"

Somers nodded his head yes. His black hair was already buzzed pretty close to the scalp, so it wasn't going to be a big deal for him. Meanwhile, I'd had wavy blond hair since I was a kid. My mom was going to kill me.

"I'm in," said naked Dennis, huffing and puffing after sprinting around the house. Then he took off again.

"Me, too," said Mendez. "If Bobby does it, I'll do it."

"Yeah," said Austin. "Me, too."

"That's all I needed to hear," I said, smiling as I sat in the chair.

"I don' know," said Austin, using this terrible Mexican accent that he thinks he can get away with because he's half Mexican. "I cuh go an gemme a do-rag at Walmartinez, but wha's Bobby gonna do to cover up that cue ball on his head?"

I laughed. "Don't you worry about it," I said, very worried about it.

Rahim did the shaving with the electric razor he uses on his own head. After the first stroke, I began to feel a cool breeze on my scalp. I liked it.

"Look at him! Dude's smiling," Mendez said, smiling back at me.

I don't know why I was so happy, but I was. These were my brothers, and now we were going to be recognizable as brothers, all bald to start the school year. I quaked with pride as Rahim's razor massaged the top of my scalp.

We were all the same. *And that means it's okay, the one way I'm definitely different.*

Right?

I'd known about the gay thing for a few years, but it was really over the summer that I'd put together the final pieces—that it mattered, that I was going to have to tell people, come out or whatever.

The dreams began in tenth grade. They were about Todd Stanhope, who pitched junior varsity. He had jet-black hair, piercing green eyes, and no extra meat on him at all, just a muscular V with a tapered waist and biceps like grapefruits.

When I dreamed about Todd for the first time, I woke up horrified, because the dream crossed some lines that I wasn't sure should be crossed.

The next day I felt really weird at school, dirty almost. And I couldn't stop the thoughts. Sitting in math class daydreaming, I yelled "NO!" really loud.

Since other people don't live inside my head, they didn't know I was yelling at an image of a soaped-up Todd scrubbing his pecs. Everyone laughed, but I didn't much feel like laughing.

The pictures in my head were the wrong ones, like the post office screwed up and sent me the ones some girl should have, and I hated it. I tried to replace each one with a picture of something normal. Carrie in a bathing suit. Nothing. The cheerleaders in the locker room, changing. Blank.

I prayed, even though I'd never been big into prayer: *God, if You'll take these thoughts away, I will do everything You ask of me.* But He didn't take them away. They just got more and more frequent, and soon I began to hate and enjoy them equally, and after a while I began to look forward to my sleep because there they'd be, my secret dreams.

"You're almost there!" Rahim said, cuffing me on the shoulder. "You're gonna be the second one in the brotherhood." He had a head start on us, since he was already bald.

"He's not smiling so much now!" said Austin, laughing. "Dude looks like he's seen a ghost."

I realized I was no longer smiling, and forced the corners of my mouth into a grin. I was still thinking about Todd.

One day last spring I saw Todd in school, and without thinking, I smiled at him and said hi. He looked surprised. Even though we were both athletes, we probably hadn't said two words to each other since junior high. As I walked past him, I recognized for the first time that what had been just dreams meant something; someday I might act on those dreams with another guy. That maybe I'd have a date with someone, and that someone would be male.

And then I would be considered gay.

It hadn't really occurred to me in simple terms like that before.

I had this feeling, this delicious sensation of excitement and fear mixed into a ball that seemed to get stuck in my throat. All day, I could hardly swallow.

"It looks good, Bobby," said Somers. "Carrie's gonna die, but it looks okay."

As I got up from the chair, Dennis flashed by in his boxer shorts, chased by about four shrieking girls.

I had no idea what they saw in that guy.

Somers squirmed his way in to be next, and as he sat down I walked behind the chair and Rahim got out of the way so I could look in the mirror.

What I saw shocked me. I stared at my head without hair for the first time, and it was like I saw who I really was, my essence, sort of.

I saw the face of a guy who looked like he had it all. But on the inside, nobody knew me.

"Can we get back to business?" said Rahim.

"Dude is so vain," said Austin.

I stepped away, flipped Austin off, and punched him in the shoulder.

What I wouldn't have given to tell people, to tell one person, that I was gay. But that was sort of tricky in a team situation. Over the summer I had three close calls with telling Austin. He and I had been best friends since we were nine. And even though he told gay jokes like everyone else, I also knew he was loyal.

I knew he would never turn on me. I trusted him like my own brother, I trusted him more than I trusted myself sometimes.

"You guys look like a bunch of fags," said this guy, Timmons, who goes to La Habra, as he peeked in the bathroom.

Usually we didn't allow guys from other teams to come to our parties, but Timmons was friends with Rahim and was a pretty good guy.

"If by 'fags' you mean guys who are gonna kick your team's ass in a month, yeah, we're fags," said Austin, winking at me.

And sometimes, I think he knows.

"This feels so weird," said Somers, who now had one bald stripe on the right side of his head.

"You're lucky you're not a senior, Rocky," Austin said. "You'd look like a pencil with an eraser head."

"Ha!" Rocky laughed. He'd gotten pretty good at dealing with the put-downs. He wanted so badly to be liked that we actually liked him. He put up with the insults because he had to.

"You'd look like, what's the one in *Popeye,* his girl?" said Mendez.

"Olive Oyl!" shouted Rahim. "Dude would look like Olive Oyl!"

Rocky had turned a dark shade of purple.

"What is he, your kicker?" said Timmons, still standing in the doorway. "You gonna let some pansy-ass kicker be part of your little fag skinhead posse?"

Bolleran stepped into the doorway, and Somers, Colby, and I were right there with him.

"Dude, what did you just say about our boy?" I said, getting in Timmons's face.

Timmons looked past them to Rahim for support. "I didn't say anything you guys weren't saying about him. I was just kidding. Chill."

Rahim didn't look up from shaving Rocky's head. "He's our teammate. He's our boy. You don't get to say that about him," he said.

It was so fast, and so united, that I knew we'd done the right thing with this head-shaving idea.

"So, Biff," Carrie said to me. "What's this I hear about you becoming a perv?"

It was Saturday, two days before the start of senior year, and we were eating breakfast at the cheesiest fifties diner in all of Southern California.

Nothing beat the Durango Five and Diner. It was really tacky in that vintage kind of way, and we always pretended to be a teen couple from fifty years ago out on an ice-cream-social sort of date. She called me Biff and I called her Annette, after Annette Funicello, who was the star of lots of those old surfer movies.

"It's the 'in' thing, don't cha know?" I answered.

"Neat!" she said, crumpling her napkin into a ball. "Being a perv is peachy!"

"It sure is, Annette."

Carrie smiled and ran her fingers through her hair. "Okay, Biff.

Truth or dare. If you had to choose only one girl in school you could have sex with, only one, who would it be?"

"Well, gosh, Annette," I said, grabbing her napkin and smoothing it out. "I don't know if I could choose only one. How's about a big orgy?"

At that moment our waitress, a woman about my mother's age with deep creases under her eyes, loomed over us with a look of alarm on her face.

"Don't worry," Carrie said. "Talking about it keeps the impulse in check."

"You kids with your casual sex," she moaned, shaking her head. "What'll it be?"

We ordered our signature breakfast of champions, hash browns and root beer floats. Carrie always wanted us to order one with two straws, but that was a little intimate for me. I always had an excuse as to why we couldn't.

"Bronchitis again?" she asked me, rolling her eyes, after our waitress left.

"Something like that," I said.

"Oh, Bobby," she said, deadpan. She said that a lot.

Carrie smiled at me, and like usual, I wondered what we were supposed to be. We'd be perfect together. We'd been friends or whatever since ninth grade, and the thing was, she was really pretty. Everyone thought so. My buddies labeled her hot but weird.

They were right on both accounts.

She had long legs and favored turquoise clothing, but tended to wear it with colors it should never be associated with. Orange. Purple. When all the girls were dressing as Lindsay Lohan and Avril Lavigne for Halloween back in ninth grade, she came wearing a black mask and a totally black outfit with tiny little eyes on her chest. She called herself "Avril Lavigne's eyeliner."

Just weird stuff that you either appreciated or you didn't, and I really did. She had indigo eyes that when she squinted reminded me of warm blueberry pie, and a wicked sense of humor that was almost unfair in a girl so pretty. We'd been hanging out all through high school, and never had a credible date.

She must think I'm a geek.

"So can someone send Finch Gozman to some third-world country?" I asked.

"Finch? Why? He's harmless. He's the definition of harmless."

"He's annoying! He's doing some Durango football preview, and today he called me to get a quote from—his words—the Bulldogs' 'quarterback supreme.' He actually said that. And every single thing I said, he laughed at. He needs to be killed."

"That may be the worst motive for murder ever," Carrie said.

"You know what I mean," I said. "He's always calling me and asking me stupid questions for his articles. It bugs the crap out of me."

"Getting all that attention must be hard. Pity party of one, your table's ready."

I laughed. "It's just the way he does it. He showers you with compliments that you don't even want. He makes me nauseous."

"That's your story, and you're sticking to it, I presume," she said.

"Amen."

"'Quarterback supreme,'" Carrie said. "That's hilarious."

"It sounds like something you'd order at a Dairy Queen," I said.

"One quarterback supreme, two straws," Carrie said. "Oh, wait. Two *separate* quarterback supremes, two straws."

The waitress arrived with our root beer floats. Foam was running down the side of mine, and I licked the outside of the glass before it could spill onto the table. Carrie rolled her eyes at me; she'd seen me do this before.

"I'm sure that glass is like sparkling clean," she said.

I shrugged. "You drink stuff that's on the inside, is that, like, cleaner?" I said.

She considered this. "By the way," Carrie said. "Your hair called. It misses you and wonders if you miss it. I told it yes, definitely."

I rolled my eyes at her. "It's a team thing, you wouldn't understand."

"Apparently not. So anyway, Shaundra has now had thirty-seven partners," she told me, changing the subject and then slurping loudly through her straw. Shaundra was her best friend from elementary school. They had been inseparable until ninth grade, when, according to Carrie, Shaundra became a total slut. Now they didn't talk and I got a daily update on her alleged sex life.

We talked about sex all the time. Or, Carrie talked and I listened.

I didn't know if that made it more like we were dating, or less. But once the subject was up again, Carrie wasn't about to let it slip away. She started talking loudly about her virginity.

"It's still here," she said, wrapping strands of her dark hair around her index finger. "And it doesn't want to be. It wants to move to Hawaii and retire, drink piña coladas under a palm tree, and get catered to by muscular Samoan boys in short shorts."

I laughed, and blushed a little. I didn't want to discuss how she was going to lose her virginity, and she was speaking so loud that the three closest tables couldn't help but be aware of her so-called problem.

"So," she said, almost as an aside, looking up at the ceiling and lowering her voice a bit. "Why don't you just take me?"

"Whoa!" I said.

"I mean it, Biff. You are the most terrible, terrible brute of a boy in our high school. I just wish you'd have your way with me already," Carrie said, her eyes wide with mock sincerity.

Amazing, how Carrie could go from serious to kidding and back without batting an eye, all sort of mixed in together. It made her vulnerable and powerful at the same time, in a way I couldn't quite fathom.

"Gosh, Annette, you know I want to, but today in health class we saw a film about social diseases. And there's this one that can make you blind if you get it, and if you have it, you get sort of a drip from your privates, and I think, well, I think I may have it."

"That's okay, Biff," she said, suddenly demure. "Gee, if that's all you're worried about. I have it, too!"

I felt a euthanasia skit coming on. Austin hated when Carrie and I performed our scenes. He always walked away when we started in on one at a party. I'd be on my deathbed with Carrie at my side, holding my hand. "Unplug me!" I'd hiss, hardly able to speak. And Carrie would respond, "What, honey? No, you're not ugly." And we'd keep going until someone in the room was in hysterics.

It was always one of us.

Carrie was only about halfway through her float when I finished mine. I called the waitress over and asked about our hash browns. Carrie took out twelve packets of sweetener, six blue and six white, and divvied them up. She gave me the blue ones, and set them up like the table was a checkerboard, which it definitely wasn't.

"Okay, you go," she said.

I looked down at the random packets of sweetener. I slid one blue packet forward about an inch and looked at her, wondering if this was legal. She showed no signs that it wasn't. She was studying the table, real serious. Finally, she picked up a white packet close to her and jumped it over each of my blue packets, in no particular order.

"Checkmate," she said, smiling at me.

I heard Austin's voice in my head: "You need help, kid."

"So how do you feel about stupid questions?" Carrie asked, loosening the tops on the salt and pepper shakers.

"I love stupid questions more than life itself," I said, tightening them back up.

"Well, here's a stupid question for you. It's really dumb," she said, addressing my chin. "So why aren't we dating?" She paused and then started again at incredible speed. "Or are we in fact dating? Is there some sort of official process one has to go through to make it official and what is it and should we be dating or is this just crazy and do you think I'm totally ugly oh just forget about it."

I grabbed a pink packet of sugar substitute and flicked it with my finger several times to see if it would break. It did not.

"First of all, you're not even close to ugly, you're completely gorgeous and you know that. You're a babe."

Carrie smiled at me, relieved. "I know! I'm just totally perfect and wonderful. So remind me, why aren't we dating?"

She'd never asked me that kind of question before and I assumed that meant she had agonized over it. She'd probably been wondering about it at least as long as I had.

I ran my tongue over the inside of my teeth, counting the top row. Some 1950s girl was singing a song about it being her party, she'd cry if she wants to. I looked at Carrie and thought about what I could possibly say.

Just blurt out the truth? I mean, she has a million drama-club friends, and some of them are gay. But with me, it's different.

Something told me that a gay Bobby Framingham wasn't a good thing for Carrie.

I swallowed and smiled at her. "I don't know, Carrie," I said. "We're friends."

"Ouch," she said, maintaining eye contact. "Friends without benefits. Peachy."

"Carrie . . ."

"No, let's stop. Discussion over. This is what we're going to do. I am going to go to the restroom, vomit, cry my eyes out, compose myself, and return. We shall then pretend this conversation never happened."

"What conversation?" I said, smiling apologetically as our hash browns arrived.

"Attaboy," was her reply as she headed to the bathroom.

Six hours later, after our final summer practice, I rolled my hand-me-down Ford Escort into the driveway and sighed, exhausted. Austin was reclined in the passenger seat. I stopped the engine, cutting off a blaring Nelly, who was in the middle of telling us how he thinks about it over and over again.

I could relate.

The car smelled like a combination of caked-in dirt and sweat. I made a mental note to get it cleaned before Monday.

"I think Coach is trying to kill me," I said, slamming the car door shut and hobbling over to the shade of the oak tree on our front lawn.

I could feel the sun piercing my skull and collapsed face-first onto the grass. Every muscle in my body felt drained.

I exhaled and continued my thought. "It's pretty clear he wants me dead."

I heard Austin's footsteps coming toward me and winced, knowing that he might sit on my back. Austin was a big guy, and kidneys are delicate organs.

Instead I heard him flop in the grass next to me, and when he spoke I could tell he was lying by my side, faceup.

"That would be awesome," Austin said, "if he really was trying to kill you."

I laughed into the dirt. "Thanks a lot. That's real supportive."

It had been a merciless practice; after running steps for ten minutes, we did an hour-long scrimmage, first-team offense versus first-team defense. Coach didn't seem to care that we were in the middle of a heat wave, that it was about two thousand and seventeen degrees out and humid. Once he had us completely drained of fluids, he tortured us with formation work. He wanted us to work out of the tier formation this season. We all hated it.

"Which is worse, the tier or the heat?" I asked, rolling away from Austin and onto my back. I looked up at the lush green leaves of the oak tree, saw the yellow-and-blue rubber football that had been lodged in a branch about twenty feet up for the past year, and beyond it, the brilliant blue sky. No clouds anywhere.

"The heat will be gone tomorrow. The tier, dude, that's forever."

I laughed. "True," I said.

"Maybe if you were smarter, you'd be able to learn it," Austin said.

"This from a guy who got a two hundred on his SATs," I answered.

"Please," he said, stretching out his legs. "I got a thirteen-ninety on that shit."

"Congrats," I said. "That's like genius level."

"Damn right."

We lay there, looking up into the sky. I didn't know what Austin was thinking about—cheerleaders, probably—but I was thinking about the coming year. I'd really played well last year, and by the end of the season there were actual scouts watching my every move.

Hopefully a Stanford scout was among them. I'd heard from two different schools—one in Colorado and one in Arizona—that were recruiting me, but my dream was to be the quarterback at Stanford like John Elway was, follow in his footsteps.

That probably won't happen.

Still, I began to see them last December, men in khaki pants holding clipboards, fervently taking notes on everything I did. Coach told me this year there'd be even more of them.

We'd been through a lot this summer. Even before the two-a-day practices all August, Coach had put us on the most ferocious weight-training program possible. I added a good five pounds of muscle for sure, and the way Austin looked, he may have added more.

"You need fluids?" I asked.

"I'm good," he said. "I'll head out soon."

I was only half disappointed. Austin's great, but an afternoon of lazing around the house alone sounded pretty good.

Austin slowly stood, and then reached down to grab his ankles and stretch his legs. "So you still not getting any from that quote unquote *girlfriend* of yours?" he asked.

"Shut up," I answered, sitting up and throwing a handful of grass and dirt at him.

"She's not even your girlfriend," he said. "You never say a word about her."

"I don't kiss and tell," I said, pulling out a few strands of grass and smushing them together with my thumb and forefinger.

"You don't kiss," he said. "I know all about you."

I looked up at him and my head began to buzz. *This is it. He knows. Thank God, he knows.*

"You don't kiss, you go right for the good stuff," he said.

I looked down at the grass and in an instant decided to just get it over with, right before the school year. Just pull the Band-Aid off real quick.

But when I looked up at him, and saw he wasn't even looking at me, was instead concentrating on stretching his left leg as far behind him as he could, I changed courses. Again.

"Did you tell Rhonda that you're doing Gabrielle on the side yet?" I asked.

"Hey," he said, improvising a little 'N Sync–like choreographed dance move that he did to disgust me. It had its intended effect, and I stuck my finger down my throat as if I wanted to throw up. He wiped grass off of his shorts and shirt. "When you got all this, you can't keep it off the market."

"Austin, the market called. They're begging you to keep it off," I said, channeling Carrie, and he laughed. I lunged for Austin's legs. He tried to jump out of the way, but I was too quick for him. I pulled him to the ground easily and pinned him. I used to wrestle, and I was good.

"Get off me, dude," Austin said from underneath me, gasping for breath. "I think you like getting on top of me a little too much."

"Yeah, right," I answered, collapsing onto my back.

We had a typical family dinner, just a little quieter. Mom served some sort of casserole thing that tasted a lot better than it looked and there were the usual "are you excited about your first day?" questions, which I grunted away.

"That's an interesting, um, hair choice, Bobby" my mother said, looking toward my father.

At least she noticed. My dad didn't even look up. Here it was, the day before senior year, and he couldn't even be bothered to ask how I was doing.

I was bald, and he didn't care. I pictured myself with a huge earring and a skull-and-crossbones tattoo on my shoulder, and him just sitting there, scooping up broccoli.

He never used to be like this.

Usually my parents double-teamed me on things, and I was already prepared with five arguments about why my naked scalp was a good thing. But my dad didn't seem too focused on my lack of hair; instead he was just staring at his food.

"It's for the team," I said, taking a bite of casserole.

"That's sweet," my mom said.

My dad picked up his fork and took a few small bites and then rested his head in his hands, his elbows on the table like I was always told not to do.

"You okay, Dad?" I asked.

He did a double take, like he wasn't even aware I'd been in the room before I asked the question.

"Fine," he said, lifting his head from his hands and smiling at me. And the thing is, it was a nice smile. He wasn't trying to be a jerk. But then he rested his head in his hands again, and it was like I didn't even exist.

My eyes focused on the mantel above the fireplace behind him, where there's a large picture of my parents when they got married. My mom was a knockout back then.

What amazed me about the picture was how my dad looked almost exactly like me. He had the same blond hair, the same wide smile, the same green eyes. Maybe he wasn't built quite as big as me, but he was pretty big. He was a baseball player in college.

I looked at the picture and then at him, balding, tired-looking, his face lined. It filled me with a momentary panic as I imagined my future. *Will I look like that in thirty years? How does that happen?* Would I look in the mirror one day and see that all the changes had happened without me noticing, or would there be a noticeable shift every day—a line forming on my forehead, my hair becoming slightly grayer?

"Donald, why don't you go upstairs and rest?" my mother asked my dad.

Her head was tilted slightly and her eyes were full of compassion. I looked down at my plate and speared some broccoli, hoping that when I got older, my work wouldn't be as stressful as my dad's. He was always so tired at night.

My dad nodded and slowly stood. And then he did this weird thing. He came over to me and planted a kiss on my bald head.

"Big year for you," he said quietly, rubbing my temples.

When he left and I was sure he was upstairs and out of earshot, I looked at my mom. "Who was that man?" I asked.

She closed her eyes and nodded, like she knew what I meant.

"C'mon! Pump those legs! Pump those legs!"

In the distance, I could see the offensive linemen doing drills. Thick calf muscles flexed and cleats dug into the dirt, sending chunks of grass flying. Though they were a good twenty yards away, I could hear the grunting and gasping and it sent shivers of recognition down my spine.

It all begins with me. When I say "hike," the ball is snapped to me and I hear the clash of helmets to shoulder pads and my heart races and the blood pumps through my biceps. Then it's my turn to make the right choice, and that's what I live for, the chance to succeed using my brain and my arm, with huge linemen bearing down on me.

"Where's your head at, Bobby?" Coach yelled.

I snapped to attention and there he was, standing in front of me, his hands on his wide hips.

"Sorry," I said. "I'm here."

We were practicing our new tier formation, and it wasn't working. Just taking snaps without a defense, it felt like we were playing underwater or something. No matter what the play call, I seemed to keep bumping into the formation's extra running back. Wherever I turned, someone was in my face.

After about four botched attempts, my face was beginning to feel hot. I threw the football down in disgust and it bounced into my ankle.

"Framingham, deep breath," Coach said. "You can do this."

"I don't know, Coach, maybe this is just wrong for me," I replied, kneeling down to scoop up the ball.

Coach looked at me through narrowed eyes and crossed his huge arms. "Are you the coach, or am I?"

I looked down at the turf. "You are."

"Have a little confidence, Bobby. It'll be tough for a while, but it'll make you a better quarterback in time."

It was practice after the first day of school, and we were preparing for our first game, at Huntington Beach, just four days away. Coach ran us through the formation a couple more times until I got off a good sideline pass to Rahim. Then he put me and the backup quarterbacks through agility drills.

D'Wayne Haskins, Richie Bardello, and I took turns focusing on our footwork. We started from our presnap stance, gave a short cadence, and simulated the snap. We then took three-, five-, and seven-step drops, and ended with a throwing motion. Coach was always stressing footwork. You do that right, or you can forget about winning.

It was true. Understanding how to survive in the pocket was everything. That was like the quarterback's safety zone, where your linemen protected you from opposing defenders. But the other team wasn't the only concern; if you dropped back clumsily, you could easily get introduced to your running back's shoulder pads. I'd done it many times.

Since I was a typical pocket passer—rocket arm, not a whole lot of speed—footwork in the pocket was extra important. When I was able to get set and throw, I was tough to stop. Anytime I got chased outside the pocket, all bets were off.

"That's it, Haskins, you got it, you got it," Coach told my backup, giving him a quick slap on the rear. "Real nice. Better watch it, Framingham, Haskins is on your ass."

I gave them a smile, as genuine as possible after a coach threatens your job. "Bring it on," I said, half meaning it.

My mind was elsewhere and it was obvious. I fumbled a simple snap, and then, recovering, nearly tripped over my own feet before handing the ball off to Mendez.

"Damn it, Bobby, get with the program!" Coach yelled. I looked away, wishing practice were over. Coach dropped his clipboard on the grass and walked to the sideline, rubbing his forehead. "Framingham! C'mere!"

I trotted over to him, a slight throbbing behind my eyes as I braced myself for the onslaught. I could feel the stares of my teammates behind me and I flushed with embarrassment. As I got closer to Coach, I could see his face but couldn't read it.

"Where the hell is Bobby Framingham at?" he asked.

"Sorry. I'm here, Coach," I said, staring at his eyebrows.

Coach sighed and studied me. It's unnerving how he can see inside me sometimes. "That's it for you today, Bobby," Coach said. "Take two laps and hit the showers."

"What? No—Coach! I wanna keep playing!"

Coach put a hand on my shoulder. "Bobby, you're our starting QB, but it's like you're still on summer break." He smiled slightly.

"You're not in trouble, I just want to talk to you and don't want you to hurt yourself. You're lost out there."

As I trotted off the field, Austin ran over.

"Dude, you in trouble?" he asked.

"I don't know," I said. "He said he wants to talk to me."

"Shit, dude."

I shrugged. "You still coming by after practice?"

"Yeah," he said, before sprinting back onto the field.

The showers were empty and every sound I made reverberated through the small, steamy room. I let the water run down my back and stared at the floor, feeling that empty feeling in my chest again, that hole that swallowed up all the good.

It was happening more and more.

I wondered if Coach was going to yell at me. I really didn't need the yelling.

I felt guilty enough; I should have been focused on the upcoming season, which would probably make or break my career. Instead here I was having the dreams.

The night before I had this dream that Todd and I were sharing a room at a hotel on a road trip. We were teammates, which didn't make sense since we played different sports. Also, none of my teammates were there. We wrestled in the hotel room for what seemed like hours, and it was the most vivid dream I'd ever had. As we lay on the hotel carpet, spent from wrestling, he brought his mouth close to my ear.

"You and me, buddy," he whispered, and I could smell his sweet breath.

I woke up feeling ecstatic, transformed. Though nothing had changed, all day I felt strange, like I was waiting for a reunion with a friend who didn't exist.

I know that's weird.

And here I was, alone in the shower room, violently aware that showering in this room was a privilege, and not one for a guy who dreamed about other guys. Guys like me weren't supposed to be in here.

One day I typed "gay NFL" into Google. A bunch of things came up about a couple guys who came out as gay, but only after retiring from the league. The number of openly gay players in the history of the league? Zero.

So how the hell can I be gay and still have a shot at making it as a pro? Hide, I guess. But isn't that sort of dishonest?

Fifteen minutes later I sat in Coach's office, across from him, and watched him wipe the sweat off his forehead with his white shirtsleeve.

Coach Castle used to be a tight end for the Cincinnati Bengals. Now he was a Durango coaching legend. We'd been real close ever since he watched me at the first practice my sophomore year. After throwing drills, he came up to me and gave me a firm handshake. "Welcome to varsity football," he had said. "You have skills. If you work hard, you're gonna be one helluva quarterback."

Coach took a sip from the soda can on his desk.

"Bobby, you need to get your head straight," Coach said. I watched as he picked dirt out from under his fingernails and flicked it down to the floor. "This is your opportunity to get noticed, and your head is not in the game."

"I know," I said, looking down.

Coach reached across the table and placed his huge left paw on my right shoulder. "Look at me," he said. I looked up at him. Coach's eyes were incredibly kind. His skin, sort of a dark mocha color, was starting to sag ever so slightly around his cheeks. "Pressure isn't easy to deal with. You can talk to me."

And I thought to myself: *Yes, I should.*

I opened my mouth to say something, but nothing came out. So I said, "I just have a lot on my mind, is all."

Coach crossed his arms, his eyes not wavering from mine. "Shoot," he said.

I could suddenly hear every noise like it was magnified. The air-conditioning chirped every few seconds, interrupting a low hum. The high-pitched buzz that goes along with the fluorescent lights rumbled through my ears.

It was just us, and I imagined the conversation we could have if I just told him. What would he say? Would he turn his back on me, or would he understand? If he didn't, would he hate me? Kick me off the team?

But it was too important. Messing up with Coach would screw up my chances of getting a college scholarship, and without one, I could forget ever making the NFL. I couldn't risk that.

"My folks," I said, and then I closed my eyes, hating myself for making stuff up.

Coach leaned forward. "What about your folks?" he asked.

I kept my eyes closed. I couldn't look at Coach. "They're having problems," I said, ashamed. I was saying something that was probably not true, but what if it was? How could I lie about something serious when I was thinking about some other stupid thing that no one even cared about but me? If something was really up with my parents, I would never be able to forgive myself. I felt a queasy sensation rise in my throat.

"I'm sorry, Bobby."

I opened my eyes and stared straight ahead, not at Coach, but sort of through him. I'd never lied to him before, and this felt like a stupid one. Why not just tell him what was really going on? But it was too late. You couldn't say your parents' marriage was in trouble and then bring up something like sex.

I held my breath. I took the feelings and balled them as tight as I could and pictured myself throwing a bomb with them from one end zone to another, as far and high as I could manage.

One hundred yards.

"It's okay. I'm fine," I said.

He came and stood by my chair. I stood up, figuring he wanted me to leave. And then he hugged me, a big, clumsy hug.

"You can talk to me anytime," he said, his ear right next to mine, muffling the words.

I stood there, paralyzed in his grip. When Coach let go I couldn't look at him.

"Do you need anything?" he said.

"I'm fine," I said. "Everything will be fine."

He nodded, and I felt like I had said the right thing, at least.

"I'm sorry this is happening. But you gotta let the feelings out, Bobby. Keeping things inside, that'll tear you up."

"Watch the master at work," I told Austin as we studied our playbooks out in my front yard after practice. I put down my playbook and picked up a football, tossed it lightly in the air to myself, twirled it in my hand until I felt the laces in the right place, gripped the ball, and threw a bullet of a pass at the tire hanging from the big oak tree on the other side of the yard. It ricocheted off the top rim of the tire.

"That's great, dude," Austin said. "Were you aiming for the house, or the street?"

"I was aiming for your face," I said.

"Well, do that in a game, maybe," he replied, stretching his legs out in front of him and reaching for his toes. "That way, maybe a pass will come close to me once in a while."

I sat back down, grabbed my playbook, and swatted Austin's shoulder, hard. He flinched.

“Hey! What the hell was that for?” he asked.

“Bug on your shoulder,” I said, opening my book again. “ know, this tier-formation thing could really work. I mean, if we get chance to play a team with just two or three players, or perhaps even more if some of the players have no legs, we should have a good shot at a touchdown.”

“You’re a really weird guy, you know that?” replied Austin, flicking the cover of my notebook.

“Thanks, man. Appreciate it,” I replied.

“Anytime, dude.”

“Where do you line up in Forty-eight Tier Gun Double-Z Flag?” I asked.

Austin gave me a dirty look. “Where I always line up in tier, moron,” he answered. “On the right side.”

“Fine, smart-ass. What do you do then?”

“Well, let’s say you actually get the play off in time, in that case, I’d fake a block on the linebacker closest to me, and then roll out and find an open space. I’m your second option. Rahim’s the first.”

“Amazing,” I said. “You get a D-minus in basic math, but you somehow know that.”

He used his playbook to swat me back in the arm. “D-plus,” he said. “And that shit was two years ago. Find something new to make fun of me for. How about Eighty-one Tier Toss Right?” Austin asked me.

I closed the book and visualized it. “I fake a toss to Somers, going left, and instead toss back and right to Mendez, who’ll have a whole bunch of blockers ahead of him. Easy.”

“You got it, bro,” Austin said, jumping to his feet and shaking out his legs.

“I still think Coach has lost his mind with this formation,” I said. “I mean, it’s not just me, right?”

You
a

'osing his mind for sure," Austin replied, rub-
like he had fleas.

ırmation would be a little better if we had a
. run like my dead grandmother—"

said Austin. "I can run." He fake-lunged at me and I
.ched.

ɪeah, from the law."

"I'd kick your ass in a race," Austin said. I turned around and watched as he again stretched his legs out in front of him and reached for his toes.

"Care to make it interesting?" I asked.

I'd attended the Nike combine in Palo Alto earlier in the summer, a day of athletic testing when scouts poked and prodded us like pieces of meat and timed us doing everything from running forty meters to getting dressed in the morning. The fastest guys ran the forty-meters in about 4.3 to 4.4 seconds. I came in just above 5, right with the linemen who weighed over two hundred seventy pounds. It wasn't good, and that was one reason I wasn't the most sought-after quarterback in the state.

Austin laughed at me—actually laughed, the prick. "Dude, you're slow even for a white guy. I'll tear you up in a race. I bet you a buck."

I loved how my friend was, like, Mexican only when it was convenient, forgetting he was half white, too. We walked across the yard to the oak tree, which we had used as an end-zone marker when we were younger. From there to the other end zone, where the house ends on the driveway side, it was about twenty yards. We decided to use the end of the house as the finish line.

"Why don't you just give me the buck now?" Austin said, shaking his legs loose.

"Because then you'd have to give me two after I win," I replied.

Austin called the race. "On your mark, get set . . . go!" We took off and I had a quick lead after a few steps, but Austin turned on his burners. He accelerated, and once again I was faced with the sad fact that I'm just not as fast a runner as I could be.

He was going to win by a lot, so I did the next best thing: I fell to the ground, grabbing my ankle and howling.

"Oh, shit!" Austin yelled as he crossed the finish line and looked back at me, writhing in pain on my back. He sprinted back over and knelt next to me. "Bobby, you okay?"

It was a trick I'd learned back when I wrestled in junior high. I quickly grabbed him by the arm and flipped him. Austin might be bigger than me, but he wasn't stronger. I pinned him easily.

"Get off me, dude!" Austin was squirming under me, trying his best to break free.

"Make me," I said, panting.

"Try this on a girl," Austin said, and I rolled off of him. He fell away and collapsed on the grass, huffing.

I stood, and wiped the dirt and grass off my arms and legs. Austin and I have been wrestling like that for maybe ten years, and it wasn't the first time he'd called me gay in one way or another. But it just hit me different this time. Maybe it was all the time I'd been spending thinking about coming out. I looked down at him, lying in the grass. Austin was more than just a teammate, he was like a brother to me. We didn't have as much in common at seventeen as we did at nine, but here we were, still together.

"So where's my dollar?" Austin said as he got up to his feet.

I turned away and looked up at the sky, which was unbelievably blue. "Calm down, I'm good for it," I replied.

I heard Austin rustling through his pockets, and when I turned and looked, he had dug a circular green container out of his pants. At first I thought it was gum, but when he pried the top off, the powerfully bitter, fruity-mint smell told me it wasn't.

"What the hell?" I said as he pinched a small amount of black gunk between his thumb and forefinger and put it in his mouth, between his bottom lip and gum.

"Tell me you're not dipping," I said.

Austin shrugged. "I like it," he said.

"Austin, that's disgusting. Not to mention how bad it is for you."

He shrugged, and put the container back in his shorts pocket. "This is the apple-flavored kind."

"Man, if only there was another, less lethal way to get the taste of apples in your mouth," I said, shaking my head.

"Shut the hell up," he said, a tiny bit of brown dribbling from the side of his packed lip.

I worried about Austin sometimes. His judgment.

"What do you wanna do?" I asked, trying to forget the fact that he had tobacco in his mouth.

"Watch TV?" he said. "We never do that."

I gave him a dirty look. I barely ever watched, unless it was a football game or maybe baseball with my dad. I preferred actually doing things, but that's just me.

He rolled his eyes. "Oh, I forgot, you're Amish."

I laughed. "I'm Amish because I don't watch TV?"

"You don't do a lot of things, dude," he said, walking to the front door. As he swung it open a blast of air-conditioning hit us in the face. It felt good. We walked in and sat on the living-room couch. My folks were out. "You hardly ever drink, don't smoke, you don't do drugs, and I don't even think you have sex."

I grabbed my dad's *L.A. Times* and rearranged it more neatly on the glass coffee table. "Whatever," I said.

"What's up with you and Carrie?" Austin asked.

I laughed, because we didn't have serious talks, like almost ever. Rahim and I did that, but not me and Austin. But he didn't laugh.

The house was incredibly quiet. My folks were both still at work. I looked away from Austin, studied the beige walls. There was a crack near the ceiling.

"You think anything could ever stop you from . . ." and I couldn't finish the sentence. *Being my friend,* I thought, but I couldn't say the words.

Austin looked over at me and raised an eyebrow. "Dude, you just have a stroke or something?"

I turned to Austin and smiled. "Could anything stop you from playing football?"

"No way, dude. I mean, like a bad injury maybe. But no way."

"Yeah, me neither," I said. "You ever think about what you'll do after?" It was another sentence I couldn't finish. How do you say to your brother, your best buddy, whose only dream is pro football, *if you aren't good enough to play in the NFL?*

"I like to talk to girls. You think I could get a job doing that?"

"You could be a pimp," I said, and he laughed.

"Yes," he said. "I have a new career. Thanks, dude."

We just sat there, looking at each other for a while.

"You didn't answer the question," he said. "What's up with you and Carrie?"

My brain was on like three tracks at once, and the thoughts tripped over one another and I realized as I struggled to think of what to say that I was exhausted.

I was tired of thinking about it alone.

I exhaled. "I don't know," I said, squirming in my seat.

He reclined, his hands clasped behind his head. "What don't you know?"

"If I should tell you," I said. "I think you know."

And when I said that, I felt like I was going to crawl out of my skin because there was almost no going back.

Austin sat up. "Know what?"

I remained still, trying not to even breathe. Maybe if I stayed quiet, we could move on to something else. But at the same time I really wanted to tell him.

"What?" he repeated, and I could hear an edge of panic in his voice.

I sat up and faced him. "Do you know what I'm going to tell you?"

His forehead was creased in a way that I hadn't seen before. I could almost imagine what Austin was going to look like as a middle-aged guy. "No," he said.

"I'm going to tell you something, but you have to promise not to tell anyone else."

"Did you get Carrie pregnant?" he said.

I laughed, way too hard. "No!"

"What?" he said.

"I'm not dating Carrie," I said. "I'm not dating anyone. I'm gay, Austin."

We sat there, staring at each other for a few seconds. His left eye twitched. Then he laughed.

"Dude," he said. "Yo. You're kidding."

"No," I answered, unable to look away from his face.

Austin laughed and pounded the arm of the couch with his fist, gently. "No, dude, yo. You shouldn't say shit like that. People will start to think it's true."

"It *is* true." My head was buzzing like a hundred bees.

Austin stared at me, with his mouth half open, sort of like an idiot. I wanted to say something that would let him close it.

"For real?" he asked quietly.

I nodded. "Yeah."

"Wow," he said, and then he smiled again. "That's, wow."

I laughed. "You already said that."

Austin laughed, too, and I felt a chest fluttering that made me feel almost elated.

"I'm totally cool with that," he said.

I closed my eyes tight and just breathed for a while. When I opened them, he was still sitting there, looking at me and smiling.

"You are?" I asked.

"Dude," he said. "I don't give a crap who you, you know. That's your business. I don't tell you what I do in bed, do I?"

I raised an eyebrow. "Um, yeah, like all the time," I said.

He laughed, way too loud. "That's true," he said. "But I mean, it doesn't matter if you're banging a girl or, you know, a, you know, a guy or whatever. I don't give a—"

"I've never done it," I said quickly.

He nodded his head like he already knew this. "Oh," he said. "Right."

"You're freaked," I said.

He stood and shook out his legs. "Dude," he said. "I'm fine. It's not a big deal. Chill. I know there's gay people and straight people. It's like, what's the difference anymore, right?"

"You're freaking me out," I said, watching him stretch manically for his toes.

He stood tall and walked over to where I was sitting. He put his hand on my shoulder. "Relax," he said. "We're cool."

I closed my eyes and exhaled. "You have no idea how long I've wanted to tell you that."

He walked to the front window and peered out the blinds. "One question," he said.

"Shoot."

He turned to face me. "You're not like, interested, in me, right?"

I laughed. "You're my best friend," I said. "No."

He pretended to wipe sweat off his forehead. "That's cool, because I'm sticking with the ladies, you know."

"Duh," I said.

"And also, I'm pretty damn good-looking." There was a familiar glimmer in his eye that made me so grateful.

"I think it's the bald head that allows me to resist you," I said, rolling my eyes. "And your odor."

He smiled. "Thank God I shaved."

We knew the first game of the season wasn't going to be a major challenge, and going into the second quarter, it appeared we were right. Huntington Beach is just not a football powerhouse, or even close. Last year we beat them 33–10. It looked like this year would be even more of a blowout.

In the four days between our conversation and the first game, Austin and I hardly spent any time alone together. On the field it was business as usual, but part of me was wondering if he was avoiding me after practice. I didn't know what to make of it, but once the game began, it was a relief to put everything else away.

We looked good, much better than in practice. In the first quarter I hit Somers in the corner of the end zone for our first score, and after a quick turnover, Mendez took a pitch out around the left side for a thirty-one-yard touchdown run.

I felt confident, completing eight of my first ten passes, and at least early on Coach seemed to have abandoned the tier formation. Leading 21–0 early in the second quarter, we huddled up at the Sharks' forty-five-yard line. I looked over our guys and felt a rush of emotion flood over me.

Here we are, the Durango Bulldogs, my brothers and me, wreaking havoc on our opponents together. Nothing's better than that.

Coach sent Rahim into the game with the play.

"Forty-eight Tier Gun XZ Flag," he said into my ear. Coach was putting us into tier formation for the first time.

"Damn," I said under my breath.

Rahim shot me a look and I buckled down and got into leader mode. You couldn't be showing dissension when you were a team captain.

The tier formation called for three guys—two running backs and a receiver—in our backfield plus me, the quarterback. Instead of a straight line behind me, we curled a bit to the left, like a dog's tail.

It was hard to know why it even existed or why Coach liked it so much, but he did.

I put on my poker face in the huddle and called the play with the same enthusiasm as any other play. I heard a few groans.

"Chin up!" I said forcefully, and the groans went away, quick. I looked over at Rahim, who was grinning at me. He winked.

The play was one I liked, a chance for me to go deep to either Rahim on the right side or Somers on the left. I nodded at Austin. He hadn't caught a single pass yet, and he was a decoy on this one. The nod meant, *Give me a chance, I'll hit you real soon.*

We stepped to the line and got set. I looked out at the crowd. Lights blinded me. It was a beautiful Friday night, a slight chill in the air. The Huntington Beach fans were pretty quiet with us leading by a big margin so early. There were plenty of people in the stands, but it almost felt like I was looking at a silent movie, looking out at them as if through a screen.

Things often felt this way when I was in the zone: no distractions, just me and my brothers doing our thing like a well-oiled machine.

I surveyed the field and saw that they'd made a change. Their linebackers were playing toward the line, looking for a running play. Their strong safety should have been closer to the middle, where Austin was lined up at tight end, but instead was doubling Rahim on the right side. Their other safety seemed to be edging toward the left, away from the middle, as if to key on Somers, who was in the backfield. It left them with little coverage in the middle of the field. It was as if they were discounting Austin's ability to make a difference.

How could they have forgotten? Austin was one of our best weapons, and that wasn't exactly a secret.

I called an audible. "L thirty-nine, L thirty-nine!" I yelled, keeping us in the tier but telling them that I would be looking for Austin over the middle.

"Thirty-three, fourteen, hut, hut . . . HUT!" Bolleran snapped the ball and I dropped back about five yards, my eyes darting left to right as I watched the play develop. I could see my left tackle was struggling to contain the rush, and my heart sped slightly.

That's when I noticed that their free safety, who I thought was going to cover Somers out of the backfield, was actually back covering Austin. He was right in the path of Austin's route. I tried to fake him out by looking left. I watched Austin's progress out of the corner of my eye, just as I sensed, out of the corner of my left eye, a defender breaking free and heading right at me.

I was forced to throw a second before I wanted to in order to avoid the sack, and I hung the pass a little high. Then I noticed the free safety hadn't bit on my fake. He was right there, and Austin was going to have to battle for the ball. He stretched up high and made a great catch, leaving his midsection vulnerable. The Oilers' free safety rammed him in the lower back. Austin held on to the ball, but crumbled to the ground.

Coach ran onto the field to attend to Austin, along with our trainer. I hurried over, feeling horrible for having caused the problem by throwing high. Austin was holding his right side and writhing on the ground. "It's his rib cage," the trainer said, instructing Austin to breathe. "We'll need to take him in, see if he broke something."

"Austin, I'm so sorry," I said, guilt flooding through me. "All my fault."

"Dude, you hung me out there," he said, moaning. "Nice audible. Next time you have the idea to change a play at the last second, leave me out of it."

"Man. I owe you big-time," I said. "Sorry."

He grimaced as he sat up with the trainer's help and got to his feet. He walked off with the trainer and Coach on either side of him.

Damn tier. My body felt cold, and I blamed the formation. If we'd just stayed with what we were good at, this wouldn't have happened.

Coach glared back at me. "You lose track of the free safety? Keep your mind on the game, Framingham," he said. He turned away from me and continued to walk Austin off the field. The crowd cheered supportively for Austin.

My head felt foggy, and in the huddle, that was obvious. I hesitated and didn't know what play to call. A teammate ran in with the new play, but I still felt a bit lost until Rahim shook me out of it.

"Part of the game, Framingham. If you're gonna be big-time, you need to deal and move on."

He was right. I shook it off and set up the play, and by the time I started the snap count, I was back. The next play was a simple fly pattern to Rahim, who streaked down the right side. Their cornerback got no help from his safety and Rahim was too fast. An easy touchdown gave us a 28–0 lead.

We won big, 44–7. After halftime, we mostly ran, since the Oilers showed no ability to stop our ground attack. In the raucous locker room, we got the news that Austin had gone to the hospital and that X-rays had been negative.

I breathed a sigh of relief, but was brought back to earth by Somers, who rat-tailed me as I bent over to dry my legs. "He's still gonna kick your ass, Bobby."

I rubbed my stung butt and shrugged, knowing that wouldn't happen. But I couldn't help but wonder how things actually would go. I'd never caused a friend to be injured before. Instead of feeling great after a win, I dressed quickly and trudged out of the locker room, thinking about what Austin was going to say to me.

Outside I found a bunch of reporters, many of whom were familiar from last year, waiting for me. I felt a little sorry for the old ones, coming year after year as if high school sports were their life. I mean, it was my life, but I was only seventeen.

"Bobby! How do you feel?"

A circle of reporters closed in around me. I was still smarting about Austin, but I put on a happy face. "Great. Not bad for an opening game."

"Do the Bulldogs have a chance to compete for the Division Nine title?" asked a short guy, one of the older ones.

"Your guess is as good as mine. You watched us play. I hope so," I said, and they all shook their heads as if this was a brilliant thing to say.

"Hoping to be recruited this year?" This came from a guy I knew wrote for the *Durango Sun.*

"Yeah, I hope so," I replied.

"Any calls yet?"

"Colorado State and Arizona. None from California yet, unless they came in to you and you're here to tell me about them."

It was an awkward thing to say. Carrie would have rolled her eyes, but they all laughed, way bigger than necessary, as if this was a great line for their stories.

As I answered their questions, I was thinking about the recruiting thing. I knew that the top players in the state were already visiting programs and talking to many schools at once. I was disappointed that more of this hadn't happened for me. I wanted to be sought after. I wanted calls at all hours of the day, and for my father to be proud of me.

My parents hadn't made it to the game. I knew they'd wanted to, had planned to go, but at the last minute they called and said they couldn't make it. It was weird—they never used to miss my games. And no matter how hard your work was, how could you be too tired to sit in the stands and watch?

The reporters droned on, asking about our game plan, and Austin's injury. I did the best I could. While answering a really stupid question about throwing on the run, I looked up and saw, behind the tight circle of press, a guy a little older than me, maybe in college, about my height, with a goatee and jet-black hair.

We caught each other's eye. He smiled and looked away.

"Word on the street has it that Austin's put a hit on me," I told Rahim as we headed to Spanish class the following Monday. I hadn't seen Austin yet, though we'd spoken on the phone Saturday. "Bruised ribs," Austin had told me.

"Mmm. Braised ribs," I'd said.

"Don't be an idiot," he'd answered. He was basically okay.

"He's gonna miss two, maybe three games. He'll get over it," Rahim replied.

Rahim was probably my second closest friend. Rahim and I could talk better than Austin and me, but I've known Austin way longer.

Rahim's family moved here sophomore year from Oregon, and I liked him right away.

"It just sucks because it's my fault," I said. "What if this costs him a good scholarship somewhere?" We walked past Rahim's locker and he stopped to drop off some books. Rahim was a pretty amazing player and had already made a verbal commitment to Berkeley.

"You need to learn about what you can change, and what you can't change," he said, fiddling with his combination.

"What does that mean? Rahim-to-English dictionary?"

"It's not that complicated. You know my mom's in AA, right? She says the Serenity Prayer every night before dinner," Rahim said. He closed his eyes and bowed his head. "'God grant me the serenity to accept the things I cannot change, the courage to change the things I can, and the wisdom to know the difference.' It's kind of beautiful, isn't it?"

Rahim slammed his locker shut and we continued down the hall to Spanish.

"What does that have to do with me? And what does that have to do with Austin and me, and what are you talking about?"

He laughed. "Sorry, B. I'll stop my preaching."

I smiled. "I mean, I get it."

We entered the stairwell side by side and took two steps at a time. "Good. It is what it is, right? He's hurt. He'll get better and the recruiters will watch him play again."

We hurried down the steps to the main floor.

"Looks like the Gay-Straight Alliance is having a dance," he said, pointing to a pink flyer on the wall in front of us.

I laughed. It was just a reflex reaction. Not that Rahim had ever made antigay jokes, but I wasn't used to my friends using the word *gay* without some sort of negative twist. Not Rahim, but a lot of the guys were always saying things were "so gay." And that wasn't a good thing.

When Rahim didn't laugh, too, I stopped. "Cool," I said, struggling to swallow.

• • •

I found Austin in the cafeteria at lunchtime and headed over to the counter, where he was buying a plate of pasta to go along with his brought-from-home protein shake. He saw me and smirked. "Oh, you're gonna pay," he said.

"Yeah, for your lunch," I said. He shrugged, putting away his wallet. I paid the woman, and when she gave me change, Austin grabbed it out of my hand.

"Wow. Free pasta and forty-five cents, this is my day!" he said as he carried his tray to a free table. I didn't have food yet, but figured hanging out with my best friend was more important at this moment.

We sat down and I waited until he settled himself and began to eat, really fast, as usual. There was a lot to talk about, and I didn't know where to start.

"Austin, I'm really, really sorry, dude. How are you feeling?" I asked.

"How are you feeling, how are you feeling?" He mimicked me, slobbering pasta. "Screw you. I'm fine, you moron. Get over it. It's football. You still owe me big-time."

"Well I'm glad you're okay," I said, boiling a bit about how he made me sound.

"Yeah you are, or else I'd be kicking your ass right now, kid," he said, and I smiled, knowing that it was all words.

"Of course," I said. "I'm scared to death of your amazing strength."

He laughed, continuing to eat. "Dude. Injure me and then talk trash. Real nice."

I laughed, grateful to hear him sound like my buddy again. As awesome as he was about things, since coming out to him a week earlier, I felt like the connection had gone down or something, like a bad cell connection, cutting in and out and suddenly it was hard for us to relate.

I got up and bought myself lunch, then rejoined Austin. Dennis had arrived and was busy devouring two heaping plates of rigatoni.

"Hey, Dennis, what's going on?" I asked.

"'Sup," he said. Dennis's communication skills were lacking. When he wasn't being funny, he was busy showing us how the world isn't cool enough for him.

His dirty-blond hair fell in wisps over his forehead, and I tried to imagine what girls saw in him. He did nothing for me.

"What are we hating today?" I asked Dennis. Getting him on one of his rants was one of my favorite things, but it could be hard to do. He was either there, or he wasn't. No middle ground with Dennis.

"You, if you keep asking questions," he said, grumbling.

"Problem solved," I said, turning to Austin to speak. Austin interrupted me.

"Don't look now, geek reporter approaching, nine o'clock," he said. I turned to my right and saw Finch Gozman loping over.

I cursed myself for not removing the remaining chair at the head of our table. Gozman took it as an invitation to join us.

"Hey, guys!" he said, and I had to suppress laughter, thinking of Dennis's imitation of Finch, which started with the same line. "Hey, guys!" Dennis would say when he saw us in the hallway. "Hey . . . hey . . . wait up!" And then he'd start following us, his arms out in front of him like Finch, his eyes scrunched up, looking like a serious nerd.

It was mean, but pretty much right on target.

"Hey, Finch," I replied, not looking at him, hoping the lack of excitement at seeing him might send him a message.

It did not.

"Great game the other night, Bobby Framingham," he said. He always called people by their full names. I didn't actually hate Finch. He was just annoying sometimes.

"Thanks, Finch Gozman," I replied, and Dennis smirked into his pasta. I prayed he wouldn't laugh. Finch, for one, was pleased to have his full name used.

"So, um, guys, what say I do my interview with Bobby now?" he said to the whole table.

I lifted my wrist and studied my watch, as if hoping the minute and hour hands would offer some sort of excuse as to why we couldn't do this right now. I didn't need the attention at the moment. I came up with nothing.

"Oh, you're doing a story about the guy who tried to have me killed by the Oilers secondary?" said Austin.

Finch laughed in big spastic breaths. "That's funny! Let me write that down!" He took out a pad, pen, and a small digital recorder. He pushed the button on it. "Interview with Bobby Framingham," he said into the recorder. He looked up at me and smiled. "So," he went on. "Who is Bobby Framingham, and what's going on with him?"

Austin looked at Dennis and laughed. Dennis laughed back, like they were sharing a secret moment. I felt a twinge of panic in my gut. "I don't know," I said. "Same old stuff."

"Why are they laughing?" Finch asked me.

"Don't pay attention to them, they're both in need of serious help," I said, shrugging them off. "I'm good. The team is playing well and I'm feeling confident."

"Is it true you want to go to Stanford?"

I smiled at the thought. "Yeah, but it's a long shot. They're probably going to recruit one or two quarterbacks in the whole country this year. Hard to imagine one will be me."

"But you could be one, you're one of the best in the state," Finch said. "I'd love to get into Stanford." I looked at Finch's big, sincere brown eyes, like those of a dog who just wanted to be petted. It was kind of nice, since my friends, as evidenced in Austin and Dennis, who were now flinging food at each other, rarely complimented me.

"Thanks, Finch. I don't know. I just do the best I can."

"Aw, perfect answer, kid," said Austin, screwing his pointer fingers into each of his cheeks and fake-smiling. "Moron."

"You have a piece of rigatoni in your hair," I said, and he violently thrashed a hand through his hair and found the offending pasta. He threw it and it hit Dennis in the eye. Dennis shut both eyes tight and swatted at the pasta as if it were a fly.

"So tell me about how it feels to be the quarterback!" Finch said, full of enthusiasm. Austin laughed, and Dennis would have, but he was still busy with the eye pasta, stuffing it in his mouth. "How does it feel to be behind center?"

"Arousing," Dennis said, jumping in to the conversation with his mouth full. My heart nearly stopped.

"Huh?" said Finch, laughing uncomfortably.

"It gets him hard," mumbled Dennis, looking at his food.

"Shut up, asshole," I said, glaring not at him but at Austin, terror in my eyes. He wouldn't look at me.

"That's what you say to the center's butt," Dennis continued, now laughing hysterically.

I felt the veins in my forehead pulse.

"Just ignore them," I told Finch, whose eyes were now wide open. Or at least they were when I looked at him at first. I looked back at my so-called friends, and when I looked again at Finch, he was totally composed and had this calm look, as if this was a normal answer and he knew exactly what to say next.

I looked down at the recorder, as if I wished I could turn it off with a simple, cold stare.

Dennis was now in fine form, and the problem was, he didn't stop when he got like this. *Why would Austin tell him?*

Dennis was playing with his food, his face red and his eyes full of peril. "Our star QB is a ho . . . mo"—and he looked at me, daring me with his smirk—". . . sapien!" And then Austin's laughing slowed a bit and he looked at me nervously. I wanted to vaporize and all I could do was allow the conversation to zip by me without affecting me. I turned myself off.

"What are you saying?" said Finch.

"That means he's a human being," Dennis said, proud. *He's such an idiot.*

Finch scratched his nose and took a deep breath. "What is this?" he asked.

"Last week he told Austin about his Homo sapien tendencies. He came out of the closet . . . Cave! The Cave! That's awesome. Bobby's out of the cave!"

I really didn't know if Dennis thought this was subtle, or what he thought at that moment. Maybe nothing.

Maybe his head was a big fat mound of mush that would put up little resistance before exploding if I, say, ran it over with my car.

I glanced at Finch, wondering how to do damage control. He was trying to ask a follow-up question, looking completely dazed.

"Moving on," he said, trying to regain composure. "What's the biggest skill you need to have in order to be a quarterback?" It was, I admit, not a bad job by Finch of getting us back on track, or close at least.

"Restraint," I said, staring directly at Dennis, who was oblivious and once again wolfing down pasta.

After a few more questions about other, less charged topics, Finch left, looking confused. I turned first to Austin, and when I could find no words, to Dennis.

"What the hell were you thinking?"

"I said Homo sapien," he said, grinning.

"And you thought that code would be tough for an honor student to break? What's your problem?"

"Dude. He's not going to write an article that says you're a Homo sapien. Relax."

I stood up and gathered my things, shaking. I kept my voice low and controlled. "Relax? Relax? You could ruin my fucking life," I said, this time directly to my so-called best friend, Austin. "What's wrong with you? Who else did you tell?"

"Rahim," Austin said quietly, not looking me directly in the eye. I thought back to the comment Rahim had made about the dance, and it all made sense.

"Great," I said. "Very nice."

"What did you expect? That's some information," Dennis said. "Yikes."

Austin just sat there, looking torn.

"Forget it, just forget it. Thanks for a terrific lunch," I said, my voice quaking, and with that I stormed out of the cafeteria.

As I headed to math class later that day, I caught myself daydreaming about strangling Austin, or better yet strangling Austin with Dennis's lifeless body.

Taking that as a sign that things weren't quite okay, I took a detour.

Coach came to mind, then Carrie. I nixed both ideas, unsure how much more drama I could take in a day. I needed someone uninvolved to talk to. I thought of Dr. Blassingame, the head guidance counselor at Durango.

Dr. Blassingame had been my ninth-grade history teacher. When I was in tenth grade, he stopped teaching history and took his current position. He also became the faculty adviser for the Gay-Straight Alliance; I knew it didn't automatically mean that he was gay, but that was the rumor around school, since he was at least fifty and not married. He was always nice, but eccentric, the kind of teacher who would be lecturing about Sumerians, go off on a tangent about the best ways to cook pork, and never come back to his point.

I'd never been to Dr. Blassingame's office before; it hadn't occurred to me to ask for help with anything. But as I walked along the hallway to his office, I felt like someone had tied a knot of rope tight inside my chest. Maybe this would help me untangle it.

The office was dimly lit and smelled slightly of vinegar. Blassingame was at his desk, gazing intensely into a book, his brow furrowed, a red pen in his left hand. He didn't look up when I knocked lightly on his door. Instead he kept his pen on the page in front of him and spoke, his voice a bit forceful.

"Please tell me this: What's a three-letter word for an ancient Hebrew coin that starts with a *Z*?" he asked, chewing on the pen cap.

"Excuse me?"

He looked up and his eyes opened wide. "Oh! Sorry! I thought you were Meg—Mrs. Moran."

"Sorry," I said, standing in his doorway.

"Don't apologize," he said. "Zid? Zid? Is that a word?"

"Excuse me?"

"A Hebrew coin," he said, exasperated.

"I really don't know," I said. "Dr. Blassingame—"

"This thing will be the death of me."

"I was hoping I could talk to you," I continued, my head beginning to pound.

"Zig? Zod? Zed? God! I'm losing it."

I took a deep breath. "Okay then, probably time for me to go," I said, turning away.

"No! No! Please. I'm sorry, you just caught me at a funny moment. Please come back and talk to me, Bobby."

I turned and saw he was smiling at me. The hostility in my chest melted away.

"How did you remember my name? There have to be two thousand kids in this school."

"Yes, but not everyone is Bobby Framingham, fearless leader on the football field," he said, standing and motioning me in. "I promise, no more crossword puzzle."

I walked in tentatively and sat in a cushioned chair facing him, my heart beating so loud I could hear it inside my ears. Blassingame was round in the middle, with tattered graying hair and a full beard. His office was decorated with Xerox copies of *Far Side* cartoons and golf memorabilia, including an iron club bent in the middle as if someone had wrapped it around a tree. It hung directly behind him.

"So what brings you to Casa Blassingame?" he asked. "I'm sure we haven't crossed paths since you were in my class a few years back, correct?"

"Correct," I said.

He reflexively grabbed for the crossword puzzle in front of him and then looked up at me and pushed it away, sheepishly smiling, his eyes wide. "And to what do I owe this great pleasure?"

I took a deep breath. "I think I'm in trouble," I said.

He tilted his head at me and raised an eyebrow. "What kind of trouble?"

I laughed, feeling completely out of my comfort zone. "I'm not sure this category of trouble is one you've dealt with before."

He pursed his lips. "Try me."

"How about this?" I said, slowly blinking and still feeling some heat in my chest left over from the cafeteria. "How about—I'm the quarterback of the football team, a college recruiting prospect, and . . . I'm gay. I told one friend, and now he told two others, and I think my life would pretty much end if it becomes public." I exhaled wildly.

Blassingame didn't flinch. "I think that's wonderful," he said, emphasizing each syllable with enthusiasm.

I opened my mouth and stared at him. "It's wonderful?"

He laughed gently and smiled at me. "Well yes, isn't it? Sexuality is a beautiful thing, and we're all different, and knowing who you are is truly a gift—"

I bolted straight up and stood over his desk. "Are you serious?" I asked. "This could ruin my life."

"Oh, I see," he said, crossing his arms as he looked up at me. "How?"

"Are you gay?"

Dr. Blassingame looked at me like I was from another planet. "Now, I must say that in usual circumstances, I'd find that to be an inappropriate question, Bobby. But in this case, I'll allow it. I am heterosexual. What difference does it make?"

"I'm sorry," I said, a little embarrassed. "I just don't think you get the significance of me, as a football player, being gay."

"Well, surely there are some homosexuals who play professional football."

"Name one," I said, slowly pacing his office.

"But that's preposterous," he said. "Surely there are some famous gay athletes. Martina Navratilova."

"Well, there are some women, yeah," I said.

"There you go," he said, as if the problem was solved.

"Can you name a single gay male athlete?"

"The diver," he said, searching for a name.

"Team sports," I said. "It's different when it's a team sport."

He gawked at me inquisitively.

"You can't name one, I can't name one," I said patiently.

"But it never occurs to me to think of the sexual persuasion of an athlete. Why does it matter?"

"Well, maybe it shouldn't, but it does," I said. "Otherwise, wouldn't there be some openly gay people?"

He seemed to be staring through me. "Zuz!" he yelled.

I protected my face with my arms, half expecting a physical attack after what sounded like a war cry.

Blassingame laughed. "I'm sorry Bobby. It was in the back of my mind. *Zuz.* A three-letter word for an ancient Hebrew coin. The doctor triumphs yet again!" He raised his hands in triumph, grabbed his pen, and filled in three blank spaces.

Anger was boiling in me, but I looked at him and he seemed so enthralled by this discovery, like a child learning how to read, that I had to laugh. He did, too.

"Forgive me," he said. "It annoys everyone. I'll try to do better."

After a beat he lightly pounded his desk with his fist. "So let me understand," he said. "You're angry that your friend betrayed you by telling others."

"Yes. Exactly," I said.

"I can imagine that. Friendships are paramount, and there needs to be trust."

I stared at him, waiting for him to tell me something I didn't know.

He studied me, as if trying to peer inside me. "Yes, I believe that's so. Also, you are angry because you are gay and this will make it hard to pursue a career in football."

"You got it."

Blassingame stood and wandered to a bookshelf, picking up a book from the second-highest shelf and replacing it on the top shelf. "I see. Perhaps the answer is to change your sexuality."

I laughed, thinking about the power of the dreams, the way they'd gotten stronger. I imagined trying to change them and suddenly it seemed ludicrous. "I don't think I can."

"Ah. So it's stronger than you are."

"Well, in some ways it is, I guess."

He took the same book down and leafed through it. "So you can't change it."

"No, I guess not."

"I see." He came and sat down again and smiled at me. "Well, Bobby. If you can't change something, I believe you have two choices."

"What?" I asked.

"You can accept it, or you can deny it."

I stared at the busted golf club and thought about this. He had a point. "So I guess I accept it," I said. "But what if I accept it, but the world doesn't?"

"I guess all you can do, then, is change the world."

I laughed. The idea of me, Bobby Framingham, changing the world was pretty stupid. It was hard enough for me to remember to change my underwear.

"Okay then," I said sarcastically. "I guess I'll do that."

He winked at me. "I know you're not serious, but do me a favor, will you? Keep that in mind. Someone has to change the world. Why not you?"

"I'll think about that," I said, wondering if there was anyone out there who actually understood what I was going through.

I was adjusting my shoulder pads before Thursdays' practice when Dennis and Austin came up to me in the locker room.

"Yo, Bobby Lee!" said Austin, clasping my shoulder. Dennis stood silently by his side. Austin called me that because my mother, who was born in the South, sometimes did. It was a term of endearment, and I usually liked it.

I liked it less when used by a double-crossing jerk of a best friend.

"What up?" I replied, focusing on my cleats. There were clumps of dirt in them from the previous day, and I tried poking them out with my fingers.

"Dipshit here has something to say to you," Austin said, and he sort of pushed Dennis at me. Dennis scowled at him.

"Monday in the cafeteria. Way out of line," he said, by way of apology, his eyes averted.

"Yeah," I said. "Way." I had avoided Dennis for three days, which isn't that hard since we don't hang out that much outside of football. The tough thing was Austin and I had barely talked either. Just football stuff, nothing personal. I was so mad at him, and Austin knew it. He'd been avoiding me.

"Finch won't write that shit," Dennis said. "If you want, I'll go tell him he better not or I'll kill him. If that appears in the paper, he's a dead geek." Vintage Dennis. An apology by way of promised violence.

I laughed, still not quite over it.

"Probably let's not do that. Just don't ever do that to me again, okay? Don't tell anyone. Please."

Dennis shrugged. "Not a problem," he said, relieved, as if everything were back to normal. Things weren't, but I didn't have the energy to focus on it. I had to think about practice and the game tomorrow. Dennis strutted off to his locker, and Austin hung around.

He wasn't in uniform, and wouldn't be for at least another week.

"Yo, I'm sorry, too, dude," he said.

"Oh, Dennis was sorry? I didn't hear him say that," I said. "Must have missed that in that great apology."

Austin sat next to me. "What do you expect? It's Dennis."

I looked up at him and saw real regret in his eyes.

He really was sorry that he had told Dennis, I could tell.

"So Rahim knows, too," I said, detaching my mouth guard from my helmet.

Austin examined his feet and said, "Yeah."

I walked toward the water fountain and Austin walked at my side.

"Anyone else?"

He shook his head.

I pressed the button, placed my mouth guard under the

stream of water, and looked up at him. I tried to say it as nicely as possible because I didn't want to fight. "Why'd you do that, Austin? I trusted you."

Austin exhaled. "I didn't mean to do something bad. I just needed to tell someone. I should never have told Dennis. That was stupid. I'm sorry."

"Yeah, that wasn't so smart," I said, waving my mouth guard in the air to dry it. "Well, it's done, anyways."

"Yeah. Done," Austin said. "And I'm sorry, dude."

"How are you feeling, how are you feeling?" I said, mimicking him making fun of me. He got it immediately and laughed.

I was glad it ended with a laugh, and felt a little bit lighter on my feet after I punched him in the shoulder and slowly jogged out to the field.

We started practice with the scrambling triangular, an agility drill. As a lefty, I dropped back, keeping the ball up near my left shoulder as if I was about to pass. I dropped back five steps, and then ran to my left at a forty-five-degree angle, as if being forced out of the pocket. I then shuffled quickly to the left and ran backward, back to where I began, and threw the ball off to my right. It's supposed to help your agility when the pocket breaks down.

Sometimes the pocket breaks down and you'd better be ready to scramble. Your feet are all you can one hundred percent depend on.

I was ultrafocused and Coach saw my intensity.

"Attaboy, Bobby," he yelled, and I felt hot, in my stomach. I like praise, especially from Coach, who can be tough.

We did formation work and I tried to keep my chin up, but the tier brought out the worst in me, as always.

The tier formation was this big, ugly, unwanted thing that was ruining my life, and I had no control over it, just had to deal with it the best I could.

I couldn't get the timing down, especially when I was throwing to Somers out of the backfield. Sometimes it meant an extra few seconds in the pocket, and it was hard to stay patient.

"Yo, Bobby, stop your dancing," yelled Rahim, after one play in which I had shimmied around the pocket for much longer than was comfortable. "You suck at it." Everyone laughed, so I did, too.

Since it was Thursday, we did our typical run-through, focusing on our opponent for the next day, La Habra. Big defensive line, Coach kept warning. We had to be aware that there wouldn't be much time to pass.

I was pretty sharp, surprising myself. On a quick five-step drop, I hit Rahim on a post pattern with a total rocket. I felt alive, powerful out there. It was the type of pass I threw once in a while that reminded me I could really do this. A few plays later I got Dennis to bite on a pump fake when we went starting offense against scout defense, no tackling. Dennis was a second stringer, which was one of those things we did not talk about. He was covering Somers, down the left sideline, and Somers did a hook-and-go, meaning he stopped short as if I were throwing to him. I sold it real well, and Dennis flew out toward the sideline, thinking the ball would be there. Somers darted past him and I hit him farther down the sideline.

Pretty slick, and it felt great.

Walking back to the locker room after practice, I caught up with Rahim.

"I know you know," I said.

"Good," Rahim said. "I'm glad you told someone."

I started in on why I told Austin and not him, and he shut me up. "I'm fine, B. You don't need to worry about that," he said.

Then he smiled. "I'm good with you being gay. My uncle is and he's cool. God loves everyone the same."

I took that information in. Maybe this wouldn't be so bad. "Thanks," I said.

The showers were boisterous, more than usual. Lots of hollering and talking about naked girls. Not my favorite thing, but I could deal with it. I usually just listened and laughed once in a while.

"Hey, moron, eyes up here," bellowed Torry Hodges, one of our offensive linemen. I froze, because I knew I could not deal with it today. We'd had a good practice, I'd had a decent day, and all I wanted to do was go home. Then I realized that the comment wasn't aimed at me. He was yelling toward one of the sophomore guys who doesn't play much, a guy named Hector Jimenez.

"Fuck you, I ain't no faggot," Hector yelled back.

"Then why is my ass all hot?" countered Torry.

"Beats me, faggot," said Hector, and everyone laughed. It was pretty ballsy of him to say that to Torry, who was a senior and about twice as big as Hector. Torry bolted over to where Hector was showering and put him in a headlock.

"What'd you say? What'd you say, boy? Fag boy?" Hector tried to squirm out of Torry's grasp, but couldn't.

This is the stuff that kills me. That straight guys will actually go over to a naked guy and put him in a headlock, no questions asked, but you make a mistake and forget to avert your eyes from their body, and suddenly you're queer.

I looked over to Rahim. The shower room was set up with round poles, six showerheads on each. He was on the other side of mine. He caught my glance and suddenly got serious.

"Hey!" he yelled. "Torry! Get off him, man." Torry released Hector and looked across the way at Rahim, surprised. Torry was bigger, but no one was more respected on the team than Rahim. Torry leered at him.

"He was lookin' at my ass," Torry said. Hector was back at his shower, his face crimson after the assault.

"You got eyes in the back of your head?" Rahim asked.

"I saw him," replied Torry.

At that moment Austin walked by the shower room. He heard the conversation, and he's not one to stay quiet, ever.

"Nobody wants your ass, kid. The hardest-up homo in West Hollywood wouldn't go near your fat sorry ass," Austin said, and the hoots came flying from every direction.

"Fuck you," said Torry, who went back to showering.

"Fags don't go for guys with elephant asses," Austin continued, and I looked over at Rahim. He was looking right at me, and I could tell he was trying to gauge how I felt.

"You would know," said Torry.

"I'm not gay, dude," Austin said, and I had that sensation in my stomach like after eating too much candy. Too much syrupy sweetness and then the nausea, and wishing you could reverse time and not have bought the candy to begin with.

If Austin had said what he'd said to stick up for me, then why was my stomach in knots?

"You guys," said Coach, his arms folded over his massive chest as he stood at the entrance to the shower room, standing next to Austin. He must have entered moments earlier.

He looked at me and I felt naked, or actually more naked than naked, as if he could peer into my soul and see the things I didn't want him to see. I was embarrassed, for all of us, myself included.

If you're gay, do you have to spend the rest of your life feeling bad every time guys joke around? Can you turn that part of your brain off? And how do you do it?

At dinner that evening, my mother entertained my father and me with stories about growing up in Birmingham, Alabama.

As we passed around dishes of broccoli and pot roast, she told us about the time she put a cat into the oven, when she was nine, to see what would happen. My grandfather saved it from the heat after a few minutes, and told her to never, ever put another living thing in the oven.

"And I didn't," she said, smiling and passing me the entrée, "until this here pot roast, today."

We all laughed. My mother's sense of humor was cheesy, but I loved it anyway.

My father seemed to be in a little better mood this evening. My dad owned his company, Framingham Refrigeration. They dealt in cooling products. The joke was that my father was successful in the field and therefore a "refrigerator magnate." My mother coined the term one night, and it got us all laughing.

"Refrigeration," he had corrected, totally ruining the joke.

My dad was usually funny, too, but lately he wasn't like he used to be. When I was little we'd play tackle football in the living room, him on his knees and me standing up. Then, when I was about eight, we took it outside. We played one-on-one, and he taught me how to throw. And those games were great, and filled with jokes that would be repeated each time we played, like how he would pretend he was John Elway and if I sacked him Elway would be injured, and his replacement would be the Incredible Hulk, meaning suddenly my dad didn't have to wait until I said "hike" to tackle me. I always knew the game was over when his tackles started getting more WWF and less football. He would tackle me, then pick me up by my feet and spin me around and it felt like I was flying.

Then he became the boss of his own company, I got bigger than him, and we turned into more of a football-watching father and son. But my dad was still pretty cool.

For a guy who sold cold air, anyway.

Driving home after practice, I'd heard my name on the radio on KXIT, the sports talk-radio station here in Orange County. "This Framingham kid, I tell you, he's a comer," the radio guy said. "I watched him last week as he led Durango over Huntington Beach, and he's probably the best high school signal caller in the area. Darned if he isn't one of the finest QB prospects in the state right now."

That kind of talk used to make my day. Now it filled me with anxiety, and I wasn't sure why.

"They talked about me on KXIT today," I said, dishing pot roast onto my plate.

My dad looked up at me. "What did they say?" he asked, a little of the old fire in his voice. I took a dinner roll and buttered it while I told him their exact words.

He pushed a piece of pot roast on top of his mashed potatoes with a fork. "Did they mention what kind of school might recruit you?"

I rolled my eyes.

"No," I said. I took a bite of the roll, which was perfect: crunchy on the outside, and hot and sweet and soft inside. I pointed to it and offered my mother a thumbs-up. She curtsied from her chair.

"I wonder if you could wind up quarterbacking at Ohio State."

I loved my dad, but he really knew how to take praise and make it into something else. *It's like, tell him you're a hot college prospect, and he'll say, "Fine, but are you good enough for the best program in the country?"*

I looked down at my plate, studied the casserole.

My father, however, was oblivious. "Don't you think, Molly? Could you see Bobby starring at Ohio State, or maybe Notre Dame?"

My mother looked at my father and said softly, "I guess I could, if he goes there and I buy a plane ticket."

I laughed. Her jokes were actually getting worse.

"Wherever he goes is just fine, Donald."

"Well, USC at the worst," my father said, exaggerating what we all knew wasn't true. USC was exactly like his other two, an elite school that had its pick of every quarterback in the country. And maybe I was pretty good, but I was pretty sure somewhere in the United States there was someone bigger, and better.

I mean, there has to be, right? Or else wouldn't I have heard from more schools? And then I started to freak out, sitting there at the dinner table, started to sweat realizing that at this moment there were quarterbacks all over the country who were opening letters and answering calls from coaches and probably had a pretty good idea where they were headed to next year, and here I was, having heard from only a handful of schools.

"We're both so proud of you," my mother said, looking at my father and then at me.

"Thanks," I said, trying to hide that I was having a little freak session in my brain.

"On to other subjects. How's Carrie?" My mother offered me a jug of water.

I took it from her and poured some into my glass. "She's good. She found out today she got the lead in *Hairspray*."

"I didn't know she sang," she said.

"She doesn't. Should be interesting."

My mother laughed. "I like her."

My father grunted. It was no secret that my father was not a huge fan of Carrie's, whom he'd never actually met, especially after her prank call a year ago. For two days my dad was walking on air, amazed that MTV executive producer Kathy Quimby had called because she wanted to do a reality show about me, the quintessential all-American California high school quarterback.

I was just confused, until the next day, when I saw Carrie in school.

She was walking toward me in the hallway and had this mischievous look in her eye. She could fool other people, but not me. "MTV, huh?" I said, and she broke out laughing. After I told my father, he always referred to her as "that strange girl."

It was not a terrible description, actually.

I looked at my dad and offered him more pot roast. He waved it away. He wasn't eating much these days.

"You should give her another chance, Dad. She's a nice person."

He concentrated on swallowing. "You can do better."

"Thanks, I guess," I said, before taking another bite of my pot roast.

My father reached for his glass, and as he raised it to his mouth, it slipped from his hands, bounced on the table, and fell onto the hardwood floor with a thunderous crash.

It was like a glass explosion. Little shards flew across the floor.

"Nice work," I said, kidding.

But when I looked at my dad, he wasn't laughing. His face was beet red. "Goddamn it," he muttered under his breath. He then pounded on the table with both fists, making all the silverware jump.

Time seemed to stand still. I didn't think I'd ever seen my father really mad, let alone table-poundingly pissed off because of a simple dropped glass.

My mother stood and rushed over to him, careful to avoid pieces of glass. "Donald," she said softly, leaning down and enveloping him in a hug. He sat there with his eyes closed, his face still red.

"Sorry," I said softly. My heart started pounding.

"It's not you," my mother said, her eyes a little dazed as she looked up at me. "Can you give us a moment, sweetheart?"

I nodded, understanding that it was time for me to take a walk, which I did, not just from the table, but from the house.

I walked out and stood in the driveway, shivering in the chilly night air, wondering if maybe my lie to Coach wasn't a lie, after all. *Maybe they're having trouble?* My dad always seemed so cold and distant these days, and I searched my memory for any evidence of problems.

I couldn't think of anything, but somehow, standing in the dark night in front of my house with my mom trying to soothe my dad inside, that didn't make me feel a lot better.

Game nights were all special, but nothing was quite like the first home game of the season. The stands got packed early, and you could feel the air. It was charged. As we ran out onto the field for warm-ups, the crowd gave us a massive ovation that shook the ground.

The La Habra Matadors, in their green uniforms and gold helmets, swarmed the field shortly after we did, and before I could catch my breath, the game was on. The Matadors scored quickly on a long touchdown run, and then stuffed us on our first drive. After a quick field goal to start the second quarter, the Matadors were up 10–0, and it was beginning to feel a lot like it had felt last year, when we lost 19–3. Their line was huge, but more than huge, they were fast; if any of them broke free, I had about three seconds maximum before I got smashed to the turf.

I got sacked three times in the first two drives, and each attack felt worse than the previous one.

We started our third drive off at our own twenty-five-yard line, and the first play Coach called was a screen pass to Mendez on the left side.

I liked the call. Their defense was beginning to overpursue, and if I could get them to bite on a play fake long enough to set up the screen, we could get a big gain out of it.

We broke out of the huddle and I felt a confidence I hadn't felt all game, the kind I felt when good things were about to happen.

Bolleran hiked the ball back to me. I dropped back in the pocket and looked right, as if I was heading downfield with a pass. It worked. I sensed the defense adjusting, the linebackers headed to that side of the field. Meanwhile, our fullback and tight end snuck out to the left, in front of Mendez. I swung left and lofted a simple screen pass to him, right on the money, and I could hear the crowd sense the big play before it happened.

Mendez caught the pass and did a stutter step, allowing his two blockers a chance to get set ahead of him. I raced out forward and to the left, hoping I could block someone and help spring him farther. I watched as Mendez raced around the left side, his blockers clearing the path, and I heard the crowd noise swell. Then I saw an arm swing out in front of my face, at neck level.

I felt the hit on my Adam's apple. It was as if someone had shut off my wind supply and snapped my head backward.

I hit the turf, hard.

I lay flat on my back, straining for oxygen. After several seconds I caught my breath and sat up, looking downfield, and saw the action was a good thirty yards away. I pumped my fist and pushed myself to my feet. Breathing was still tough, but I dusted myself off and trotted downfield.

Then I saw the yellow flag.

It was thrown much closer to the play than to me, but I clapped my hands, knowing that we'd be tacking on extra yardage. You couldn't get away with cheap hits on the quarterback in this league.

I hustled to where the ref was making the call. He signaled face mask, and I was confused, because the defender hadn't hit my face mask.

Then he signaled with his arm the direction of the penalty, and I was truly shocked when it was against us.

The referee called it on number 81, Rahim, a flagrant foul. Already smarting from the hit to the Adam's apple, I felt my face heat up. Rahim was not capable of a flagrant foul; he was strong and powerful and talented, but a gentle giant.

No damn way.

I started to run at the referee when for the second time in less than two minutes my progress was stopped by a stiff right arm. This time it was Rahim himself.

"Leave it alone, Bobby."

"No way! Their lineman threw me to the ground," I said, nearly hyperventilating.

"Leave it. Can't change things now."

I calmed myself down and we huddled. Coach signaled in a short pass, and my gut wrenched. We were already down by ten, and now we had twenty-five yards to pick up. What was he thinking with this short stuff? No way were we going to break anything against these guys.

I wanted to go deep.

I looked at Coach, and decided to change the play. No one in the huddle would be any the wiser. I called for a long pass down the sideline, hoping to test their cornerback's speed against Rahim's. More often than not, Rahim would win those battles. In case he didn't, I could look short over the middle to Somers. In that case, Coach would get what he wanted anyway, no problem.

It was a win-win.

The ball was snapped and I took a deep drop, seven steps. Somers was open over the middle, about eight yards downfield.

I wanted more. Rahim was racing down the sideline, about even with their defensive back. I waited two extra seconds and threw it as deep as I could.

As soon as I threw it, I knew it was wrong.

Rahim didn't have the guy beat at all.

If it was catchable, it would be for either of them, and it could be my first interception of the year. I'd lost my cool, and it would cost me. Luckily, I overthrew both of them by a good five yards.

I sighed, relieved.

"Framingham!" Coach yelled from the sideline. "What the hell was that?" He signaled for a time-out, and violently motioned for me to come over. "What the hell, Framingham? You see something I don't see?"

"No, Coach." I took out my mouthpiece and waved it in the warm night breeze.

"So what were you thinking?"

"I wanted to test them deep."

"Why?" I could see the veins popping out from Coach's forehead.

"Because I was pissed off," I said.

Coach shook his head as if he'd never been more certain of anything in his life. "Unacceptable, Bobby. You don't cost this team a chance to win because you feel something. No damn way. Next time you do that, you're out of the game. Not to mention a thousand stadium steps a day for the following week."

"I'm sorry," I said, looking him directly in the eye.

I felt confident. I'd made a mistake, let a momentary emotion get the best of me, and I was taking responsibility.

Coach nodded at me, accepting my apology, before he turned away to tend to the game plan. I trotted back out to the field, confident that this new change of character would result in a win, and be the major story of the game.

It turned out I was half right. My change of attitude did help the team, and it was one story of the game.

Not the only story, however.

Some of the others involved a hard-nosed Durango team that overcame a bunch of early mistakes to take a fourth-quarter lead at 17–16. Our stellar defense really clamped down on their running game, keeping it in check. Mendez scored once and Rahim scored on a short touchdown pass in the right corner of the end zone that culminated a long, patient drive for us.

Rocky had kicked a thirty-yard field goal to give us a lead early in the fourth quarter.

With less than three minutes remaining, we were trying to run out the clock, driving toward midfield. The crowd was loud and I felt their energy in my hamstrings. On a third-and-long call from our own thirty-five-yard line, I got set in the pocket and saw their biggest defender, number 99, bearing down on me.

My feet froze.

I saw a quick flash of maroon jersey behind him, near the sideline. It was Mendez, and I quickly lobbed a pass toward him. It was a smart idea, but he didn't see me throw it.

One of their linebackers saw the gift pass and received it gracefully. Had he not inadvertently stepped out of bounds with his next step, he would have returned the interception for a score.

The crowd got quiet. It was the first real mistake I'd made all game, all year. I expected all hell to break loose from Coach and the other guys on the team. I ran to the sideline slowly, deliberately, petrified.

"That's just a miscommunication," Coach said, slapping me on the rear. "That happens when you don't get good protection. Head up, Bobby."

I looked around. Was he for real? I'd probably just cost the team the game, and I wasn't being screamed at? Who was this coach?

When I saw my teammates weren't cursing at me either, but were focused on the game, I bucked up and stopped thinking of myself.

La Habra got to our fifteen-yard line as time ran under thirty seconds. We were out of time-outs, so they let the clock run down to about five before bringing their kicker out. Basically, Roger Gordon was money.

I watched as Gordon lined himself up, talking to himself, settling himself down. I prepared myself for how I would feel after the kick, knowing he wouldn't miss, and that my senior season wouldn't end with us undefeated, as I'd hoped. It was prayer time.

The long snapper snapped the ball back and I watched as the holder received it cleanly and placed it under his finger at the correct angle. I watched Gordon stride toward the ball.

Then out of the corner of my eye, I saw a disturbance around the left side of the line of scrimmage.

I saw the maroon-and-gray jersey first, couldn't make out the 81 on the back, but knew it was Rahim.

He flew untouched past the right-side blocker and extended fully, aiming his hands not toward the ball exactly but toward where it would be a moment later. In the silence, I could almost hear the scrape of ball against bone.

The ball continued upward and I held my breath, wondering if it was possible that Rahim had blocked the kick but that it would still be good. I imagined Rahim's finger attached to the ball as it sailed through the uprights, but was relieved seconds later as the trajectory changed and the ball wobbled well short and to the right of the goalpost.

Sometimes you feel like you might explode out of your body. The power of your happiness overwhelms your body and can't be held by it, and you feel it rush out of you through your fingers, your hair, every part of you.

This was one of those moments.

The scream from our sideline was nearly deafening, and it was joined quickly by a roar from our home crowd that threatened to carry for miles. I rushed out to find Rahim, who was underneath a pile of our guys who were screaming and hollering and beating down with celebratory fists. I looked for other bodies to envelop, and found, first, Mendez. We tangled into each other and jumped up and down, ecstatic. Then I saw Austin. I lunged toward him.

"Careful of the ribs, dude!" he yelled.

I finally found Rahim, who was exhausted from the pileup and soaking from the Gatorade shower the guys had given him. "I owe you one!" I yelled as we hugged.

I was psyched up after the game, talking to reporters, when my mother and father found their way to me.

"Yahoo, Bobby Lee! Sensational!" my mother shouted, throwing her arms around me. I hugged her hard, laughing with giddiness into her shoulder.

"Thanks, Mom!" I yelled, over the blaring noise of the crowd around us. I looked to my father, who was standing by her side, smiling contentedly at me.

"Hey, Dad," I said, hugging him hard. He felt warm and wet.

He hugged me back for a moment before pulling away. "What a game! Other than the one play, you were perfect."

"Can you believe Rahim?" I said, pointing to where the other guys were hoisting him up and carrying him around the field.

"You almost lost it there. What you should have done," he said, "is tried a pump fake on him. If he bit, you could have gone right around him."

My father was a great guy, but he had lots of stupid ideas. He was wrong. No way could I have done that. I just stared at him.

"All's well that ends well," he said as he started walking toward the car. "See you back at the house." And with that he was off.

My mother turned around and offered a subtle, silent apology for my father—a shoulder bob and a certain way of creasing her eyes that says, *Don't Take It Personal, Bobby Lee. He's Just Like That.*

Carrie was there. She hated football but sometimes she came to my games. She came up behind me and placed her chin on my neck. "That was one of the finest basketball games I've ever seen," she said. I turned to her and smirked.

"Hockey," I corrected.

"Look, I may be white, but the name-calling is totally out of place," she said, kissing me on the cheek and heading out toward her car. *She's so weird. I love her.*

"What were you thinking when you threw the pick?" The usual suspect reporters had come to form their circle around me. I was a little relieved to see them flock to Rahim this time. But sure enough, they found me, too.

There were about seven of them looming in front of me, including Finch who was waving a tape recorder in my face along with the rest of them.

What kind of questions are these? What do you think I was thinking? What would you think if a six-foot-six mammoth in a helmet was running at you, full speed, with a look somewhere between homicidal and maniacal in his eye?

"I was thinking, 'Holy crap, I'm about to be mauled,'" I said, and the laughs came pouring out, as if from a comedy faucet.

That's me. Just turn my crank and I'll gush stupid jokes at you all night.

"Did you throw to the right place, and Mendez got messed up, or was it your fault?" asked a short guy, new to me.

"Just a miscommunication," I said, echoing Coach. "It happens sometimes." They all nodded, as if this answered, rather than restated, their question.

"Did their guy, Levy, get in your face today?" asked a tall, skinny guy, maybe fifty, who was standing to the right of Finch.

"I have no idea who that is," I answered.

He rifled through his notes. "Number fifty-five," he said. "Linebacker?"

"Well, I got knocked down a bunch, so probably," I said. "Mostly it was number ninety-nine. I saw his number a lot from the ground." A couple of them laughed.

The man smiled thinly. "I'm doing a feature article about Gus Levy. He's one of their linebackers, and he's Jewish."

I laughed, feeling a little high from the adrenaline still. "A Jew in Southern California? Stop the presses!" I said. A huge laugh.

I should do stand-up. Or more truthfully, when I'm punch-drunk on adrenaline and dealing with pesky reporters, I should do stand-up.

"A Jewish football player who's being recruited all over the country," the man said patiently, his thin smile barely remaining.

"Oh, okay," I answered. "Cool. But there are some Jewish players in the NFL. That quarterback for Houston. Sage Rosenfels? He's gay, isn't he?"

It took about two seconds for the sirens to start going off in my head.

I meant Jewish, of course, but I don't think in my whole life I'd had a conversation with anyone about Jewish athletes, let alone thought about it. Gay ones, though, I'd thought a lot about that. It just slipped out, and there was no way to slip it back in.

"Pardon me?" the older reporter said, his ears seeming to dance as they perked up.

"Jewish," I said. "Did I say? Wow. I don't know why that was in my . . ."

I looked at Finch. I didn't mean to, but subconsciously I thought of our interview and I just looked at him. He had this expression on his face, like he was deep in thought, and I wanted to yell out, *No! No! Stop thinking that.* But I was already looking strange enough to the group of reporters.

I looked away, and that's when I found myself, once again, staring deep into the eyes of the goateed stranger whom I'd seen after our first game, at Huntington Beach.

He had this glint in his eye that made me blush. He smiled big, a flawless row of white teeth showing, and I lost my train of thought completely.

"You think you have a shot at a perfect season?" said Finch, and I came to, thankful for the question.

"I think if we win all our games, we have a good shot," I said, and more laughs.

"You're Yogi Berra!" shouted one of the old-timers, a guy with chronic bad breath and even more chronic bad suits. He shouted as if he were threatening me, though in a happy sort of way.

Totally demented.

I smiled, fielded more inane questions, and headed to the showers.

I took my time showering and changing, and when I left the locker room, all my buddies were already gone. There was some party at Colby's, and I just didn't feel like dealing with it. I was glad to escape to my car, alone.

But once I got outside, I realized I wasn't quite by myself yet. There was Finch Gozman, standing alone under a streetlight in the parking lot, his head hung low.

He was standing right in my way, and I was like, great. There was no way I could get to my car without walking near him, unless I took some insane circular route that only a person with OCD would take.

So I exhaled, counted to ten in my head, and approached him.

"Hey, Finch," I said.

"Hey, Bobby Framingham," he answered, looking at his cell phone. He stared at it for a few seconds, shook his head, and put it in his pocket. He looked sad.

"You okay?"

He looked off in the distance. "Define *okay,*" he said.

Finch wasn't a friend, obviously, but I had sort of a soft spot for people like that, who didn't fit in. That's probably why Carrie was my—whatever she was. We stood silently under the streetlight for a few moments while I debated with myself whether I had enough energy to take on someone else's problems.

It surprised me a little that I was very okay with it. The game had left me in a pretty good mood, and Finch's issues seemed like a welcome break from my own.

"What happened?" I asked.

Finch looked into my eyes and it was like he was searching to see if it was okay to talk to me. Sometimes I was reminded that I was not just another guy to a lot of people at school. People, especially ones like Finch, looked up to me. He studied me for a while, like he was trying to psych out my motive, before he finally spoke.

"My mom, she just won't stop," he said.

I nodded.

"It's Friday night. And I didn't even go to the game for fun. I went because it's my job. She just picks and picks. 'Will you have enough time to study over the weekend? How do you expect to get into Stanford if you waste your time going to football games?'"

"Wow," I said.

"It's like, if I don't get into Stanford . . ." He closed his eyes and for a second I panicked because I thought he was going to cry.

But he didn't cry. He just looked beat-up, so I put my hand on his shoulder.

"There's just a lot of pressure," he said, regarding my hand as if I'd just put an exotic parrot on his shoulder.

"But you have, like, perfect grades, right?" I asked, removing my hand. "And you write for the school paper and your SATs are probably, like, insane."

He half smiled. "They're pretty good," he said. "But you never know with a place like Stanford. You never know."

"That's true," I said. "It sucks that your folks put all that pressure on you."

Finch sat down on the concrete, and for a moment I wondered if we were done. But I knew the right thing to do was sit down, too, so I did. We faced out toward the mostly empty parking lot, and it was sort of nice.

"You probably want to be out with your friends," he said.

I shook my head. I needed several hours to decompress after games. Guys like Austin and Dennis and Rahim always went out afterward, and I didn't get it.

"This is kinda nice," I said.

Finch smiled and turned a little red, and for just brief second I looked at him and realized that under the nerd he was not a terrible-looking guy. And then I blushed.

"So who cares?" I said. "So you don't get into Stanford and you go to another really good school. What's the big deal?"

He crossed his thin, slightly hairy legs Indian style. "I'm sure it seems stupid to you," he said. "But it's more than that. I'm just so tired of being me, you know?"

I shrugged. I didn't know. I mean, I had lots of stuff going on, but I never really felt like I didn't want to be me. I just sometimes wanted to be me with fewer problems.

"I just feel like I'm stuck being me," he said. "And I don't want to be."

I chuckled a little and shrugged again. "Come on, it's not that bad."

Finch turned to me, his face very serious.

"She checks my homework," he said.

I snorted. You know how some people snort when they laugh, and it's cute? This wasn't that. It was totally involuntary and real, because I had just played an exhausting football game, and I was secretly gay, and this nice, nerdy kid I'd known since we were like twelve had just told me that, at seventeen, his mom still checked his homework. The snort was about as appropriate an answer as I could come up with.

Finch frowned. "She does. She makes a photocopy of it, and marks my homework up with a red pen, and makes me redo it. Every night, I do my homework twice." He was gripping his knees with his hands.

I took a deep breath so that I didn't snort again. But this time I laughed. I wasn't trying to be mean, but I couldn't help laughing.

He frowned again and I could tell he was sorry he had confided in me.

"Thanks," he said, and he was about to stand up, so I put my hand on his shoulder and held him down.

"Finch," I said. "I'm sorry. I didn't mean to laugh."

"Yeah, well," he said.

"Oh, come on," I said. "We all have weird things. About a year ago my mom asked me if I had a playdate with Austin. And she totally didn't get it when I laughed at her. She's a mom. That's what they do."

Finch closed his eyes and I could see his cheeks puff out a little in amusement. But he composed himself.

"Come on, Finch. It's a little bit funny."

I watched the smile slowly pour over his face, and then he laughed, and I laughed, too, and there we were, the weird duo of Finch Gozman and Bobby Framingham, cracking up while sitting on the concrete of the parking lot on a late Friday night.

"Playdate," he repeated, laughing in that spastic way he has.

"Mommy, my homework's done," I said, doubling over.

When we finally stopped laughing, Finch looked like a different person.

"Thanks," he said. "You really cheered me up. I didn't think you'd be the kind of person who would waste your time with me."

"Nice self-esteem," I said, and he laughed, and I did, too, and it crossed my mind that Finch and I were sort of friends now. I imagined what Austin would think if he were watching this. His head would like totally explode.

I softly punched his shoulder as a good-bye and walked toward my car. It was dark now, the only illumination coming from sporadic streetlights, every ten yards or so.

I was thinking about after the game, how we'd gone nuts in the locker room, with music blaring and stuff flying around the room: water bottles, chairs . . . Coach was right there with us. It was so cool to see him joking around for once. He had gone up to Rahim at his locker and said, "Hey, Bell! I'm takin' you out of the starting offense. You're a full-time kick blocker now," and Rahim had looked at him like he was crazy for a second before realizing that this was Coach's idea of a funny joke.

"Good thing, 'cause I'm done with this offense anyway. Got a QB can't throw, and a coach can't even call plays right. Never givin' me the damn ball!" and the room was silent for a split second before everyone exploded with laughter.

It was the most unlikely sentence for Rahim to say, ever. I was walking in the dark parking lot, thinking about that, when I realized that I was going to tell Coach. What harm could it do? I mean, I'd be telling him the truth, right? And I knew he cared about me, so he'd try to help me out. I thought about timing, and decided to do it soon, maybe that coming week.

For once, elation overcame my fear, and I felt like sprinting to my car, and driving really fast.

Austin, Dennis, and Rahim were basically fine with me being gay. Why wouldn't Coach be fine, too? Telling the world, maybe that was a bit much, but Coach was smart and maybe he'd help me figure out the right thing to do.

Every squeak of my sneakers along the concrete parking lot told me that if I played this right, it was all going to be okay.

"I'll take Jewish ballplayers for one hundred, Alex . . ."

The voice came softly from my left, maybe ten feet away, so I turned slightly and saw that there was a figure leaning against the bed of a silver truck. I'd been daydreaming and hadn't seen anyone around, so hearing a voice startled me. There were fewer than thirty cars remaining in the entire parking lot. My car was ahead, about forty feet on the right.

I squinted, but couldn't quite see who it was.

"Hi?" I said tentatively, not breaking my pace.

The voice laughed, not a nasty laugh at all, more amused and playful. "Okay, here's your clue," he said. "He was a premiere southpaw before arthritis took him out of baseball in the mid-1960s."

"Huh?" I slowed my walking. He laughed again, and slowly his face came into view for me through the shadows.

It was the mystery reporter whom I'd first seen at our game at Huntington Beach, the dark-haired guy with the goatee.

I'd forgotten momentarily that I'd seen him again earlier that night. "Oh, it's you," I said, realizing that meant nothing. I might as well have said, *Oh, it's a homicidal maniac.*

"We're playing *Jeopardy!*," he advised me, smirking. "As I said, he was a great lefty before arthritis ended his baseball career. Mid-1960s."

I felt somewhat safe with this strange stranger. "Sandy Koufax?" I asked.

He buzzed at me. "Zzz. Wrong answer," he said.

"Huh?"

"The correct answer is, 'Who is Sandy Koufax?'"

I raised an eyebrow at this strange guy. "The correct question is who are you?"

"Who is Bryan Paulsen?" he said.

"What is nice to meet you," I responded, and I couldn't help but smile as my heart continued to pound.

"Sandy Koufax is a total jerk," he said. "I couldn't believe how he severed ties with the Dodgers just because of some rumors that he was gay."

Sirens again. "I don't know anything about that," I said, trying to figure out how to say good-bye to this weirdo and get to my car.

We stood in the silent parking lot, looking not quite at each other but sort of past, as if we weren't alone. It was only us, and that was a little close for comfort.

"It was on Outsports, the gay sports Web site," he said.

"What?" I couldn't look at him.

"You've never been there?"

"No!"

"Hey, don't get defensive, guy," he said, rubbing his elbow and approaching me. I shrank back. "I just wanted to talk to you, finally. It's always so hard when the other reporters are around, but you keep sending me the message, loud and clear."

All I wanted to do was sit down and digest what was whizzing around my head, way too quickly. "Sending you the message?"

"Yeah, you cruised me."

"I what you?"

"You . . . looked at me," he repeated. "The first time I saw you. Huntington Beach. And today again."

He's gay, and he thinks I am, too. Is this a good thing, or a bad thing? Is he setting me up? It's all too much.

"Dude, I didn't even see you today."

"No?" He grinned and raised an eyebrow.

"No. You're way off base. Sorry."

"Am I?"

"Yes," I said, trying to look him in the eye and flinching as soon as contact was made. I was suddenly chilly. "And now I have to go. Good-bye." I hurried to my car, nearly breaking into a sprint but avoiding that out of fear that he'd take it as a sure sign I was gay, and hiding.

"Hey, wait," he called, and I battled my urge to turn back and talk to him. I was hyperventilating. I fumbled for my car keys, hit the button on my keyless entry, and climbed into my car, slamming the outside world out as quickly as I could. I got out of there and didn't turn back, praying he wouldn't follow me.

"This is such an L.A. date. Drive separately, communicate by cell phone along the way, then play virtual games together. No need to physically interact at all. I love this," said Carrie.

We were entering the Laser Tag Amusement Center in Newport Beach, about a twenty-minute drive from Durango. It was a typically warm Saturday morning, a day after yet another win, 35–17 over Point Linda. The first thing I noticed as she got out of her car was that Carrie had dyed her hair flaming red.

The effect was that she now looked like a beautiful girl whose hair was on fire.

"I just can't believe you're into this," I said. I'd never thought of Carrie as the sporting type, but she had suggested it.

"I am SO into this," she said, using her best Valley Girl accent. "Are you kidding? A chance to shoot you repeatedly? Count me in!" Carrie scurried ahead of me, impatient to get going.

“Next thing you’ll be joining the NRA,” I said, following close behind her. “Carrie and guns together, just what the world needs.”

We were ushered into a dark area with neon signs and black lights, a type of waiting area where this geeky girl, really tall with braces and a face full of acne, her voice high-pitched like that of a squealing pig, explained to us what was about to happen.

“Now listen up!” she whined, every syllable stressed, raising the pitch at the end of every sentence, as if it were impossible to talk without the use of exclamation marks. “I’m going to tell you how this works, so listen very carefully!” She glanced at us expectantly. “Find a laser pack and strap it on! Then go and find the gun you want to use!”

She said this as if telling young people to grab guns was a time for great enthusiasm.

I glanced over at Carrie, who was looking at her with an intense seriousness that I have come to understand is a form of mockery, and suppressed a giggle.

Carrie raised her hand and didn’t wait to be called on before asking her question. “So should we get the guns first, or the laser pack?” she said, her eyes scrunched up like this was confusing.

The attendant girl was blessed with an obvious gift for enthusiasm, even in the face of people who ask really dumb questions. “Pack first!” she said, beaming.

“The pack, then?” Carrie asked, confused.

“Yes!”

“Should I just hold it in my outstretched hands, or strap it on?”

“Strap it! Strap it on!” She walked over to the packs, put one on, then drew the strap around her and buckled it. “See! It’s just like a seat belt in a car!”

“Oh!” said Carrie. And just like that, she dropped the dumb routine and followed instructions. Our attendant thought nothing of Carrie's quick change of character.

She must have seen weirdness all day long.

"Run through the maze and shoot anyone you see," she yelled.

I thought of Dennis, suddenly wishing he were here.

"Fifteen hits and you're out!"

Carrie looked down at her hands and began to count her fingers. She began to raise her hand, but decided not to. I could tell she was going to ask for more clarification.

"Other rules: You can't try to hide the lights on the front and back center of your laser pack, the part that registers when people have shot you! You can't lie down on the floor!" the girl yelled.

"Darn, a perfectly good filthy floor, and I can't even lie down on it," Carrie muttered.

"You have to leave the playing area immediately once you're out, following the neon exit signs," she screamed.

"Also a darn, sounds like a place where I could really settle down," I responded.

"When you're shot, your pack will vibrate and go dead for a few seconds. During this time, you can't shoot and no one can shoot you. So it's a good idea to run! Fast!"

I looked over at Carrie, who seemed very intent on all the information, a girl on a mission. "Okay, guys," the girl said, at the peak of her manic enthusiasm. "Are you ready! Go go go!" She flung open the black door leading to the maze and shouted after us that we had two minutes to find a place to hide.

That's basically what it is, I realized. Hide-and-go-seek for the over-six crowd.

It was a three-story maze. I discovered this as I ran toward the other end of the maze, where I encountered first stairs leading up, and then stairs leading down. Seeing metal grating in the ceiling, I headed down, figuring it would be easier to not have to worry about being shot from a floor below. Blaring guitars seared into my brain as loud rock music pounded through the corridors, Kelly Clarkson screaming that she would never believe some guy, never again. My thought was to hunker down low, crouch, make myself small, and stay where I was. The more you moved, the more likely you were to get shot. It didn't take a brain surgeon to figure that one out.

After a few minutes I began to hear screaming and feet scampering above me. I looked up and watched people sprint across the floor above me, scampering legs and flashing laser packs. One kid stopped and stood still right above me. I watched as he carefully looked both ways and felt the same adrenaline I feel on the football field.

I quietly, precisely, raised my gun and shot his pack. Bull's-eye.

I watched from below as he looked around, no clue what hit him. He didn't look down, but hurried off, in search of a target. All seemed quiet on my level. Of the ten or so of us, I wondered if I was the only one in the basement.

Then I felt a buzzing around my midsection, and my first thought was that I'd put my cell phone on vibrate. Then I realized I'd been hit, and I looked around, but saw no one. My laser pack stopped shaking after a few seconds, the lights on it died, and when I picked up my gun and fired it, nothing happened. A few seconds later the pack lit up again as if someone had recharged the battery, but only for a second before I was once again shaking.

"What the hell?" I said, and then I heard laughter, from above and behind me. I turned around and looked up and there was some kid, maybe twelve, with his gun pointed down at me through the grating.

No way was he going to hit me again.

I jumped up and moved positions, raised my gun, and was about to shoot him when once again I shook. Anger flooded through my veins, and I could feel my head pounding. I hated losing.

The kid took off running when he saw me move toward him.

It reminded me of my tenth birthday party. My parents rented out a gym and we played dodgeball, the sport I lived for at the time, all day. I was feeling invincible until my friends ganged up on me. They waited until I threw the last red ball on my side, and then I noticed that five of them, all on the other side of the middle line, were holding onto red balls and smirking at me. They all attacked at once, hurling the balls at me. The plastic orbs collided with each other and ricocheted into different parts of my body—one got me in the nose, one in the chest—and I fell under the impact of them. My so-called friends then crossed the center line, against the rules, gathered the balls, and proceeded to pummel me. My fists clenched with rage as I lay on the ground. My eyes welled up, my head pulsed and I screamed at them to stop. I ran to the bathroom and locked myself in, and didn't come out for hours.

So as I felt myself hit for the third time in less than thirty seconds, I felt the same emotions simmer and begin to rise to the surface. This time I turned and saw it was Carrie, behind me, grinning, the bitch. She looked a little demented with the laser pack on, very intense.

"Dead meat," she said, and then she turned, grabbed her gun in both hands, and hustled out of the area. At that moment she became the only possible target.

I ran after her, actually angry. She could hear me running right behind her, and I could see her slowing and I knew what she was going to do. I beat her to the punch. She flung around at me, wildly, and tried to aim her gun, but I was too quick for her. I grabbed it from her hands and tossed it aside, and proceeded to shoot her, point-blank, in the gut.

It felt good.

"Jerk," she said. She stormed past me and picked up the gun. The bravado was in my chest now, the strange pride that I could feel in my lungs, coupled with an anger that at once enveloped and embarrassed me.

"You shot me, I shot you back."

"No. I shot you, you chased me and threw my gun, and shot me. Bullshit," she said, bending down and picking up her gun. A guy, maybe fourteen, with a Mohawk appeared in the doorway, and quickly set our packs ablazing.

"Fuck you!" we both screamed at him, and he saw that there was something beyond a game going on and booked it out of there. Carrie's face was red, and I could feel the same heat rising in me.

We stared each other down. This was a new thing for us; we never raised our voices with each other. There was never any reason. Carrie picked up her gun, placed it against my rib cage, and pulled the trigger.

I felt the pack and its buzz, again, and it sent unusual shock waves through me, into my pelvis. I waited a few seconds and fired back, and we stood there, taking turns shaking.

Finally Carrie laughed. "What's wrong with us?" she said. I wasn't quite ready to laugh. My gut was in knots and a primal roar far beyond the game was welling up within my belly. "Maybe we should just get it over with and kiss," she said. "Make love, not war." She was leering at me. She didn't get it, didn't see that something had broken in me in the midst of a stupid game.

I just stood there, looking at her.

For a moment I was lost in thought, and then I saw Carrie's lips, a dark shade of red, and plump like overripe fruit, coming toward me. She pressed her lips against mine.

I searched myself—for arousal, for anything good, for proof that

I'd made all this gay stuff up—and for a moment I felt a pressure on my upper groin but not the kind I'd expected. I pulled away and looked down, and saw it was her pack pressing awkwardly into mine.

We stood there, connected by our packs and staring at each other. I imagined Carrie standing there topless, and shivered at the thought, her breasts like alien bumps on her chest where no bumps should be. A guy about our age ran by the corridor we were in and shot Carrie in the back. She laughed, softly, her eyes huge orbs of innocence and wonder, and I loved her at that moment, not sensually but emotionally, loved her and wanted to protect her from bad things. *From me.*

Our midsections shook together.

"See what you do to me?" she said, raising one eyebrow, and she tilted her head slightly once again, made her eyes into slits, and moved her overripe lips to mine.

I jumped back.

It was involuntary. I'd meant to stay with it, but whatever power deep within me that I couldn't control pushed a button and I pulled away from her before she could get me.

Carrie seemed to galvanize at that moment, her eyes registering comic disbelief and a level of injury I'd never seen before. She opened her mouth to speak, but could say nothing. She looked away, up at the ceiling, as if the answer were there, and then back to me. She shook her head in disbelief and sighed in a manner I hoped never again to hear, ever, in my life. A sigh of resignation and pent-up rage, if you can believe one might sigh with rage. She marched right past me. I stood still, facing away from her, unsure how to help. Then my pack began buzzing again. No one was above me or in front of me.

I'd been shot in the back, and when I turned around, no one was there.

I stood there for a few moments, paralyzed and not knowing what to do.

Then it hit me: *Tell her.*

The thing to do was to find the exit, and find Carrie, who had probably stormed off. I'd talk to her, tell her the secret that might hurt her, but at least would explain why I didn't want to kiss.

A sign pointed me toward the exit, and I headed that way, my heart beating very fast. It would all be okay once I told her. I hadn't done anything wrong.

After a few minutes of winding through dark hallways, I found the exit, pushed open the heavy black door, and was back in the lobby, the waiting area. I was alone, no Carrie.

The geeky girl was sitting on a bench, reading a magazine.

"Did you just see a girl with flaming red hair—"

"She just left," she said.

I ran out to the parking lot just in time to see Carrie's red Jetta peel away.

"You see what Vince Young does? He keeps his options open," my father said to me as we watched a game one Sunday in early October. We were sitting on the couch in the living room. He reclined, I sat forward, wolfing down chips from an open bag and dipping them into an open container of salsa. "If no one's open, he's not afraid to run. That's what you need to do."

"Sure, Dad. Good idea." I wiped salsa off my chin.

My father acted as if I'd never watched a pro football game before, let alone played quarterback.

He never had; he'd played baseball in school, yet somehow he was the football expert.

"I never see you scramble," he continued as we watched a replay of Young, the Tennessee Titans quarterback, running for a first down.

There was, of course, a reason for this. I was a total drop-back passer. I was slow as molasses and I had a rocket of an arm. He should have been comparing me to Peyton Manning, not Vince Young.

It was one of those fall Sundays that I loved so much. Sometimes the best thing was just to relax, hang out, not have anything expected of you. It was so rare for me, especially in the fall. We were now 4–0, having beaten Los Altos handily, 34–10. I'd played well, three touchdown passes, two to Rahim. My folks showed up, which was nice. After the game, Bryan had once again been there, and this time I just smiled politely. I avoided more weirdness by leaving with Rahim and Austin, going to a party even though I didn't really want to go.

I'd almost told Coach on Wednesday. I went to his office and sat down, but all that came out of my mouth was more stuff about my parents. It was shameful, getting Coach to feel sorry for me and not telling him what was really up.

Yesterday, as I was doing homework, a call came in. It was an assistant coach from Stanford, telling me that he wanted me to visit Palo Alto to talk about the program. My spine tingled, but I acted all calm and collected and told him that I would, and that I would be taking trips to visit schools when the season was over. When I told Dad, I thought he'd go nuts, but instead he sort of smiled about it, didn't get up at all. *Hello? The one thing you seem to care about when it comes to me? Can I get a reaction? My dad is so weird.*

As we watched the late game, Tennessee at San Diego, my father, who used to scream at the television through a game, kept dozing off. He'd be awake for a while, make his commentary, definitive statements no one should ever challenge about who the best running back in the game was, and then suddenly I'd hear snoring. My father never used to sleep through games. I didn't say anything about it when he'd wake up and look around for a moment, and then close his eyes again.

My father nodded off and I watched Young in the midst of a pretty impressive drive against the Chargers. I was studying his footwork in the pocket when the doorbell rang. Mom was out. I paused for a moment to watch Young throw an incomplete pass before I hurried to the door.

Standing there, wearing an ugly purple windbreaker and a black fanny pack, something that hasn't been in style in our lifetime probably, was Finch Gozman.

"Hey," I said, less than thrilled. The talk we'd had two weeks earlier had been nice, but were we buddies now? We'd talked maybe twice since then, just "hey, how are you?" kind of stuff in the hallways at school. Couldn't we just be people who talked in a parking lot after a game once and leave it at that?

"Hey, Bobby Framingham," he said, a wide smile on his face. "Can I borrow you for a few minutes?"

Borrow me? Why couldn't he just talk like a normal human being? Who went to someone's house and borrowed the person who lived there?

Finch Gozman, apparently.

"Well, I'm kind of busy with my father," I said. "Watching a game. Actually I'm watching and he's asleep."

"Well, if he's in there, maybe we'd better talk out here."

I sighed. I hadn't agreed to talk to him, and now here I was, backed into a corner. "Fine," I said.

We walked out to the huge oak tree at the foot of our front yard. When I was a kid, I sometimes used to try to climb up and sit on a branch. I broke several branches that way. We stood beneath it, and I leaned on it as Finch paced beside me.

"Stanford called," I told him.

He adjusted his fanny pack, fumbled through it, before turning and looking at me and smiling. "Wow! How excellent. Are you going to sign with them?"

"No offer was made, Finch. I'm going to wait until December for all of that."

"Wow. I doubt I'll get in. Mrs. Markowitz said I need to write something great, something that'll get me noticed." He rubbed his neck.

"You'll get in," I said.

"Well, we'll see," he said.

And we stood there, awkwardly silent.

"I wanted to thank you for last weekend, listening to me whine."

I laughed. "You weren't whining. Well, not much, anyway," I said. "No problem."

"Thanks," he said, and there it was, the silence again. I looked at Finch and wondered if all he wanted was a random conversation with me.

"The thing is," Finch said, "I kind of have to ask you a question."

"Shoot." I leaned against the tree.

"Remember our interview? I've really been thinking about it a lot. And there's this one thing that I don't know how to . . . I don't know. What I'm trying to say is . . . are you gay? If you're not, please don't hit me."

He sort of jumped back, as if he were afraid of me.

I kept still.

Inside, I felt the pulsing of my heart, the wheezing of air through my lungs. I said nothing. A flurry of thoughts flooded my head. I thought of Dr. Blassingame: *If you can't change something, you have two choices: you can accept it, or you can deny it.*

I couldn't change being gay. And now I couldn't change the fact that Finch knew. No one would ask you something like that unless they were pretty sure about it. I pictured a football field, and saw Finch there with me, in the backfield. He was already there. Would I rather have him on my team, blocking for me, or the opposing team, chasing me down? I studied him silently.

"I didn't come here to cause you trouble, Bobby Framingham. You know I consider you a friend."

I continued to observe him, thinking back to the time in ninth grade when Dennis pinned a sign on Finch's back that said I'M A FAG. The popular jocks were always picking on him. It was right after history class with Dr. Blassingame and everyone was laughing and pointing at Finch, and I could see the pain on his face. He didn't know what was going on. When none of my friends were looking, I tapped Finch on the shoulder, peeled the sign off his back, and handed it to him. He turned bright red. I said, "People are stupid," and walked away.

"Bobby?"

"Yes." I scraped at the bark of the oak tree with my middle finger. I listened to the sounds around me. Silence could sometimes be so loud. The wind hissing through the rustling trees, some chirping birds, I almost never heard any of this, because I didn't listen.

"So I'm sorry to ask you a personal question, but are you? Gay?"

I looked around to make sure my father wasn't standing there. "I just said yes."

"Oh," Finch said, and then his eyes lit up. "Wow."

"Shut up," I said, miserable.

I sat on the dirt under the tree and rested my face in my hands. Finch stood above me, and it was like this major power shift.

Finch smiled and knelt over me. "That's okay," he said. "I'm cool with that."

I looked up at him, surprised, but not shocked. "Really?"

"Sure." He stood up and looked at the branch about two feet

above him. He sort of jumped up, trying to touch it, but never actually left the ground, as if his feet were glued to the dirt underneath him. I can touch the branch. He didn't get close.

"Thanks, Finch. It's new; I'm just figuring it all out." I found a twig and began tracing a pattern in the dirt, a circle. Was Finch becoming someone I could talk to?

"I think it's an amazing story."

I looked up at him in amazement, and shook my head, hard. "No. No no no."

"Think about it Bobby. I did some research. Did you know that there's not a single openly gay athlete in any of the four major sports? You could be the first! That's incredible, that's like, Jackie Robinson incredible. Don't you see that?"

I stood back up and began to pace. "No, Finch. I'm not ready for that at all."

"But—"

"No! I'm serious Finch. We're four-and-oh, and I got a call from Stanford. This is my dream. You really think I want to ruin that?"

"How would you ruin it?" he asked.

Now I was pacing fervently in front of the oak tree, and he was standing still, watching me like he was watching a tennis match. "I can't do that now. If Coach found out, I have no idea how he'd react."

"Coach Castle? He loves you," he said.

I registered that. "Yeah, well."

"I know it sounds difficult, but I think you're missing out on a big part of it."

"What?" I stopped in front of Finch, hoping that he had some magic words for me that would make it all better.

"You'd make a difference in a lot of people's lives. There are so many people out there who think all gays are wimps or something, and you're not a wimp. You're, like, the coolest guy in our school."

I blushed. Actually, I hadn't really thought about that before. *How can who I want to sleep with and love have such an effect on other people?*

It seemed so dumb, but it made a lot of sense when he put it that way.

"Finch?"

"Yeah."

"Thanks. You're a friend and I appreciate that."

He smiled and looked down, embarrassed. "Thanks, Bobby Framingham."

"Maybe I can make a difference in people's lives. I don't know. I'm not ready."

"I thought that might be the case," he said. "It's too bad, 'cause it's a great story. I've been thinking about it and researching it for a few days now."

"So you knew?"

Finch laughed. "Well, Bobby Framingham, if you don't want people to know, you'd better tell those friends of yours not to make it so obvious. It wasn't just what they said, it was how they acted. Of course I knew."

"Damn. I'm gonna kill Dennis."

"That would make the world a better place," Finch said. "Sorry, just kidding. I know he's your friend."

I laughed. "No, you're right." I looked back at the house, turning away from Finch. "Are you?"

"Am I what?"

"Gay?" I turned back and looked at Finch.

He looked up at the sky. "There was a time when I thought I was, but nah, I don't think so. I like girls too much."

I wasn't sure if I was disappointed or relieved. "Do me a favor, Finch?"

"Sure. Anything, Bobby."

"Please don't tell anyone. I'll make you a deal. If and when I'm ready to come out publicly, no matter when or where I am, I'll call you and let you do the story."

His eyes registered this and I imagined the victory parade in his brain. Score one for Finch Gozman. "Thanks! You think you could time it before my application to Stanford is due?"

I looked at him like he was crazy, and then he laughed.

"Just joshin' ya," he said.

"Yeah, that's funny," I said. "Anyhow, I gotta go back to my dad."

"Sure, Bobby. Take care of yourself. If you ever need to talk . . ." I nodded and he got in his green Nissan. He turned on the ignition and drove away, the radio blaring. I watched as his car disappeared, thankful that he wasn't a jerk.

On Wednesday afternoon during my free period, I decided to do it. My secret was coming out, little by little, and I thought about how Coach would feel if I didn't tell him.

He'd be hurt, and I didn't want to hurt him.

I walked to Coach's office with long, self-assured strides, the theme from that Eminem movie playing in my head. I imagined telling Carrie that. She'd have a heart attack. I wasn't a rap kind of guy, and she really hated Eminem.

But I had to stop worrying about Carrie's reaction to stuff. She wasn't talking to me, wouldn't even look at me. People kept on walking up to me and asking if we broke up.

I just shrugged.

I'd seen Carrie in school just once since the laser-tag disaster, and she'd ignored me. I tried to approach her in the cafeteria, but she was with friends, and they'd all glared at me, while she put her head down in a very deliberate way. I pivoted quickly and walked away. Impulse. Very much like being in the pocket when I didn't see or hear anything behind me but instinctively knew to get rid of the ball.

The gymnasium was loud and busy and I saluted half a dozen buddies who were there playing a pickup game of basketball, before heading down the hallway to Coach's office.

Coach was in the middle of scripting plays on his computer. I could tell, because I know how he spreads everything out all over his desk when he does that—stats, scouting reports, play diagrams—and it made me think that maybe I should wait. The game against Laguna Hills was just two days away, and even if that was one we'd probably win, I'd hate to screw things up. But then I thought, if not now, when?

Is there ever a good time for a personal issue when you're on a team?

I stuck my head into his office and quietly knocked on the door.

"Is this important?" Coach asked, looking up slightly.

"I don't know," I said.

Coach looked up from the computer. "Well, either it is or it isn't. Come on in, Framingham."

I quietly sat down across from him and leaned forward, resting my elbows on my knees and folding my hands under my chin as if to pray. On the desk in front of me were piles of articles chronicling the team's victory over Los Altos. One had a picture of me dropping back to pass. I hadn't seen that one. There was also a Cincinnati Bengals schedule, a testament to Coach's fixation with the team he once played for. He was nothing if not loyal, and the guys gave him crap for it.

"Life is weird," I said, after a short silence. Coach raised an eyebrow.

"Uh-oh, looks like someone's been hitting the philosophy textbook a little hard again," he said.

I laughed and rolled my eyes. "Sorry," I said. "I think too much."

Coach turned to face me, giving me his full attention. He smiled. "What's on your mind, Bobby?"

"I'm having dreams about men." It had come blurting out easier than I'd thought, as if it had been hanging on the tip of my tongue. I'd figured it had been sort of stuck in the throat somewhere, figured it would take a long time, lots of stalling, but here I was, and my secret had popped out with very little prodding.

Coach remained expressionless, adjusted himself in his seat, and kept his eyes focused on me.

"What kind of dreams?"

"You know," I said.

He adjusted again. "Have you acted on these dreams?" There was an urgency in his voice that scared me.

"No."

"Good," Coach said, clenching his hands together. "I don't think you should."

"Really?"

"Yes, really," Coach said forcefully. "Look. Thinking things is one thing, acting is another. That's not a good lifestyle, Bobby. Maybe you're a little confused right now, but that won't work for you, you're not the right kind of guy to do that."

"So what do I do?"

"Ignore it, Bobby. Look. What do you do when you go up to the line of scrimmage and you don't like what you see in the defensive backfield?"

"I call an audible."

"Exactly. Do that here. This is a bad thing goin' on in the backfield." He laughed, a strange, weak laugh. "You don't like what you see, change it. You're not a homosexual, Bobby. I know you. Just ignore those thoughts and get some new ones. What about Carrie?"

"She's great."

"Well, great. There you go."

"But—"

"No buts . . ." said Coach. "Pun intended." He laughed, and I just stared at him. "Bobby, how many gay quarterbacks do you see in the NFL?"

"None."

"Exactly. And another thing. Don't tell people. These are private things, Bobby. Do I tell you about what I do in bed with Mrs. Castle?"

I blushed. "No . . ."

"Well, there you go. Now, what else can I do for you?"

The conversation had not gone the way I had wanted it to. I wasn't sure how it was supposed to go, but now I felt worse.

I was pretty sure that Coach was wrong about this, that it wasn't the same as him telling me about having sex with his wife. Of course that was inappropriate. But he was asking me to lie.

Isn't that different?

I wished I could rewind the clock, back to the second before I entered Coach Castle's office, and call an audible there.

Later in practice, I screwed up my progressions as we were practicing a new play in tier formation. Rahim was covered, and instead of looking to my secondary target, Austin, who was playing again, I went directly to Somers, who was supposed to be a decoy on the play. This would normally have been a time for Coach to go ballistic on me—he'd done it hundreds of times before. But instead, he was quiet on the sideline. He looked down at his notepad, made a mark, and said, "You'll get it next time," without looking up. The entire offensive line did a double take. I just shrugged it off and headed back into the huddle.

After a few more plays, we took a water break. On the sideline, Austin ran up to me and punched my shoulder. "Something's up," he said.

"What do you mean?"

Austin crooked his head at me and took a quick squirt of water from a squeeze bottle. "You look weird today."

"Thanks. Thanks a lot, dude."

"No, I mean weirder than you usually look. Usually you're just plain ugly, but today you look, I dunno, ugly and weird, too. What up?"

I looked around, saw that Coach was busy working with our defensive line. "I told him," I said, looking away.

"Who?" Austin raised his voice.

"Coach."

"Coach?" he said, laughing. "You crazy? You have to be crazy if you think that's a good idea."

I took a squirt of water and looked at him. Austin shook his head.

"Man, you are crazy. You tell your friends, that's one thing. We're young and we understand this shit. You can't be telling Coach, he'll probably drop you off the team. Damn. No wonder he didn't yell at you." And with that, Austin put his helmet back on and ran back onto the field. I watched him, the way his upper body barely moved, how he carried all his weight so effortlessly just with his legs. For a moment he looked so different to me, foreign.

This was my best friend of the past six years, and as he ran away from me it made me think how random our friendship was. What did we even have in common? History, maybe? I watched him run and imagined him continuing to run, farther from me, getting smaller and smaller, until he was just a useless speck on the horizon.

And the anger built up in my veins like venom, and I grabbed my helmet and stormed back onto the field, hoping to have a chance to throw a pass to Austin that would sever him at the neck.

I arrived in the locker room for my usual pregame one-on-one with Coach, but his door was closed. So I waited outside of his office for a few minutes. Minutes passed. Other players started to arrive and change. No Coach.

After about twenty-five minutes, an assistant defensive coach came out of Coach's office. I started to stride toward it, but the guy closed the door behind him.

"Castle can't meet with you today," he said.

I nodded, wondering if he knew, if Coach was telling people. I felt like I'd been punched in the gut. Our meetings were a pregame tradition. An hour before every game I'd ever started, he and I would sit and chat for about ten minutes. We'd go over the game plan, talk about the opposing defense, sometimes even joke around.

So I walked over to my locker and began to change into my uniform, feeling vacant inside. I tried to reason with myself. Maybe he was focused on the defense. Perhaps because Laguna Hills was not supposed to be a real challenge for us, Coach figured he didn't need to focus on me.

Yeah, right, the other part of my brain said. We hadn't spoken one-on-one since our conversation two days earlier. That's what this was about.

The team was busy getting rowdy, which is what we did before games. Rahim was leading our breakdown, Rocky was breakdancing, and everybody was hooting and carrying on. I was, too, except it didn't feel the same. It was like the shouts were coming out of my mouth, but they weren't connected to me.

I looked over to Austin, but he was joking around with Dennis and I didn't have the energy to deal with Dennis right now. So I sat by my locker and tried to get my head in the game.

As we took the field in front of our home crowd, I felt totally unprepared, and scared. I stood on the sidelines, adjusting my helmet strap, and felt like I wasn't quite there, like the boisterous crowd around me was an illusion.

I walked over to the stands to give my mom and dad a hug. My mom grasped me and said, "Give 'em hell, Bobby Lee."

My dad hugged me, but it felt like he wasn't paying attention. When I pulled away, I saw his eyes looked sort of hollow and unlike him.

"I'm thinking five touchdown passes," I said, because that's the kind of thing my dad likes to hear from me before games. But he didn't say anything back, he nodded and smiled a weak smile and I wanted to say, *Dad, snap out of it! What's wrong with you?*

I mean, sometimes people got busy and preoccupied. Sometimes they were really tired. Did that mean they got to stop paying attention to the things that mattered to *you*?

I turned and trotted back toward my teammates.

It's all wrong. The game is wrong. My coach, teammates, friends, family, everything is wrong.

As I ran across the field, I shivered and felt tingles along my sides, like an iceberg had formed there, on the inside. No one could touch me.

The first play was supposed to be a deep pass, and I knew Rahim was too fast for any of their cornerbacks. I took the liberty of waiting an extra second for him to get a step on the defender, and just as I cocked my shoulder to throw, I was blindsided. A flying shoulder, with the weight of a two-hundred-pound linebacker behind it, pummeled me directly in the small of my back. The ball flew out of my hand and I hit the turf, face mask first. My neck absorbed some of the shock of the surprise hit, and I felt a quick jolt down my spine.

I stayed down, even as I heard the crowd roar in a way that made me guess that we'd recovered. I wondered if, when I moved, something would begin to pulse along my spinal cord. I tightened my stomach, frightened. But when I sat up, there was nothing, just a dull pain in my back where the guy had hit me. I stood up, wiped dirt and grass off my jersey, and headed back to the huddle. We had recovered the football. In the huddle, Rahim grabbed a handful of turf out of the top of my face mask. "Thanks," I said. He nodded and cuffed me on the shoulder.

We were a little off, or at least I was. At halftime we went into the locker room down by a touchdown to an inferior team, and Coach was savage in his pep talk.

"I don't know what's going on out there. We're in the hunt for a state championship," he said, looking right past me and frowning, "and you guys are letting a lot of meaningless shit get in your way. It's unprofessional. You can't do that, you're letting everyone down when you do that."

I knew his comments were directed at me, but he wasn't making eye contact. I felt the block of ice shift in my stomach and reverberate into my throat, chilling me and making me wheeze.

He went on to attack our defense. I shut my eyes and tried to will myself to be more intense, more focused, but it just wasn't working. Something was off.

The universe had taken some strange turn and I could sense it in my bones. If something didn't change, we were going to lose the game to Laguna Hills, a not-so-great team, on our home field.

As Coach continued his rant, the door leading from the tunnel to the locker room opened and Principal Morris stepped in. Coach stopped speaking and looked at him. Morris surveyed the room and sighed, heavily, something weighing on him. His eyes darted from player to player until they settled on me.

"Bobby Framingham," he said.

Was he going to yell at me, too? Was it against the law to have an off day? And then, as I looked at him closely and saw the pain on his face, I realized, with horror, what was about to happen. The word had gotten around.

He is going to humiliate me. He's going to shame me in front of my teammates. He is going to kick me off of the team, here, at halftime.

"Come with me please, Bobby," he said. I felt my lungs sear with rage.

"No," I said. "Just say it. Say it here. I don't care, just get it over with." There were some surprised murmurs throughout the room, and the boiling blood raced to the edges of my face. "Shut up," I yelled.

He exhaled and looked at Coach. Coach shrugged. Morris looked back at me. "You need to come with me, Bobby," he said. "It's your father."

The emergency-room waiting area was too bright. Everything was so shiny, from the bright yellow vinyl-covered couches to the TV, which was playing some stupid dating show.

Who thought to put fluorescent lighting in a waiting room? It gave the room a false cheeriness, bright and cold like a fake smile. Nobody stood in a hospital waiting room feeling cheery. They should've just made it real dim and gloomy—the lighting, the furniture. That way you'd feel comfortable in your misery. My head pulsed, a nasty pain behind my eyes. I couldn't get my head around it. My dad. Something was wrong with him.

Standing in a waiting room was never fun, but doing it on a Friday night in a football uniform was worse. I wasn't so selfish that I wanted to leave and play football, but it made me nervous, thinking that our perfect season was on the line and we might lose because

I wasn't there. I wondered which would be worse—losing, or them winning without me—and that thought made me feel awful.

My mother was sitting up very straight, her eyes not really focused on anything. Every time I looked at her I felt pressure in my chest, like a balloon expanding and ready to pop. I paced and sat, sat and paced. Sitting was hard, when you were waiting for news about your dad, who'd just fainted at your football game.

My father had fainted on the sidelines, and was out for about a minute. My mom called 911. Some other parents offered to help and sat with my mom, who was freaked. When Dad sort of came to, he was completely disoriented. They waited for the ambulance, and once it arrived, they had Principal Morris get me.

"How're you holding up, Bobby Lee?" my mother asked me, squeezing my hand as I sat down beside her. I stroked her arm.

"Okay," I said, my eyes on the television.

"He's going to be fine," she said, and I nodded, translating in my head from mom-speak to what was real. I had no idea, and I had the feeling she didn't either.

"He's just been so tired, and I couldn't get him to go to the doctor. Now we'll know why, and then we can fix it," she said, and I knew she was basically talking to herself. I nodded and gripped my mom's hand.

We sat in silence for a few moments.

"Mom?"

"What, honey?"

"Am I an awful person?"

She rubbed my arm. "You're one of the best people I know. Why would you ask that?"

"He hasn't been well, has he?" I asked.

She paused for a moment. "No, he hasn't," she said.

“I didn’t notice,” I said. “That makes me a bad person.”

My mother hugged me tight. “We didn’t want to worry you. You’re very preoccupied and you have every right to be,” she said.

I felt my jaw heat up. *They don’t want to worry me? How could they keep something this important from me?*

“We didn’t really know that much,” she said, as if reading my mind. She reached up and stroked the back of my neck. “If he’d have gone to the doctor and there was something to know, I would have told you. We would have.”

“Huh,” I said, trying to take this all in and wondering how I could be so clueless.

“Don’t ever think you’re a bad person,” she said. “Your father and I can’t believe how well you turned out.”

She kissed me hard on the head and I smiled as she mashed my face into her shoulder. “Especially given the crazy parents you have.”

I didn’t want to ever let go. My mom was one of those totally normal people who talked about how zany she was all the time. I usually got irked when she did that, but right then, I just wanted to hold on forever and never pull my face away.

At ten-fifteen, an hour and a half into our stay at Durango Medical Center, a doctor came out. My mother stood up, so I did, too.

“He’s alert and he’ll be fine to sleep at home tonight,” the doctor said, and my mother exhaled deeply. I shut my eyes and thanked God. “You can see him in a moment.”

“Do we know what this is? He hasn’t been right for months,” my mother said.

“We ran a whole battery of tests,” the doctor said. “He fainted because his blood pressure is so low. Why that happened we don’t know. Some people just run low.”

"He's been so tired," my mother repeated. "Could that be related?"

The doctor smiled. "Most definitely. We're giving him fluids by IV right now, and we'll want him to rest for a bit, but there's no reason he can't go home tonight."

The tears streamed down my mother's face, and I could feel the sense of relief in her body, could feel it in my shoulders and chest. I allowed myself to breathe, and it felt good. Good like it hadn't felt in a long time.

My dad was going to be okay.

17

I was in bed, studying calculus, when my dad appeared in my doorway, wearing a Dodgers cap, an old ragged-looking tan baseball glove hanging off his left hand.

"Knock, knock," he said.

It was like looking at a stranger. I hadn't seen my dad with a baseball glove in years, and he was smiling, full of life. I hadn't seen that in a while either.

"Hey," I said, sitting up.

"You up for a catch with your old man?" he asked.

It didn't matter that I was still sore from the game against Laguna Hills, two days earlier. Was I up for a catch with my father? Nothing could have sounded better.

As I rifled through my closet, looking for my own glove, I could hear my dad snapping his mitt repeatedly.

"Still nice and broken in," he muttered.

"I don't think 'broken in' goes away, Dad," I said. A beat-up purple Frisbee, a jump rope I hadn't used since I was a freshman, a red dodgeball. I flung these things aside as I dug through my sporting equipment. I couldn't remember the last time I'd used my baseball glove. My dad and I used to throw the ball around, but that was like eighth grade, maybe. Maybe once with Austin for kicks, a couple years back.

Finally I saw the black leather finger of it and pulled it out. A dingy-looking baseball dropped and rolled onto the floor. It must have been sitting inside the webbing for years. I picked it up and rubbed the palm, knelt down, and grabbed the baseball.

"You ready?" I asked, and my dad smiled, almost euphoric.

He'd been a different man since we'd gotten back from the hospital two days earlier. His eyes looked different, more like his old eyes, full of life again, and he'd gone out for a long walk the day before, Saturday, around the subdivision. He never did that.

"Is this bad for your throwing arm?" he asked as we got outside and walked to opposite ends of the front yard.

"I won't throw that hard," I said. "Don't worry."

He dropped his mitt in front of him and did windmills with his arms, which is what he always used to do when we played catch. When I was a kid, we did it every weekend before I got into football.

I watched him as he warmed up and I could see that there were changes to his body, recent changes. His arms and legs were thinner, and he had developed a little paunch in his gut, something he didn't used to have. And the upper-body tone that he used to be so proud of was all but gone. His face was thinner, too. But then again, he was like almost fifty, so what do you expect? He bent over and picked up his glove, put his hand inside it, and slapped the glove against his leg. "Let's do this," he said.

It felt good, palming the baseball for the first time in a while. I slowly wound up and threw it to my father. The ball whistled through the air and hit his glove with a satisfying *pop*. I'd forgotten how much I used to love that sound.

My father's eyes bulged and he dropped the glove off his hand with the ball still in the pocket. "Holy . . ." he said. "Jeez. You're gonna kill me!"

I blushed, because I hadn't really thrown it all that hard. Either I was a lot stronger than I was back when we used to play, or he was more brittle. Or both. "Sorry," I said. "I'll cool it a bit."

He tentatively leaned down and picked up the glove. "Jeez," he repeated. "Maybe you should go out for the baseball team this spring. Be a pitcher. I guarantee you'd be great with that arm of yours."

I momentarily flashed to Todd Stanhope, and felt this curious heat over my body. But I was playing catch with my dad, so I blocked that thought away.

"Great," I said. "Because I have all this extra time these days for new activities."

He squinted at me. "Where's all this snarkiness coming from?" he asked. For a moment I thought he was serious, but then I saw he was smiling and I felt like I'd met up with my best friend from many years ago.

"Jeez," I said. "Sorry."

"You will be," he said, winding up exaggeratedly. And then he let one fly, a pretty decent throw that surprised me a bit with its velocity. It was high, too, and I had to jump to make the catch.

"Nice," I said.

"Man, this feels so good," he said, and I wanted to run over and hug my dad, hard.

"That's great, Dad," I said.

"Hell yeah," he said.

I grinned. My dad and I used to have our best talks while throwing the ball around. This was years ago, when the topics were less intense than they would be now. Back when it was about him playing college baseball, or him advising me about how to handle a situation with a friend.

Soon he was throwing me pop-ups, like we used to do, and I was throwing back ground balls. He was bending his knees, his hands hanging down low in the correct fielding position for an infielder. It wasn't graceful like it used to be, but you could tell, watching him, that he used to be pretty darn good. Then he had me down in a catching position and he was trying his curveball. It used to break almost a foot, but now it just sort of spun out of his hand and otherwise went straight.

He wound up and threw me a fastball, pausing on his follow-through. I could tell he was winded but was trying not to show it. So I caught it and jogged over to him.

"Let's take a break," I said. He nodded, breathing heavily, his eyes a bit puffy. I led him to the shade of the oak tree.

"I'm an old man," he said, sitting down.

"Nah," I answered, sitting down next to him.

"I think I'm still just a little tired."

I nodded. His blood pressure was mostly back to normal now. He was taking it with a digital cuff every few hours, and if it was low, he was eating something salty, which sounded like a pretty good medicine to me.

"Okay, new rule," I said. "Next time you're going to get all old and tired out of nowhere, go to the freakin' doctor, okay?"

He cuffed me on the shoulder. "Man oh man," he said, shaking his head and laughing. "I can't wait till you get old yourself, Bobby Framingham. I just can't wait."

I lay down and looked up at the tree, and then my dad did the same thing.

"You ever feel happy to be alive?" my dad asked, his voice sort of quiet, peaceful.

I thought about that. I mean, I'm generally a happy person, and that means I'm usually happy to be alive, but I guess he meant like focused on it. I thought about how I felt in the hospital after the doctor told us he was going to be okay. "Sure," I said.

"That's me today," he said.

I smiled. "Good, Dad."

We were silent for a few minutes. I stared up into the branches of the tree, thinking about how there wouldn't be many more of these moments now that I was a year away from college. When I turned to say something to him, he was looking at me and smiling.

"Whoa, you startled me," I said.

He smiled.

"I'm just so damn proud of you," he said. "You're a success."

"Great success," I said, imitating Borat. He ignored me.

"You're the quarterback of an undefeated team, and you're a good person."

I didn't have the heart to tell him we weren't undefeated anymore. We'd lost the game against Laguna Hills by a touchdown.

"Thanks," I said, careful not avert my eyes even though I wanted to. "You okay?"

"I'm better than okay," he said. "I feel like I have this whole new goddamn lease on life and I want to change things. Do you know what I mean?"

I nodded, because I did.

"I want us to talk more," he said, raising up and resting on his elbows.

"Okay," I said, and of course I began to think about my secret.

What would my dad think? I mean, he hadn't really been much of a sharing kind of guy, and now here he was, sharing, and I was thinking, would he be okay with it?

He talked, and it was different than I'd ever heard him speak before. My dad's not exactly an open book. Back when things were normal, it would be hard to get basic information out of him. Now here he was, telling me about his life.

He told me about growing up in New York City, about my grandfather, who had been a gambler, how it had ruined his life, and about the time my grandmother pulled Grandpa out of a racetrack by his ear. Then he talked about how they sent him to sleepaway camp when he was just five. He was the youngest camper by two years, and during baseball games he would stand out in right field picking flowers. The other kids made fun of him because he couldn't swing a bat yet. At night he would pray that in the morning his parents would come to take him home, but they never did.

"Wow," I said.

"I think that's why I've always been so cold to you," he said, his eyes focused on me.

"You aren't cold," I said, reaching over and squeezing his shoulder.

He didn't say anything, just looked at me and smiled.

"You weren't," I repeated.

He sat up and mussed my hair, which was still pretty short from shaving but had grown in and was now sort of spiky. "Things are going to be different from now on," he said. "We're gonna do things together again."

"I'm all for that," I answered.

"And I want us to talk. I want to hear about what's going on in your life. I'm not going to let a little fatigue run my life anymore, okay?"

"Okay."

"I want to hear about Carrie. And you know what? If you like her, I like her."

I laughed. "Okay, Dad. Fine."

He laughed back. "I know I'm being weird. Just give me today, okay? I'm so goddamn relieved to be feeling like myself again."

I peered at my father, and it was freaky, like I was seeing my future. Someday I'd be older, but that didn't mean I'd have it all figured out. My dad sure didn't. That was sort of scary, in a way.

"I'm glad, Dad," I said. "But can we come back down off the moon for like one second? I miss the dad that used to say, like, normal things."

He doubled over laughing. "Oh man, I can't wait till you have kids of your own who cut you down to size. I cannot wait."

"Yo, Framingham needs to think twice before running with the ball," yelled Haskins from the sidelines as we huddled on the field. "Boy thinks he's Michael Vick. Runs more like Vick's VapoRub."

"That's cold," said Rahim.

"Yo, that last play took five minutes!" Haskins said back. "Thinks he's Vick. Next thing you know, dude's gonna be into dog-fighting."

There was laughter on the sidelines and in the huddle. I laughed, too. On a play where no one was open, I'd rolled to the left, tucked the ball in, and headed for the first-down marker. Unfortunately, I'd miscalculated something, maybe not taking into account the curvature of the earth or the speed of light, because defenders came quick and what had at first looked like an easy ten yards wound up with me sliding after a long two-yard gain. I'd run about fifteen yards, but almost all of it parallel to the line of scrimmage, and I'd still not even made it out of bounds.

My speed just wasn't where it needed to be.

I turned from the huddle and yelled back, "Yo, Haskins, learn to throw," I said. "It's a football, not a purse." There were a couple hoots from the sideline, and I heard Coach's laughter, too.

"C'mon, boys, back to work," he yelled. And with a smile, that's what I did.

It was a warm, sunny Wednesday, and we were going first-team offense versus first-team defense. For the first time in a while, Coach seemed to be warming up to me again. He'd slapped my butt after a good timing pattern to Somers worked, just like he had hundreds of times in the past. Then I called a "Waggle" play, where I'd roll left, fake a handoff to Mendez, and then all but one of my receivers would flood the left side of the field. I loved throwing on the run, and that play always seemed to leave someone wide open.

I barked out the snap count and we sprang into action. My fake to Mendez wasn't perfect, but a couple defenders stayed to the right, where he was heading. With Somers and a fullback coming out of the backfield, the defense looked confused. Their reaction left Austin wide open on a crossing pattern, and I fired a rocket into his hands about twelve yards down the field. He looked upfield and with a quick juke got rid of Dennis, the only guy standing between him and six points. Perfect execution.

Coach was pretty animated. "Excellent! Framingham, you got it now! Quick six if you play it right, Bobby. Sell the fake better, okay? Way to go, Rivera," he said to Austin, slapping him on the butt as he ran to the sideline.

• • •

I was changing after my shower when Coach came to my locker and motioned me into his office. I got goose bumps on my arms. We'd barely talked at all since the coming-out conversation, which had happened exactly three weeks before. I towel-dried my wet head, threw on a shirt, and hustled into his office. Coach was sitting at his desk, peeling an orange. He looked up when I walked in and began speaking immediately.

"I wanted to ask about your father."

"He's doing good," I said. "Seems a lot better."

Coach offered me a section of orange and I declined. He jammed several pieces into his mouth at once, and I watched his lips as he savored the juice explosion before swallowing. "I'm glad," he said, his mouth full. "Give him my regards."

"I will," I said, looking at the chair in front of me.

"Sit," Coach said, and I did. "That's not the only reason I wanted you to come in. How's Bobby?"

"I'm okay," I said as I sat, my face feeling warm.

"Good, that's good," he said. "You're looking good out there, today especially."

"Yeah, it felt good today," I said.

"Good, that's good." Coach rolled the orange peel between his fingers.

I scanned my brain for any safe topics of conversation. "Other than the tier, it's all coming together," I told Coach.

Coach smiled and seemed relieved to have a comfortable topic. "Bobby, I instituted the tier formation for you."

I looked at Coach, my eyes wide. "For me? How is that good for me?"

Coach crossed his arms over his massive chest, then uncrossed them. "This team is built around you, Bobby. Not Mendez. He's a good back, but it's your team. The tier gives you more receivers, not less, but you don't see that."

"I guess I don't," I said, eyes locked with Coach, intent on his every word.

"Bobby, the three backs behind you, are they possible receivers?"

"Sure," I said.

"Well, picture it from the perspective of the defense. There are three possible receivers behind you. What do you do if you're covering a guy out of the backfield?"

"You cheat toward the line."

"Yes! And do you cheat toward the line out wide, or in the center?"

"Depends, I guess."

"Yes again. They can't get used to anything, and what we have in the backfield is like a swarm of bees. All three guys can go in any direction. It's confusing. You ever wonder why you keep finding Mendez open this year? Or why at least a couple times a game we got a guy open deep? It's the formation. And with your arm, I wanted to give us a chance to be dangerous on every single play." Coach smiled and made a throwing motion as if he were throwing a bomb.

I thought about that. All this time I'd been seeing the tier as my enemy, but what it really allowed was the chance to take my skills to the next level. I'd balked at it because it was different, and different things were always hard to handle. "Cool. I didn't get that," I said.

He nodded at me. Coach was one of the most humble people I'd ever been around. He never took credit for anything. "Otherwise, you okay?"

"Yes," I said. "Doing better."

"Me, too," he said, nodding his head again, and it took me a moment to realize he was saying he was doing better with what I told him. I smiled at him, and he offered me a tight-lipped grin back.

The phone rang early on Saturday morning. I was still in bed, not sleeping exactly but not awake either, just zoning, in a fantasy world after the game last night. We'd won and I'd played well. I was replaying the highlight reel in my head. The best play had been a simple hook-and-go to Rahim. I'd rolled out right, chased by a blitzing linebacker who almost sacked me before I could throw. I threw just in time, a perfect spiral that I watched drop into Rahim's hands like a cherry off a tree. A painless six points.

I'd heard my mother leave for her morning run half an hour earlier, and I figured my father was still asleep, so I darted across the room to my desk and picked up my cordless extension.

"Hello?"

"Bobby?" The voice on the other end was faintly familiar, reedy and slightly nasal. I couldn't place it.

"This is me," I said.

There was laughter on the other line. "This is me?"

I had no idea who it was I was speaking to. "What's so funny about that?" I took the phone and sat on the edge of my bed.

"This is he, this is him," the voice said. "I've heard those. 'This is me' just sounds . . . totally wrong."

I picked at a frayed string on my comforter. "Okay . . ."

The laughter stopped. "This is Bryan Paulsen."

Heat. In my brain.

I curled up in my bed, feeling shivery and jittery yet somehow in complete control. "Who?"

"Bryan. The reporter? We spoke after the La Habra game. Saw you last night at Garden Grove, but I'm not sure you saw me?"

"Oh . . . yeah, right," I said, all nonchalant. I had seen him, but had pretended I didn't. "What's up?" I anticipated his compliment for the game last night. When you're in the public eye, and you do well at something, there's always the matter of praise, and how you deal with it. I promised myself I'd always be real humble, but at that moment I had to catch myself in order not to say, *Did You See Me Last Night? I Was Awesome!*

"Now you remember. The tall guy who chased you off the parking lot by assuming you were gay," he said.

There was nothing like getting right to the point.

I exhaled. "How could I forget?" I said, rubbing my thighs together. It was toasty under the blanket, just like I like it.

"I'm actually calling because I want to do a piece on you," he said. "For the *Orange County Register*."

I stretched out and enjoyed the tingling sensation all through my body. Things were on fire. But for once, there were no sirens.

"Sure," I said.

"Can we meet later?"

I made sure there was no trace of excitement in my voice. "I guess so."

Bryan asked me to meet him at a coffee shop in Fountain Valley, which was about ten minutes from me. He lived in Long Beach, he said, went to school at Cal State there and was interning for the newspaper. It would be a longer drive for him.

After breakfast I showered and dressed and told my father I was going for an interview. Part of me felt like a criminal, as if what I was doing was illicit.

I drove there around lunchtime, excited and scared out of my wits. The sirens in my head only began once I got in the car. I was having lunch with a gay guy. And not just any gay guy, but one who was good-looking and liked sports.

This could be very interesting.

When I got there, he was waiting at a table inside, drinking a latte. Bryan was wearing a dark blue T-shirt that made his deep hazel eyes really stand out and showed off his build. He smiled and I tried to smile back, but probably came off looking pretty stupid.

"Thanks for meeting me," he said.

"Sure," I said, staring hard at the table. I sat down, and when the waiter arrived I ordered an iced tea. Then we sat across from each other and tried to find things to say.

"Great day," he said, and I nodded emphatically like he'd just said the most brilliant thing ever.

Excellent. I go out with a sportswriter, and suddenly I'm the one who's an idiot.

"Totally," I said, wide-eyed and smiling vacantly.

"You played well last night." Bryan gazed into my eyes and I held his look. I could feel my eyelids flickering and wondered if

I looked constipated the way I was staring at him. I couldn't even breathe.

"Thanks," I said to his forehead. I found if I looked at his forehead, it was easier to say actual words.

"That pass to number eighty-one, really great," he said.

His forehead had a sort of design to it, the creases. If I looked closely enough, it was almost like hieroglyphics. "Yeah," I answered.

"The other team was all zombies, intent on devouring your soul."

Hieroglyphics. I wondered if it amounted to a complete sentence or thought, like maybe a message to me about how to keep my heart from jumping out of my mouth. "Totally," I said.

Bryan laughed. I refocused, and saw his was a kind face. His teeth were slightly uneven on the top; it made him imperfect and that made me like him more. I laughed. "You're really nervous," he noted.

"Maybe a little," I replied, tracing a circle on the table top with my pinky.

Bryan touched my shoulder and I flinched before willing myself to look back at him. "Relax," he said. "I won't bite. Why don't we put off the interview for just a little bit? Just talk for a while."

I returned his smile. "Probably a good idea," I said. "At this rate, I'm liable to sound like a complete idiot."

"That would *never* happen," he said sarcastically, laughing and lifting his hand from my shoulder. "Actually, I need to go next door and pick something up. You mind?"

I nodded, and gulped down the rest of my four-dollar iced tea. The coffee shop was in a mall area, and what he meant by next door was actually a walk across the massive parking lot to a Sports Authority.

"I need new cleats," he said as we walked.

"Cool," I said.

"I play in the gay flag football league in L.A."

I took that information in without commenting, trying hard to glance at his body without turning my head. Did he have really strong legs? I couldn't remember.

I got a nice look as he tried on a pair of football cleats. His legs were thin but solid like a runner's, matted with a light fur.

As he paid for his cleats at the register, Bryan told me he wanted to be a news reporter, not a sports reporter. His internship was his foot in the door at the paper. He said he liked sports, knew a lot about them, but they weren't his passion.

He was only a year older than me, but Bryan seemed to know things about life, about the world. I felt like I knew nothing.

"How do you feel about Caesar salad?" he asked as we left the sports store and found ourselves back in the sun. I was beginning to feel comfortable with him.

"As? As an emulsifier? A means for attaining world peace? Help me out here. Be more specific."

Bryan laughed, and put his hand on my shoulder. I stayed deadly still as he touched me.

"How do you feel about it as a lunch item?"

"Mixed," I said. "But if you need it to live, I could probably find something on the menu, too. I guess we're going for lunch?"

"It doesn't take much to clue you in. A few hints like salad and lunch, and you get it almost right away." Bryan took the lead, and I realized we were walking toward his truck. "I have a place in mind. I'll drive." He unlocked the passenger-side door and threw the bag with his cleats behind the driver's seat.

I didn't have to be asked twice.

We drove to Laguna Beach, where I'd only been once with my

parents as a kid. We parked on a side street near the main drag, about a block away from the Pacific, and I could almost taste the salty air.

"Where are we going?" I asked as we got out of the car.

"Just don't you worry about it," he said. And I didn't.

We walked to a café near the ocean. Inside, we sat at a window table. I could feel Bryan's hazel eyes on me.

I stared at the menu, and when I glanced up there were those eyes. I looked away, turned the menu over, and stared at the empty back of it.

"Anything interesting?" he said.

I looked up and he was smiling at me. I didn't want to smile back, but it felt like someone was tickling the inside of my chest with a feather. I shrugged, looked away.

"So you like football," I said weakly, trying to bend the menu. It wasn't a bender.

Bryan laughed and took the menu from my hands. I let it go and studied the table. There was no place left to look.

"Okay, we need to deal with the invisible elephant," he said.

"Excuse me?" I took a sip of water and settled into my chair.

"The invisible elephant? That's, like, pooping all over the place and no one is mentioning it?"

I wrinkled my nose. "What are you talking about? Are you insane?"

Bryan laughed. "I'm gay, Bobby," he said.

I grabbed my paper napkin and tore it into little pieces. "I know," I said quietly.

"And?" Bryan's voice was insistent. I knew he wasn't going to let me go on this.

"Congrats?" I said weakly.

"Nuh-uh," he said, shaking his head, a smile still there.

"Um . . ."

Bryan reached over and cuffed me on the head gently. "Come on, Bobby. Just say it. It's okay."

I thought about my life the last few years, the ways I'd changed, the dreams that wouldn't go away, the conversations with Austin, Rahim, Coach, Blassingame. I'd never expected to have conversations like these. When I was younger I could never have guessed that my life would take this turn. I looked at Bryan and realized there was nothing to say but the truth.

"I guess we may have something in common," I said.

"Guess? Maybe? Hello!" Bryan laughed a bit too loud and I felt a little embarrassed.

"You're one of the only people who know," I said.

He raised an eyebrow at me. "Yeah, I know."

"You can tell?" I asked, sipping my water.

"Well, yeah, but I also know because of my cousin."

I wanted to say, *How can you tell?* But there were more important questions.

"Huh?" My heart was beating so hard I worried I'd have a heart attack.

"Bobby," Bryan said, his arms crossed. "Dennis Fowler is my cousin."

I sat in dazed silence for a moment, wishing my food would arrive so I'd have something to do. Then Bryan explained to me what had happened.

"My dad told me after my aunt told him," he said. "Otherwise known as—"

"Dennis's mom," I said, leaning my head back and staring at the ceiling.

"He told me to keep it on the down low," Bryan said. "I'd just started at the *Orange County Register,* so I had access to their photo archives and I did a little search one day."

He lowered his voice and leaned forward. "You're very sexy," he said, suddenly a little shy. "I decided it was absolutely necessary to cover all your games. Didn't you think it was a little weird that I was always covering your games? Did the *Orange County Register* do that in the past?"

"Hell if I know," I said, floored by this revelation. "You're related to Dennis Fowler? How come you're not an idiot?"

Bryan laughed. "You don't know that for a fact," he said.

I looked him over, and raised one eyebrow. "You know what this means?"

"No idea," Bryan said, and right then our food arrived. I was suddenly not hungry for my Oriental chicken salad.

"It means that you're a stalker. Do I need Mace?"

We both laughed. "I think you're safe for the time being," he said.

Bryan paid the bill, and I looked at my watch. It was nearly four o'clock. "Are we going to start the interview now?" I asked.

"In a bit. I need to work off that meal. How do you feel about minigolf?" he asked as we got up from the table.

"'Bout the same as Caesar salad," I said.

Bryan grinned and shrugged. "Good enough for me."

He was terrible at minigolf, but decent in the batting cages. I tried not to show him up—aw, the hell with that. Of course I tried to show him up. And I succeeded. We drove back from Laguna Beach as the sun set. I'd totally lost track of the day, hadn't called home, hadn't done anything. It felt perfect.

"This gay stuff is difficult, isn't it?" I said as we drove.

Bryan glanced over at me and smiled. "What do you mean?"

"I mean, my life would be a lot easier . . . never mind."

Bryan put his hand on my leg and I nearly jumped. "Who's to say, Bobby? Don't you think some good things come out of being gay?"

His hand was still on my leg, and I was beginning to be glad it was there. It had warmed up and was now pretty comfortable. Just two guys driving, one with a hand on the other's leg. "I don't know," I said, thinking about it. "Like what?"

"Like sensitivity," he said. "Being gay has made me more sensitive." I almost laughed, because it sounded so, I don't know, gay. But as I pondered that I realized it was true. Being different was a big part of it. I knew what it felt like to feel different from my friends and family. To be isolated and alone. And that's not something that someone like Austin or Dennis could relate to.

"And of course, there are other things, too."

I raised my eyebrows at him.

"Well, like the sex-with-guys thing," he said.

"Yeah," I said, my face flushing. "Well, I wouldn't know."

He stared ahead at the road, taking the information in.

We got back to the parking lot at about five o'clock. The two of us sat in awkward silence for a few moments. I was trying to figure out ways to make this day never end.

"So maybe we can do this again?" I said, adjusting my seat. "Well, maybe not this exactly."

"Yeah, something different. Maybe an interview," Bryan said, and I laughed.

I turned and looked at him. "I'm going to ask you out on a date, how about that?" I said, feeling very close to him. He smiled and raised an eyebrow. "But this needs to go slow, okay? I mean I've never even been out on a date with a guy."

"Yes you have," he answered.

"No, I haven't."

"You've just been dated, Bobby."

"I have?"

"You have." Bryan smiled, a cute, boyish smile, his mouth curling at each end. "Thanks to my unique guerrilla dating tactics."

It was a mob scene at the Five and Diner after school on Monday. The smell of grease wafted into my nostrils as waitresses hurried past carrying overloaded trays of cheeseburgers and fries.

While I waited for a table to open up, I fiddled with the bowl of wrapped toothpicks and wondered whose job it was to wrap them.

Was that what life amounted to for some people? If that was your life, how did you deal with it, how did you tell yourself that it had meaning?

This would have been a good time to turn around and ask Carrie, but my usual companion was at *Hairspray* rehearsal, hated me now, and had been replaced by a clumsy but well-meaning journalist nerd. Over the weekend Finch had asked me where he could interview me further, and I chose my favorite fifties diner. It sounded especially good now, since I had a major hankering for a root-beer float with whipped cream.

A couple of girls from school were in a booth near the door. I recognized them as cheerleaders. One, blond, wore a maroon-and-gray ribbon in her hair, our school colors. The other, dark-haired and olive-skinned, wore a pink halter top that revealed a huge chest. They eyed me as if I was some kind of celebrity, and out of the corner of my eye I watched them whispering to each other.

I wondered if they thought it was weird that I was with Finch. Was it weird? Were we friends now? *Is this what life has come to, and how can I turn back time and make it turn out another way?*

We were seated in a booth in the back, and as I picked up a menu Finch began to arrange his interview things: a digital recorder, a spiral notebook, and an array of pens. Finally organized and oriented, Finch looked up at me and the left side of his mouth curled up. "I really appreciate you redoing the interview," he said. "Obviously I need more if I'm going to explain to the world who Bobby Framingham is."

"We're friends, Finch. You can call me just Bobby," I said, smiling back at him.

Finch looked down. "Okay, thanks."

We sat there in awkward silence for a moment. I had an urge to play sugar-packet checkers, but figured Finch would think there was something seriously wrong with me and would write about it. The humor would be lost in the translation. I held off.

"So," he said, turning on the tape recorder and grabbing a green pen. "Talk to me about your future, what you want to do, where you want to be."

I rubbed my chin, hoping that made me look mature and introspective. It probably just made me look like a dork. Without Carrie around, it was often hard to get the needed feedback on my physical actions. "I don't know. Playing football somewhere."

Finch scribbled a note in his pad. "Any sense that you'll wind up at Stanford?"

"I really don't know, Finch. I mean, I have enough on my mind without worrying about next year, you know? I'll focus on that in January maybe."

"I'd kill to get in," Finch said, his eyes narrowing.

"Yeah, I remember, your crazy mom."

I figured he'd laugh, given how we'd laughed about things after the football game that time, but he didn't. It was like the window had closed and Finch was no longer laughing about his family life. I looked over at him and felt bad that his mom was putting all that pressure on him. "You'll probably get in," I said. "And for me, I don't care that much, wherever I wind up is fine."

Finch snapped out of his sudden funk. "That's really great, I mean, that's really cool that you're so together about everything," he said.

I gasped. "Together? Finch, have you seen me lately?"

The waitress came over and I ordered my float. Finch ordered onion rings and a Coke. He gathered our menus and placed them in the menu holder on the side of our booth. As she walked away he said, "You look fine to me, Bobby. It's probably all in your mind."

"Let me ask you something," I said, flicking a sugar packet. Carrie or not, those packets couldn't survive a visit by me. "Do you think it's weird?"

"What's weird?" he asked.

"That I'm gay." I paused and looked behind me to see if I'd said it too loud. No one was paying any attention. "It's still pretty new, this being gay stuff."

Finch squinted at me. "Weird? Are you serious?"

I sighed and drummed my fingers against the table. "Nah, I guess not."

"Bobby, you're a cool guy. Who cares if you're gay or straight? It's all the same, I mean, either way you love someone. That's all there is to it. Anyway, I think it's sort of cool. If you ever decide to be open about it, you're going to change the world, Bobby."

I looked down at the tape recorder and was bothered to see it still running. "Maybe we should turn that off?"

Finch laughed. "Okay," he said, turning it off.

"Maybe we should get back on topic."

"We can talk about whatever you want, Bobby," he said, wiping white flakes off the left shoulder of his blue shirt, before reaching down and starting up the recorder again.

"Football, then," I said. He nodded, searched his notebook for a moment, and asked me the first question. During our twenty-minute interview, Finch asked typical questions, ones I'd dealt with before, about what it's like to play the position, and about my best and worst experiences. He told me he was writing a feature article that would be in Wednesday's school paper.

Finch's eyebrows twitched, and I realized he was looking up at someone behind me. Turning, I saw the two girls who had been sitting up front. The blond girl was rail thin and wearing tight low-rider jeans. The other girl was about to fall out of her pink top.

"Hey, Bobby!" the blond girl said, and as she said it, both girls smiled.

"Hey," I said, wondering if I should know their names. I had noticed the cheerleading girls about as much as Austin would notice the guys on the baseball team. "How are you?"

"I just wanted to ask you . . . can we sit down?" the blonde asked.

"Sure," I said, glancing over at Finch, who was rearranging his pens obsessively.

Both girls sidled into the booth on my side. I moved all the way in. There was more than enough room, but the blonde wound up pressed against me, so close I could smell her perfume, which smelled like an obscenely powerful rose. She moved toward me until my hand actually rubbed against her leg. Remembering Carrie and the laser-tag disaster, I resisted the impulse to pull away. I looked over at Finch, who was staring down at the table, looking really uncomfortable. I felt bad for him. Here he was, the only one at the table who'd appreciate this sort of attention, and he was getting shut out. "So what's up?" I asked.

Blond girl smiled at me. She looked like she'd just stepped out of a *Cosmopolitan* cover photo. "I was just wondering, are you and Carrie Conway dating?"

My neck flinched. "No, not really," I said. And as soon as I said it, I wished I hadn't.

"Cool," she said, and suddenly her hand was on my knee.

I couldn't swallow. I could feel the muscles in my left eye contracting, and I wondered if I was about to have a seizure or something. "My friend Beth is having this party on Saturday night. I'll give you the address."

"Sounds great," I said, hoping they'd both leave, quickly, which they didn't.

A few agonizing minutes later, they got up and left Finch and me alone. I felt like taking a shower. Not because the blonde was so close to me, but because I felt like a liar, a fraud. I knew this was one thing Finch wouldn't get. We were silent for a moment.

"Are you okay?" Finch asked.

"I don't know," I said. I just wanted to sit there, no talking, for a bit, and somehow Finch seemed to get that. We sat that way until our food came, and then he picked at an onion ring while I ignored my float.

"You didn't do anything wrong, Bobby," he said after a while.

I craved the warmth of my bed, a blanket, silence. I wanted to be with Bryan. He was the one person who got me, who maybe understood what my life was about. "I sit there not saying anything, and it might as well be a lie," I said, a headache forming along the sides of my skull. "I should just come out."

"Well, Bobby, you can do that," Finch said, and I looked at him and realized, for a moment, that he was right. I could do that.

I could also rob a 7-Eleven or dance naked in the cafeteria.

"Maybe someday I will," I said, only half meaning it.

"There you go," Finch said, gulping down some Coke and looking energized.

"Maybe I should just do it, come out of the closet, get it over with. Something has to give," I said.

"Just say the word," Finch said, his voice cracking slightly.

I thought about the big picture. The team, Coach, my dad. I sipped my float and wiped my mouth before speaking again. "This just isn't the right time, not yet," I said. "Thanks for your support, really. And I know you want to write it. But can you just give me some time?"

Finch nodded. "Doesn't matter to me," he said. "Whatever you want to do."

It was a warm Southern California Wednesday morning and I was feeling good. My homework was done, I was just a few days removed from my first-ever date, and I'd just woken up from a dream in which Bryan had played a stunningly key role. I woke up feeling invincible, even though I was running slightly late, and another tardy on my record would mean a detention. I could deal with everything that was happening in my life, all of it. That's how I was feeling as I made the turn off our street, Palm Court, toward Durango Avenue, the road that takes me all the way to school, two miles north.

I turned on sports radio and thought, if the world was a whale, sports radio was kind of the blowhole. I laughed to myself, since the analogy broke down quickly once I thought about it harder. Still, it was a lot of hot air and sometimes I liked to listen, for kicks.

"Coming up next," the announcer said, "a local high school

quarterback comes out of the closet. How's that for a wake-up story!" There was laughter, and then they spliced in this really effeminate voice saying, "Oh mah goodness!" Then they went to a commercial.

My shoulders jerked. A gay high school quarterback coming out? Where? My head pulsed and a huge air bubble filled my chest. I needed to hear that story, but I knew I was going to make it to school about one minute before the morning bell sounded. They'd have to hurry right into that story or I'd miss it.

The Athlete's Foot commercial wasn't too long, but the one following it, for a product guaranteed to restore lost hair or your money back, went on forever, testimonial after testimonial. "End!" I screamed as first Powell and then Warner Road flashed by. I was just about a minute away from school, and the clock read 7:58. Finally, the stupid commercial for bald guys ended, and the familiar voice returned. "Two minutes till the top of the hour. Time for a quick look at the weather . . ."

"It's Southern California! Who cares?" I yelled at my stereo, pounding the dashboard as I waited at the stoplight on Reed. "Hurry up!"

As I pulled into the parking lot, they went from weather to traffic, and I gave up, knowing I'd have to sprint just to make it inside the building on time. I slammed the door and pivoted into a full-on sprint, dragging my backpack behind me in my left hand. The story would have to wait until after school.

I made it to the doorway literally seconds before the bell rang, and sighed, relieved. The policy was that you had to be in before eight on the dot or you were marked tardy by the officer who stood by the door every morning.

Is this high school, or jail?

I headed down the long main hallway to homeroom. Coming

toward me was this guy with a buzz cut I'd had a math class with junior year.

"Congratuations, man!" he said, and he slapped me on the shoulder. I looked back at him, and he saluted. I didn't just climb Mount Everest, I thought, I just made it into school before eight. I continued down the hallway and saw a guy and a girl talking by the lockers. As I got near they stopped talking and looked at me.

"That really took a lot of courage," the guy said, smiling warmly at me. "Wow."

"Yeah," the girl said, coming over and giving me a hug. She had an orange ribbon in her hair, and I recognized her as one of the theater girls. I'd seen her in a play Carrie was in. She clasped me and held on tight. "That's about the bravest thing I've ever heard of."

Everything froze. The hug, the hallway, time itself. I gasped and my whole body shook. I don't remember letting her go, or her letting me go. All I remember is running as fast as I'd ever run, football games included, down the hallway and to the right, to the journalism office.

I bolted through the door and a senior named Phil Johnson, the student editor, was standing in front of the main desk, reading a paper. He looked up. I thought my head was going to explode.

"Is there something in the newspaper today about me?" I asked, trying to catch my breath, as I approached him. The office was empty other than us.

Phil was a small guy, dark hair, acne. He studied me and smirked. "Very funny."

"What the hell do you mean, very funny?" I got in his face and repeated my first question. I wasn't a violent guy, but the images in my head were beyond real violence. They were more like cartoon clips of severing people's heads, pushing them into oncoming traffic, and watching the bodies explode.

"Bobby . . . have you read?" Phil stood up and stepped backward, as if to get away from me. He had no chance. I felt my fist clench and realized that I was about to hit this guy.

"What? What did you put in the paper about me?"

Phil's eyes were wide as saucers and he sputtered. "I heard the recording . . . Finch . . . he wrote . . . oh God."

I took a deep breath, and allowed the reality to enter my brain. I wanted to scream. Why would Finch do something like that? This had to be a mistake. Phil rummaged through his desk. "You need to hear this . . ." he said. He found a digital recorder and showed it to me. "Isn't this you?" he asked as he pressed play. After a couple of seconds I heard my own voice. ". . . *it's new, I'm just figuring it all out . . .*"

"Are you kidding me? Are you absolutely kidding?" I started to pace. "This is unbelievable. You put that I'm . . . you put it in the newspaper? Without asking me first?"

Phil shut the tape off and stammered, "Finch vouched for you. He played me the recording."

"He taped that without me knowing it, you idiot," I said.

"No, he didn't," Phil said, shaking his head with confidence.

"What?"

"In the tape, Bobby. You mention the interview. Being on tape. You knew."

Finch. My head swam with memories of talking to Finch. *What did I do?* Then I knew. He didn't just tape me in the cafeteria and at the diner, he was taping me outside my house, when we talked by the tree! Wasn't he like fiddling with his fanny pack? Was that a digital recorder in there? Why the hell?

"You want to hear?" Phil asked.

"You think?" I answered.

He pressed the play button, and there was my voice. *"I sit there not saying anything, and it might as well be a lie,"* I heard my voice say.

Then Finch: *"I think it's an amazing story."*

And my response: *"It's still pretty new, this being gay stuff . . . Maybe I can make a difference in people's lives."*

The feeling was like I'd just been punched in the throat, or like someone had just reached down my mouth and yanked words right out of me. My whole body felt violated, and if I hadn't had a burning desire to read the article, I'd have been out the door and away, far, far away from that school, from anything in my life.

The truth was out, and I had no control over it. I scanned to the bottom of the piece.

> For Bobby Framingham, it's bound to be a long and hard road, but it's one he's well equipped to handle. And his decision makes sense, since he hates lying.
>
> "I sit there not saying anything, and it might as well be a lie," says Bobby, reflecting about his silence to this point. As a community, we should stand behind such bravery one hundred percent.

It didn't matter that it was nice. All I could do was shake my head at the betrayal by a guy I'd let into my life, trusted as a friend.

Really juicy news travels fast.

I found that out as I sprinted around the entire school, trying to swipe every single copy of the paper. I wondered if the papers were spawning other papers, or what, because everywhere I went, I got seriously strange looks from people. After about twenty minutes I gave in to the fact that the news was out there, and wasn't ever going to go away simply because I deposited a few hundred papers in trash cans.

I thought about ditching Spanish class and going to see Dr. Blassingame. At least he'd be supportive, but as I passed his office I didn't go in. Instead I decided to catch Rahim outside of Spanish class. I took the stairs three at a time as I climbed to the second floor, my heart pumping fiercely. I opened the door to the second-floor hallway and almost smacked into the one person I was least ready to see.

Carrie's eyes were bloodshot, the color of her dyed hair. I just avoided a collision with her, and when she saw it was me, her hand went up, the Stop Sign.

"Now you, you need to be killed," she said, holding her ground in the hallway. A circle of strangers formed around us, intent on seeing this drama play out.

"I . . . I was . . ." My voice shook in a way I'd never heard before, chattered as if I'd stepped out of a freezing ocean into a chilly wind. I closed my eyes and tried to make myself calm. It wasn't working. My eyes opened and tried to focus on Carrie. And then came the heaving in my chest, and I couldn't stop breathing, faster and faster, harder than a person should ever breathe. The hallway became blurry. I latched on to certain faces—a girl with eyebrows that joined at the center of her face, a short kid, maybe a freshman, with braces glimmering—faces looming above me, and then they were in my eyes, then on the inside of my lids, and down, deeper, until I couldn't breathe.

The room was very white. There was a ceiling fan above me, and as I rose onto my elbows I saw that all the walls shared the same blandness. I wondered how I'd gotten to the infirmary, what had happened, and in the midst of wondering that, I was again hit in the chest by the reality of what had occurred. I was gay, and everyone knew it. My chest felt heavy, but my brain was suddenly very clear.

The news is out about Bobby Framingham. Where to now?

A woman my grandmother's age looked into the room and smiled. She wore white, which made me feel for a moment like I was dead, in some weird version of heaven.

"You're up! Are you feeling better?"

My mouth barely moved as I spoke. "Yeah, I guess." She raised a finger at me as if to tell me to wait, I had company. I didn't really want to see anyone.

Carrie walked in. Her eyes were still red, but she was calmer now. She walked over to me and I looked away, out the one window in the room, which led to an alleyway I'd never seen before. She sat down on the side of my bed and sighed. "I'm sorry if I caused that," she said, and she put her hand on my shoulder. I couldn't look at her.

"It's not your fault," I said, concentrating on counting the specks on the window. There were fourteen. "It's all on me."

"What happened, Bobby?"

I took a deep breath and told her everything. I told her that I loved her, and I had for a long time wished I loved her *like that,* but I just didn't. She winced when I said that, and then collected herself and lay down on the bed with me and held me.

"I'm so sorry," I told her. "I—"

"Shh . . ." she whispered. "Not now."

Carrie ducked her head and nestled it in my chest, and I could hear the echo of her voice in my chest cavity. "I'm gonna be fine, okay? I mean, I sort of love you *like that* and that part sucks, and obviously telling me in person would have been good, but I get it, Bobby. I'm still your friend. Nothing's changed there."

The nurse walked in, saw us on the bed together, and frowned.

"Please get up from that bed, miss," she said. Carrie sat up, looked at her, looked back at me, seemingly asking permission, and then spoke.

"Don't worry, he's gay," she said, matter-of-fact.

The nurse had this strange look on her face, and as soon as I saw it, there was laughter where the tears would have been if I'd let them come. Laughter poured from my tear ducts, this sound, this vibration, first softly and then really hard, and Carrie began to laugh, too, while the nurse stood there, confused.

We walked out together, Carrie holding my hand. "Oh my God!" she said, halting her stride and looking at me, dazed.

“What?” I was dead tired and didn’t know if I could take any sentence that started with “Oh my God.”

“I’m your fag hag. Oh my God,” she said. “I’m gonna be the woman with twenty cats in my apartment. I’ll wear shawls and live in West Hollywood and never get married. And all for the love of a football player. Please say this won’t happen to me.”

“Aren’t you allergic to cats?” I asked as we paused in the empty hallway.

She was staring into space wistfully. “I’ll have to get weekly allergy shots.”

I put my hand on the back of her neck and rubbed, something I’d probably never done when we were so-called dating.

“I think you’re going to be okay,” I said.

She continued walking, her head down. “I hate shawls,” she said.

I missed my first three classes that day. Carrie went with me to Dr. Blassingame’s office, where we sat, mostly silent, every once in a while offering random comments about my situation.

“This is a wonderful opportunity. You don’t have to lie anymore,” said Dr. B.

“Football today will be really tough,” I said.

“You’re free to love whom you choose to love,” Blassingame said.

“My folks . . .” I said, trailing off.

“Truth never hurt anyone, only lies.” Blassingame again.

“You can finally stop dressing like a straight person and show us your flair for style,” offered Carrie. I looked at today’s outfit, chosen in about three minutes before the dash to my car. Beat-up white sneakers, jeans, and a green polo shirt. I’d forgotten a belt. Not horrible, but certainly not real fashionable either. I guess I didn’t get that gene. I looked at Carrie, and when I met her eyes, I saw she was kidding. We giggled.

"That may be a little beyond my level of gayness," I said.

"True," offered Mr. Blassingame, and we all nodded.

We three trudged out of Blassingame's office at lunch hour and I wondered if maybe Carrie and I would do better to walk without him. Dr. Blassingame seemed pretty concerned about me and really "wanted to support me," as he said. I let him.

The cafeteria was crowded. I paused at the door and took a deep breath. "Are we ready?" I asked Carrie.

"I don't know, are we?"

I thought about this. "No," I said. "Not even a little bit."

"If Finch is there, may I kick him repeatedly?" she asked, squeezing my arm.

"If Finch is there, kicking him repeatedly is a requirement," I said. "Then we'll set his withered body on fire."

"There will be no violence," said Dr. Blassingame, missing the joke entirely.

I took the first step, feeling a bit scared about what was out there waiting for me. I could feel it as it happened. First, a couple eyes on me, followed by pointing and whispering. I felt this, eyes averted, intent on food, anything to make me feel less woozy. Then there was a hoot, not a nasty one, but the type a rock star might get, followed by a random "yeah!," and then there was the clapping. First just a few people closer to the entrance, and then it traveled to the back of the cafeteria, in waves, and suddenly I was receiving a standing ovation in the lunchroom. I wanted to run. Carrie had her hand on my shoulder and she squeezed, as if reading my mind, telling me to stand my ground. Dr. Blassingame gently pushed me forward in a show of support.

What does the gay quarterback of the football team do to acknowledge a crowd? A wave? The Wave? A Queen Elizabeth Wave?

I put my hand up meekly, as if to say hi to maybe one or two friends, and felt ridiculous. The cheering got louder. "Bob-bee, Bob-bee," began a couple chanters, but mercifully that ended almost as soon as it began.

I looked around, half savoring the moment, relieved that it was clapping, and not flying food, sent my way. That's when I saw them: Austin, Rahim, and Dennis. I fixated on Austin, wanting, more than anything, him to look at me. He was looking at his feet.

The sign on the door to the locker room said VARSITY FOOTBALL PRACTICE CANCELED—MANDATORY TEAM MEETING, 4 P.M., LOCKER ROOM. Interesting, I thought. Advertise a meeting at the meeting place. I opened the door and, sitting in our meeting area in street clothes, was most of our team. As I entered, many of the guys looked up, Coach included. I couldn't read his face. The room got quiet, and I resisted the urge to bolt. I walked to my locker, through the circle, very still, careful not to show any sort of emotion. I wanted to tell them everything at once, but I didn't know where to start.

It was quiet. I sat down tentatively, glancing around to see who was there. I tried to catch Austin's eye from across the room, but he refused to look at me. I searched out Rahim, who did hold my gaze and nodded. I wanted to smile, but couldn't.

"Dude," said Somers, straddling the bench in front of his locker. "What the hell were you thinking?"

"Shut up, Somers." This came from Rahim. I was grateful, and tried to show him that with a sort of half smile that may or may not have expressed it.

"Wow," Somers said, looking around. "Bobby comes in and people change fast." I felt a twinge in my abdomen, like a muscle cramp. I took a deep breath.

"Look, guys," I said. "This is all a mistake. Finch Gozman wasn't supposed to write about that. He totally screwed me over."

"Wait. Are you saying it isn't true?" asked Bolleran.

I saw Coach sitting at the head of a broken circle of players. He nodded to me. I didn't know what the nod meant. Tell them? I support you? Hi? It was vague.

"It's true," I said. I couldn't look at anyone. Silence.

"So you're gay, and you told a reporter, but it wasn't supposed to get in the paper?" This was Somers again. "Good thinking, Bobby."

"It wasn't like that," I said, shuffling my feet back and forth. I was used to feeling confident with these guys, like a leader, and now that was in serious jeopardy. They all turned to face me. "I told Finch as a friend."

"Well you screwed everything up," said Bolleran. "We got homecoming in a couple of days and now we're going out there with a quarterback who's a homo. Your timing sucks."

I felt my face getting red. "My timing? I told you already, there was no timing. I didn't want to come out, okay?"

"Hey, all's I'm saying is, if you didn't open your mouth to a reporter, of all people, it wouldn't be in the paper." I heard some people quietly agreeing with him.

"Okay, okay," said Coach, stepping in. "I also question your timing, Bobby. But you did what you had to." I wanted to say, again, *It wasn't my timing,* but he didn't give me a chance. "What do we need to do to put this behind us and get ready for Friday?"

"If he's playing, I'm not playing," said Mendez.

"Say what?" Coach asked.

"I ain't goin' out on the field with no faggot. No way."

Coach looked around the room. "Anyone else feel this way?"

Bolleran raised his hand. "I'm not gonna be center for this freak! I don't want Bobby touching my ass," he said. A couple people laughed, including Dennis. I narrowed my eyes at him, but he wasn't even looking my way.

"He should have to work from the shotgun," said Dennis, and there was more laughter. He mimed it, me standing way behind center, and then he ran forward and pretended to squeeze the center's ass, all the while licking his lips. That brought a roar from the room. I just sat there, unflinching.

"Goddamn it, Dennis!" Coach yelled.

Dennis sat down. "I don't like it," he said. "We shouldn't have to worry about how the gay guy feels. I hate this PC bullshit. I don't want to have to worry about what I say all the time."

I felt the rage pulsing through my clenched jaw and neck. "You're a lousy excuse for a human being, Dennis," I said.

Dennis flared his nostrils. "Dude, you've seen me naked," he said.

"Dude"—I sneered back, raising my voice—"maybe if you stopped taking your clothes off at parties, I wouldn't have."

Austin cracked up. "Oh, snap!" he said.

"Shut up, Rivera," Dennis said. "It isn't funny."

"It's a little funny," Austin answered.

Coach cracked a smile. "I know this is off topic, but I'm curious. Fowler, why are you taking your clothes off at parties?"

The room erupted. Dennis looked down and for a moment he looked ashamed, but then he broke into a smile. "I'm just giving the ladies what they want," he said.

"Just trying to lighten the mood a little," Coach said, smiling slightly. I wasn't in a smiling mood.

When the laughter died down, Kyle spoke up. "He's our quarterback, and we need him," he said. "But the thing I don't like is the locker room thing. He should have like his own locker room."

Coach scanned the room. "What do people think about this?"

"I think if you're worried about being in a locker room with someone who might be gay, you need to move to another planet," said Rahim. "There's gay people everywhere."

"What, are you gay, too?" said Somers. "This day just keeps getting better."

"My uncle is gay," Rahim said, staring down Somers. "And so are a lot of people. And they aren't all after your body, okay? You're being stupid."

"Exactly," said Rocky.

Somers shook his head. "Screw this. I know I'm not the only one who feels this way, but I'm the only one who has the balls to say it."

"This is everyone's chance to speak their mind," Coach said. "Speak up if you have something to say."

"You're our leader. You can't be gay!" said Torry. "That's just . . . wrong!"

"Exactly," said Somers. "This is like a big-time violation of trust, you know? All this time, you've been lying to us about who you are. That ain't right."

My face felt like it could explode. "Wait. First you're mad because I came out as gay. Now you're made because I didn't come out? Which one is it? Because this doesn't even make sense."

Somers shrugged. "Hey, that's how I feel."

"I already said it," said Mendez. "If you choose to be gay, we can choose to kick you off the team. That's the way it is."

"You want me off the team?" I shouted, standing. "Who else?

Because I think you all know I'd die for most of you. I figured there would be some loyalty, but I guess not."

"This would be a good time to die for us," said Dennis.

"I swear to God, Fowler, keep your mouth shut for the rest of the meeting," said Coach. Dennis stiffened.

"I think he should apologize," said Somers.

Coach looked at him. "What for? For being gay or for the story? I didn't like the gay thing either, to tell the truth, when he told me—"

"You knew?" Somers asked.

Coach ignored him. "I didn't like it at first either, but I thought about it and realized this is Bobby Framingham, and I know Bobby and I trust him as part of my family. So I thought about it and figured maybe I didn't have all the answers. I went to the library and did some reading, and what I read made me understand a little better."

So that explains Coach's turnaround.

"And anyway," Coach continued. "So what if Bobby is different. It's none of my business what he does in bed."

"But I haven't—"

"It's not your turn to talk," Coach said to me sharply. I shut my mouth, my gut twisting into a painful knot.

"He should apologize," said Mendez. "That shit ain't right."

"This is a betrayal," said Bolleran. "I mean, we were like brothers and now it's like one of our brothers plays for the other team. The party is over. This sucks."

The room went silent. I wondered if I'd ever get up from that spot, because at that moment I was pretty sure I was paralyzed. Every part of my body felt lethargic. I wondered if my legs would even work if I tried. Rahim broke the silence.

"I don't see the problem," he said. "That's my boy over there. I got his back, and if you're a teammate, you should, too."

Once again there were a few garbled sounds of agreement. I tried to see who they were, to see who my allies were. Then Rocky spoke.

"I don't see how anyone on this team can turn their back on a teammate. Bobby always supports me, so I'll always support him," he said.

There were a few murmurs of consent.

"Thanks," I said, looking around to see who would make eye contact with me.

"Being homophobic is just as bad as being racist," Rocky said. "Of course we should support Bobby."

"Shut the hell up, dude. You're a kicker," snapped Somers.

Coach stepped in. "He's a teammate, and he's got a right to speak his mind."

When no one else spoke, Coach started talking again. "Well, I'm surprised it has come to this, but here we are. I think we need to have a vote. Are we going to support our teammate, or not? Because we're a team here, okay? We are all for one, one for all, and if we can't support a teammate who is gay, then I need to know that now."

"We're teammates. We're supposed to back each other, no matter what," Rahim said, shaking his head. "We protect each other."

"Yeah, well. I'm not protecting Bobby. He's on his own," Somers said.

I began to shiver. It was like my whole world had disintegrated. It wasn't supposed to happen like this. I had imagined telling a friend, I had even had dreams about everyone knowing, but never once had I expected a vote about whether I should be allowed to stay on the team.

"Let's do it," said Rahim, who obviously felt more confident than I did.

"All in favor of supporting our teammate Bobby Framingham, raise your hands," Coach said.

I didn't want to look, but I had to. A bunch of hands shot up.

Rahim, Rocky, and about fifteen others went up right away. My heart pulsed as I slowly looked toward my best friend.

Austin had his hand raised high. I closed my eyes and felt my tear ducts burning. I held my breath.

"All opposed," Coach said.

Somers, Bolleran, and Mendez were among the six who held their hands up. I gripped the bench I was sitting on.

"That's twenty-eight to six," Coach said. "Bobby stays. And of course he should stay. We are a team here. If anyone has a problem with that, you come talk to me, but I'll tell you right now, don't think you're going to give our teammate over there"—and he pointed to me—"any kind of trouble. Okay? Okay."

When the meeting ended, Rahim, Austin, and a bunch of other guys came over to me.

"I can't believe those guys," I said, standing at my locker, unable to look in anyone's eye.

Austin put his hand on my shoulder. "Yo, B, sorry to tell you this, but those were my thoughts when you told me, too."

I forced myself to look in his eyes. What I saw there confused me. Sadness, regret, and what looked a little bit like kindness. It surprised me a little. "Are you serious?" I asked.

He nodded. "It was pretty rough on me, kid. It was like, you get that shit off your chest and it's 'have a nice day' for you. Then I got it on mine."

I wanted to say, *You said you were fine!* But there was no need. I got it. He had done the best he could with a tough situation. I nodded.

"You just need to give people a little time. You want everybody to be cool with it right now," he said. "That's not gonna happen."

"I just want people to realize it doesn't matter. Is that too much to ask?"

Austin shrugged. "Like it or not, it looks like it does matter. How long until you realized it didn't matter?"

My head buzzed. *Maybe it does matter. I keep waiting for people to just accept that I'm gay, like gay and straight are equal. But they aren't equal. Otherwise, would we be having this conversation? Would we have voted on whether I could stay on the team?*

As I looked at Austin, I realized I was seeing him in a new light. It was the smartest thing I'd ever heard him say. I almost made a joke about it, but instead closed my eyes and nodded my head to show I got it.

"Just give it some time," he said. He squeezed my shoulder and walked off.

I kept my eyes closed and imagined how nice it would be to disappear.

"You okay?" I opened my eyes and saw it was Rahim. He tapped my shoulder with his forearm.

"Not really," I said, feeling dizzy. I steadied myself by holding on to the locker.

"What do you need?" Rahim's dark eyes were filled with compassion.

"A new life," I said.

"You got the one you were given, can't do nothing about that," he said. I nodded. That was true. "You want to come over? Play Xbox? No practice, got to do something."

I did want to, but I knew that I had to go home and talk to my folks. I was sure they knew by now. I'd seen a few television cameras in the parking lot. I was news.

"Well, if you change your mind, just show up," he said.

I nodded again, hoping that my gratitude showed in my eyes. I wasn't sure what was showing at this point.

The house was dark, but my mom's car was in the driveway, so I knew she was home. I walked in the front door and my first instinct was to bolt to my room and ignore the situation, hope that she hadn't heard and pretend nothing had happened. But I heard noises from the kitchen, so I went to check it out.

She wasn't in the kitchen, but once there, I could see the faint light leading to the porch. I wandered back and found her sitting on her peach love seat, reading, an open container of cottage cheese with a spoon sticking out on the coffee table in front of her.

"Hi," I said tentatively.

She looked up at me and put her book down.

"Hi," she said, her face betraying no emotion I could read.

"Hi," I repeated, like an idiot.

She took a deep breath and blinked a few times. When she finally spoke, her voice was lower than usual, very controlled. "I'm not sure I can talk to you right now," she said very evenly.

"You heard?"

"Yes, Bobby. The Associated Press called here and asked me to comment about my gay son. It's a goddamn national story."

I hadn't ever heard my mother curse. It made me want to go to her and hug her and tell her everything would be all right, but I wasn't sure it would be.

"I was set up," I said, and she looked up at me, her eyes pleading with me, as if I'd just offered her some hope.

"So it's not true?" Her eyes told me very clearly: *Say It Isn't, Bobby Lee*.

I sighed. She had taught me not to lie. "It wasn't supposed to be in the article. Finch double-crossed me. Finch Gozman?"

She reached for the cottage cheese, and as she picked it up, her spoon dropped to the floor. "It's not true," she said, her eyes locked on mine, frozen.

"What?"

"You're not gay, Bobby." She bent down and picked up the spoon.

"Yes, Mom. I am."

My mother wiped off the spoon and stuck it in the container, scooping out a dollop of white gook. She wouldn't look at me. Before she put the spoon in her mouth, she repeated herself. "You're not gay, Bobby. It's just a phase. Plenty of people go through this. You're confused."

"I don't think so, Mom."

She wiped her mouth with her finger and looked up, not at me exactly, but at least near me. "You don't know everything, Bobby. You don't know . . ."

I sighed, exasperated. "What do you want me to say?"

My mother stood, dropping the cottage cheese container onto the coffee table. It capsized, oozing its contents onto the table. "I don't want you to say anything, Bobby," she said. "Nothing. Your father is finally feeling better. Couldn't you give him a couple days to just feel good again?"

She marched out of the room.

I stood alone on the porch, feeling nothing. I'd figured she'd be my biggest supporter. She always was. Without her on my side, who was left? I imagined myself as a speck of dirt on the floor, and envisioned a huge broomstick coming at me, at lightning speed, and I shut my eyes tight. And suddenly there was nothing. No light, no sound. Just me standing on the porch with my eyes closed.

My dad must have had a late meeting, because he didn't come home for dinner. Then I began to worry that maybe he didn't come home because of me. Maybe he was so upset that he couldn't come home.

Or maybe that had nothing to do with it. Maybe he didn't even know. How the hell was I supposed to know?

And how long was I supposed to live like this?

The phone rang at seven-thirty. I was sitting on my bed, not moving much. I realized I hadn't moved in a long time, maybe an hour, since coming upstairs. The phone rang, and it was in reach, so I picked it up and answered as if everything was normal.

"Is this Bobby Framingham?"

"Yup," I said, frozen inside.

"Luke Hutchens, *L.A. Times*. How're you doing?"

I didn't answer.

"Hello?"

"Hi," I said, devoid of emotion.

"What you've done is sensational, Bobby. You should be proud.

We're running an article tomorrow. It's mostly written already, but I need a few words from you, okay?"

"No, it's not okay," I snapped. "This was a mistake; the reporter tricked me and printed the story without my permission."

Luke was silent for a moment. "That's a strong accusation, Bobby. And I've heard the recording myself. I spoke with the young reporter earlier. You told him you were gay, and it was during an interview. I heard it myself."

"Look, I don't know what he did, but he doctored something," I said. Please don't publish anything more about me."

Luke sighed loudly. "Bobby, the cat's out of the bag. You can't take back what you said, it's already out there. Finch told me today that you'd changed your mind."

"Finch? I didn't even see him today! What does he mean, 'changed my mind'? Nothing to change! I didn't want to come out right now! Understand?"

"My strong suggestion to you is to bite the bullet and do this," he said. "Your story is out there, whether or not you changed your mind. It doesn't matter. You're doing a great thing. Relax and enjoy it."

The laughter began softly, low in my belly, and then it rose into my chest and throat and it got loud, and ugly. "No one is listening to me! You want me to relax? My life is totally out of control and you want me to relax?"

"Look, you can answer the questions and have your say, or I can publish my column without you, all right? Your choice."

In the thick of my anger I realized he was right. *Nothing I can say is going to stop this speeding train. It's in motion and way beyond my power.*

"Fine," I said. "Ask away."

When my dad finally came home around ten, I braced myself for the conversation. But then I just sort of stood at the door, paralyzed. It was just too much. I figured I'd tell him another time, or maybe not.

Maybe I'd fly away to a land far, far away, where none of this mattered. Wherever that was.

It didn't matter. He just went to their bedroom and I went to bed, where I barely slept at all.

Driving to school on Thursday, I felt wasted. It seemed like years since I'd heard on the radio about the gay football player coming out; it had been only twenty-four hours. My head hadn't stopped pounding, and I'd slept for about twenty minutes. I considered staying home for the day, but being home didn't sound like a picnic either.

I pulled into the parking lot and saw a grouping of trucks at the front of the lot. I saw a big Channel 8 logo on one.

Wonderful, perfect.

I parked and walked slowly toward the media fray, head down. As I approached I heard someone scream, "That's him!" and as I glanced up a half-dozen reporters charged toward me, along with a bunch of cameramen.

I stopped walking and braced myself for the assault. I felt their manic energy approach and I felt as if I were in a bubble, not part of the scene but watching it from above. A sticklike female reporter with bleached blond hair got to me first. "Bobby, how are you doing today? We need you for a few minutes, okay?"

I nodded, giving in to the inevitable. I'd thought about it after the reporter called last night. I could come across as the crazy guy who came out and then changed his mind, the guy who kept screaming that he'd been duped by a nerd reporter, or I could be the quarterback who had come out of the closet and was bravely doing a controversial thing.

"How are you feeling today?" she asked again.

"I'm okay; tired, I guess."

"I bet!" she said, a saccharine-sweet smile on her face. "Do you think that your coming out will send a message to the rest of America that 'gay is okay?'"

I had to think about that one. Beyond the point that I hadn't wanted to come out in the first place, I did think there was some good to be done here. "I hope it will," I said. "I didn't choose to be gay, all I did was tell the truth, and suddenly I'm news." I felt dizzy with exhaustion, and I wondered if I was making any sense. "What I mean is, the only choice I had was whether I would be honest about it, and, well, here I am."

The blond chick gave me this sort of "oh, isn't he a sweet pet" look, pursing her lips and tilting her head. A male reporter, a Latino guy, spoke up. "What do your teammates think?"

"Ask them," I said, and immediately I wished I hadn't. They didn't want to be bothered with this. I was supposed to be doing damage control, and here I was granting interviews and encouraging the media to seek out teammates. "I guess they're mostly okay," I added, hoping they wouldn't bother anyone on the team.

"Do you think this will affect your status as a big-name recruit?" a mustached guy holding a microphone that said ESPN asked.

I froze. In the craziness of the previous twenty-four hours, that hadn't crossed my mind. "I don't know, I hope not," I said, kicking the concrete with my right sneaker.

The reporters ran off to file their stories after a few more questions. One asked if he could follow me around for the day with a camera. I told him that was up to the school, not me. That, I figured, was as good as a no.

About five minutes before the bell, as I walked toward the main doors, someone tapped me on the shoulder and I jumped, tense. I turned and saw it was Bryan. I tried to smile, but it probably wasn't the best smile ever, because he looked concerned. "Oh my God, what happened?"

I looked at him and felt, for the first time in twenty-four hours, a slight slowing in my heartbeat. Calm in the storm. I was so relieved to see his face. I told him the whole story, including how my mom freaked out, and he held my eye contact and listened to me. He told me that he was there for me, whatever I needed.

I smiled and bit my lip. Everybody seemed to want something from me, but Bryan came along and made me feel better just by looking at me. I didn't care that other kids were looking at us as they walked past. I needed the comfort Bryan was giving me.

"So how's school?" Bryan said after a short silence, and we burst out laughing. As we stood there, at the side of the front door, I caught a glimpse of Finch heading right toward us, maybe twenty yards away. He looked downward as he walked. I shushed Bryan and pointed at Finch.

"That's the weasel," I mumbled. "Hey!" I barked.

It felt good to let it out at the right person. Finch looked up, saw me, and didn't react, didn't stop walking. He glanced at Bryan, and it seemed to make him more comfortable that we weren't alone. "Hi, Bobby," he said to a spot somewhere above my forehead as he approached.

"I can't believe you, Finch. Why would you do that?"

Finch looked at me and opened his eyes wide. "Do what?" he said.

"Out me, you moron."

"I don't know what you're talking about," he said, looking at Bryan for support.

"I swear to God, your ass is dead. What's your problem?"

"No problem, just a journalist doing his job," he said, heading toward the front door. I stood in his way. "Thanks for allowing me the exclusive. I actually broke a national story. Stanford will love that."

"That's it? That's all you have? When this comes out, you're going down."

"Your word against mine," he mumbled, his voice low enough so Bryan couldn't hear him, and he continued toward the door. I pushed him toward it, hard enough so he'd stumble, but not so hard that he would crash into it. He looked back at me, fear in his eyes. "You don't want an assault charge on your hands, Bobby. Stay away from me."

He went inside and I turned to Bryan, furious. "Can you believe that guy?"

Bryan nodded, agreeing. "That outfit is horrible," he said. "That purple windbreaker should be burned."

It was so unexpected and stupid that I had to laugh.

"Hey," Bryan said, turning toward me and staring into my eyes. "You're gonna be okay. You're a strong guy."

I felt tired, in my bones. Everything was sagging and I couldn't imagine that it would ever feel better. "I don't know," I said. "I don't feel so strong."

He didn't speak, just rubbed my elbow. There was no tingling. I was just too tired. Then Bryan put his arms around me. I just stood there and allowed him to hug me, feeling frozen until something in his grip melted the fear away. I hugged him back, finally, moments before he let go. "Call me," he said. I nodded and went inside.

As I walked into homeroom, once again people applauded me. There on the wall I saw the big picture of me on the front of the *Times* sports section. It felt nice and I smiled. I finally read the article.

THE KIDS ARE ALL RIGHT

by LUKE HUTCHENS

October 23, 2007

Los Angeles Times Sportswriter

The kids are all right.

They knew all along what we adults managed to completely miss, that the sports world had to reconcile its themes of fair play and inclusion with the stark reality that not one single openly gay man has ever actively competed in one of the four major American sports.

All of our great sports heroes, and the best we could do was a handful of brave men coming out after the fact, in retirement. Billy Bean. Dave Kopay. Esera Tuaolo. John Amaechi.

Shame on our sporting heroes, whom we love for their integrity as well as their prowess. Shame on their counterparts, the heterosexual sportswriters.

We have held the power. So why have none of us had the courage to say, "Something isn't quite right here? Maybe the world we've created isn't quite conducive to true diversity."

No one said, "Of course there are gay men playing sports. They should be allowed to be open and honest. We should create an environment that will help them to be so."

Instead it was a brave, talented seventeen-year-old quarterback named Bobby Framingham who decreed that he should have the right to be open with who he is—a homosexual—while playing quarterback for his Durango Bulldogs at an extremely high level.

Of course, it was not done by a professional athlete, with millions of dollars in salary and endorsements at stake (again, a system we adults screwed up), but by a member of this new generation of hipper, wiser kids who grew up with gay characters on TV, in movies.

They know, at seventeen, how important inclusion is and how hypocritical the current "gay is fine, just don't tell me about it" model is.

And Framingham's revelation will lead to another student athlete deciding to come out, and another. And soon it will be happening at the college level. Then, and only then, may we begin to bring the sports universe into the twenty-first century.

That's the lesson we're learning from this brave Bobby Framingham.

If only we'd known sooner.

Luke Hutchens thought I was a hero, and now everyone wanted to talk to me, and I thought about Dr. Blassingame, when he told me to change the world. It made me shiver.

Later in Spanish, Señorita Vasquez said something I didn't understand, beaming at me and enunciating, very carefully, the word *homosexuales*.

The Day of Horrors turned out better than I'd thought. Carrie and I hung out at lunch, during which she listed her new prospects for dating, since I was out of the picture romantically. There were four such prospects, apparently, and she wanted to know my opinions about each of them. I laughed.

"Carrie, I've been openly gay for, like, two minutes. Maybe we could talk about something else?" I asked. She shrugged it off.

"Well, okay, but if I get pregnant by the wrong man and wind up a teenage bride, it's on you," she replied.

All day I dreaded the locker room before practice. Things had gone much better than I'd expected in classes, but I didn't feel like dealing with whatever the guys were going to throw at me.

It turned out to be a lot quieter than I anticipated.

A couple underclassmen said "hey" when I walked in. Usually the younger varsity players are pretty quiet around me, but I guess my coming out gave them the courage to talk to me, which I didn't mind at all. I never understood why anyone would be intimidated by me in the first place, since I'm not exactly like a yeller or anything.

Austin was already in his pads. He jogged over and slapped me on the back of the head.

"'Sup?" he asked.

"'Sup," I answered, opening my locker. I got it. Austin and all my friends were trying to show me that it didn't matter that I was gay. The result was weird, like everyone was trying too hard. I just wanted everything to be back to normal.

Austin faked out the bench in front of him with a quick start and stop, and then clattered into the lockers next to mine, shoulder pad first. Then he raised his arms and looked around, as if he were open and looking for a pass.

A football flew in his direction. I turned and saw that the throw came from Rahim, who was changing down the aisle from us. Austin caught it in one hand and then, since there was no crowd, went crazy *for* them, simulating the roar he'd get for catching a big touchdown pass.

For an encore, he spiked the ball, which banged into the bench and spun to a rest on the floor. Austin ran off to the water fountain, arms in the air, the adoring fans in his head cheering for him.

"How was the day?" asked Rahim, walking up to me while we changed.

"Not terrible, actually," I said. "Not so sure about how practice will be, though."

He smiled. "It's gonna be good," he said. "It's always good to get out on the field and sweat a bit."

Sure, Somers and Mendez and Dennis and some other guys kept their distance. But the locker room sure didn't seem that much different than it had been before my secret was out.

I was able to forget about things during practice, and it was business as usual in the huddle. I concentrated on footwork and timing my throws and handoffs. Maybe Mendez was a little more quiet than usual, but he still looked fast dodging defenders when we went first-team offense versus first-team defense.

We were going to crush Los Amigos at homecoming tomorrow.

I got so intensely into practice that when Bolleran flinched before I finished my snap count for a hike, I reacted like I would have before, almost forgetting for a moment that he was flinching because I had my hands next to his flabby ass.

"Hey," I barked. "That's five yards right there. Get your head in the game."

I looked over at Coach and he nodded at me. And when we tried it again, Bolleran stayed real still. Things were going to work out just fine.

I actually waited out on the field for a few extra minutes, hoping to get to the showers late to avoid any kind of weird scene.

Once most of the guys were gone, I noticed that I wasn't alone, doing extra stretching. So were Somers, and Mendez, and a few underclassmen.

I passed them as I headed in to the locker room. Somers saw me walking their way and started talking really loud.

"The NO GAYS ALLOWED shower room should be open in about fifteen minutes," he said.

"Cool," answered Mendez, stretching his hamstrings by bending forward with a straight back. "I'm not showering with no faggot."

I had the urge to say a bunch of things, but I let it go. No use arguing, I figured. They were going to dislike me regardless of what I said. As I walked away I even chuckled a bit, thinking about how Mendez had used a double negative, which really means he was going to shower with a faggot.

I got to the locker room, hoping people would be getting dressed already, but when I got there, it was still pretty crowded.

I undressed and walked into the shower area, and it was strangely quiet.

"We gonna take it to Los Amigos tomorrow?" Austin yelled, and some other guys yelled back "hell yeah," but it was pretty weak, like everyone was being really careful with what they said.

I closed my eyes and let the water pour over my back, wishing I knew what to say to defuse the tension. I really wasn't interested in ogling my teammates naked, thanks very much. I'd been to a summer retreat with these guys, where everyone acted gross for a week and there were no doors on the toilets. I felt no lust for my teammates. I just wanted to win a damn football game.

"Hey, guys, I got an announcement." It was a naked, skinny Rocky, walking with his arms wide to the center of the shower room.

Kind and quiet Rocky, who had supported me the day before. But I couldn't help the way my face heated up anyway. I was afraid he was going to make a seriously weird situation worse. The shower room got very quiet.

"I just want to let you know there's an article coming out tomorrow about me. I'm . . . an openly . . . Vietnamese kicker."

Silence. For a good three seconds, all that could be heard were pellets of water slapping the tile floor like a rainstorm.

I snorted. I couldn't help it. It was so ballsy, and out of character, and downright stupid, that I lost my ability to hold it in and just snorted really loud, and then the laughs came, from my belly, like I was having a seizure.

And once I started, I thought, *Oh, great, the naked gay guy is having a seizure in the shower with his horrified teammates,* and that made stopping impossible.

Luckily, the naked-gay-guy-laughing thing made someone else laugh, too. I wasn't sure who it was, because my eyes were closed, but I heard some laughter near me and felt a wave of relief flood through my chest.

Then the laughs started coming and then they wouldn't stop. I wiped the water from my eyes and looked and there was skinny-ass Rocky in the center of the room, beaming, loving every second of it.

"I'm openly tall!" yelled Colby, who is like six-foot-six.

"I'm an openly Latino tight end!" yelled Austin. "No, wait. I'm an openly sexy tight end."

"Look at me, I'm an openly hung-like-a-horse defensive back," yelled Dennis. "Hands off, Bobby."

"Yeah, right," I said. "Get that thing disinfected first." I got a lot of laughs for that one. Dennis even smirked a little in response.

And amid all the hooting and hollering, almost all of the guys came out in one way or another.

"I'm openly black!"

"I'm openly French-Canadian!"

"I'm openly Chinese."

And by the time I left the locker room, the openly gay guy was feeling pretty damn good.

I started laughing again when I was alone in my car, a mixture of fear and excitement making my chest tingle. All over America, I realized, people were watching TV and learning about me, and this could all be okay, I thought. *Except . . . except?* As I drove down Durango Avenue, there was this tiny pocket of something in my gut. I tried to suffocate it, but it wouldn't leave me alone, as if I'd forgotten something terrible.

My phone was sitting on the passenger seat. I had left it in the car all day, I guess. I picked it up and it said I had missed a call. I clicked a button to see who it was and saw the word DAD. There was no message. My dad. He must have heard about it in the news. How come I couldn't keep my mouth shut until I told him first?

I hit the accelerator. I had to get home as quickly as possible.

My parents were up in their bedroom. I took two stairs at a time and barely stopped to knock at their door, I was so anxious to talk to him.

He'd felt like his old self for three days, and here I was ruining everything.

They were sitting on the bed, my mom facing the door, my dad facing her. The flat-screen television on the far wall was on. As I walked in, my mom stood, gently, and walked over to me. She paused for a second, then squeezed my side before walking out. I didn't have time or energy to try to decipher what the squeeze meant.

What if my dad hates me now? I stood, frozen, unsure of what to do, until he finally turned around. His eyes were glassy.

I tentatively sat down next to my father, unsure of what to say. I looked at the television and there I was, a clip of me throwing a touchdown pass to Rahim. Then it cut to me being interviewed that morning. I looked like a moron, all wide-eyed and goofy. I could hardly recognize myself, and immediately hated that the world had seen me like that. I opened my mouth to speak, but he beat me to it.

"I . . . am . . . so . . . proud . . ." he said, and a tear rolled down his cheek and I started quaking inside.

I can't speak, I can't move. All I can do is look at him and listen and allow my body to quake silently.

"That was the bravest thing . . . I've ever heard of." His words were beginning to come easier, and I stared at him, hoping my eyes could tell him what I could not, that I loved him and that I was sorry if I'd hurt him. "You are so strong."

"Dad . . ." I said, a thousand thoughts blurring into less than one in my brain.

"You're the best son I could have ever asked for. I love you, Bobby."

"I love you, too, Dad." He smiled and I felt a tenderness for my father that I had never felt before. He was crying, for me. Proud, of me. I could never have imagined.

He put his arms around me and then the sobs began, and I didn't know what to do but sit there and hold him while he cried. I couldn't remember ever seeing my dad cry before.

"It's all gonna be fine," I whispered, but he cried right through my words and it scared me, how emotional my dad had become.

"Well," he said.

I laughed. "Well what? Of course it's gonna be fine. My teammates are cool with it, mostly. I mean, some of them aren't, but mostly they're cool. I just know it's gonna work out."

My dad pulled away from me and wiped his eyes with the back of his hand. "I'm so glad, Bobby. I'm so glad to hear that," he said.

"Thanks, Dad."

He kept wiping, but the tears kept falling. "There's something else, though."

"What now?" I asked, too quickly. Because as soon as he had said "something else," I realized his tears weren't all about me, but my mouth was faster than my brain.

"I'm so sorry about the timing of this, kiddo. I called you before, but then I thought, let Bobby have his day. My news will still be, you know, news in a couple days. But your mother, she's a smart woman. And she's right. You have a right to know."

No, I thought. No more news. "What?" I repeated, unable to swallow.

He swallowed. "You've been so brave. And that's the kind of . . . inspiration . . . I needed right now . . . to face . . . because . . . well, it's my turn now to be brave."

"What?" I asked, not wanting to hear any more.

"The tests came back from the hospital," he said. "Actually, they came back Monday. My blood counts were all messed up. They called me in for a biopsy and I got the results today. I have lymphoma, Bobby."

I always hated when people said say their lives flashed before their eyes. It had always sounded stupid as hell to me. Life wasn't just one thing, so how could it flash? Except that's exactly what it did. My life, all the things that made up my life, flashed like a series of photographs in my mind's eye.

And I was unable to talk. I tried counting to ten. My head felt so full of things, like I could pop.

My dad rubbed my back. "We caught it pretty early. I guess that's why my appetite has been so lousy these last few months and why I've lost some weight. It's also why my blood pressure was so low. I'm going to a hospital in Arizona that specializes in a new type of radiation therapy. I'll stay maybe a week or two. They think if we do it now, I have a pretty good chance to beat this. Not a hundred percent, but pretty good."

I started to tremble. And the stupid, asinine first thought I had was, *Are you going to miss my homecoming game?* I knew that wasn't the right thing to say and I hated that it came into my mind at all.

"I'm going tomorrow," he said. "Your mother and I talked and we decided to do this up. I could go in for radiation treatment as an outpatient, but I'm going to the place in Arizona where they'll really work on me."

"Oh," I said.

"I'll leave early tomorrow morning. I'm so, so sorry I'm going to miss your game, Bobby. You know I want to be there, but I feel like I have to get this going. Knowing I'm sick makes me feel like I need to get going on getting better right away."

I nodded, because that made a lot of sense. "Of course. You have to do that."

"This can get me better, Bobby. And you'll have plenty of big games in college, and the pros." He smiled when he said that, so I did, too.

"Right," I said, a stabbing pain behind my eyes. "Okay. Right."

"God, am I proud of what you did yesterday and today," he said. "That's just about the bravest thing I've ever heard of. If I can be half that brave . . ."

I started to roll my eyes, but he stopped me. "No, I mean it. Putting yourself out there when you know it could put a big wrench in your dreams, that's . . . that's something, Bobby. You have great character and people will see that."

I didn't have the energy to correct him, tell him how it all had happened. "And you're fine with it?"

He took a deep breath and shrugged. "I've never had a gay friend before, let alone a son," he said, laughing ruefully.

"That's what Austin said. I mean, not the son part. He said he'd never known a gay person and I was like, well, you've known me for a long time."

My father took this in. "Right," he said. "I guess that's right. You have an interesting path ahead of you, that's for sure."

I realized then something that until that moment I'd never fully understood. I realized that I was my own person, separate from my dad, separate from my mom. And I was gay. I was alone in this no matter how much other people cared, or supported me. This was my thing. *We aren't going to make it better. Like it or not, I'm going to get through this, or not. Myself.* The pain behind my eyes throbbed.

"We don't need to talk about this. It doesn't matter," I said. "Let's just focus on you getting better, okay?"

He wiped his eyes, sniffled, and rubbed his nose. "I think we can do both," he said. "This is really all going to be okay."

I nodded, praying he was right. I gave him a hug and he put his chin on my shoulder and kissed my cheek. "I love you, kiddo. Let me get some sleep now, okay?"

I kissed him back and walked out of the room, feeling entirely lost, unsure if I was sad or happy or what I needed to do to make the throbbing in my head go away.

I went down to the porch to talk to my mother.

"Hey, Ma." I said, sitting down on the other end of the peach love seat from her.

"Hey, Bobby Lee," she said. She was staring into space.

I inched closer to her. "You okay?"

"I'm not sure," she said. "I'm medium."

"He's going to be okay," I said.

"God, I hope so," she said. "God, I hope so."

I rubbed her knee. "Are you still mad at me?"

She massaged my fingers. "No, Bobby. I'm not mad. I mean, I'm glad your father took it all so well. I'm surprised, frankly."

"Me, too," I said.

"Your father . . . surprises me all the time."

"I know," I said. "I thought he'd have trouble with it and you'd be fine."

My mother laughed a little. "I guess I like to surprise you sometimes, too."

We sat in silence for a moment. I was playing back Dad's words. He loved me. He was proud of me. I could never have predicted. And now he was sick.

"Why'd you do this, Bobby Lee?" I turned toward her and she looked at me in the way she does when she really doesn't understand something. Her lips tightened, and her eyes became tiny slits. Her face looked so small.

"I didn't mean to, Mom. Really. Finch outed me."

"I know, darling. But all the interviews?"

I sighed. "If I didn't, I'd look like the gay quarterback who wasn't brave enough to go through with what he started. I guess the world will never know that this wasn't planned. Now I just have to live with it. I mean, I can't deny who I am, right? And now I guess I can do it up right, I can start being the brave guy Dad thinks I am."

My mother paused for a moment, as if she was taking that all in. "It's good your father reacted as he did. I think a lot of my reaction was fear that it would really hurt him, Bobby."

"Yeah," I said. "Are you okay?"

My mother laughed softly, a sad laugh. "I don't know, Bobby Lee. This isn't what I had planned for you, you know." I knew my mother was half joking. She often claimed to have planned every aspect of my future. I laughed sadly, too. "I guess I'll just need to deal with it, won't I?"

"Yeah, I guess so."

She sighed. "I think I was just full, you know? You probably don't know what I mean by that."

"I think I do," I said. "I'm full, too."

She smiled and nodded at me.

"Mom?"

"That's me." She reached for my hand. I crawled over to her and we hugged.

"I love you," I said.

"I love you more," was her response as she cradled my head in her chest.

The phone rang at about nine-fifteen, and I rushed to pick it up, fearful it would wake up my father.

"Bobby Framingham, please."

"This is me—he," I said, correcting myself, thinking of Bryan.

"Hi, Bobby, my name is Vincent Morley. I'm the executive editor of *Out & Proud* magazine."

"Don't know it, sorry," I said.

He laughed. "We're the largest gay and lesbian magazine in the country. And we're about to make you a gay icon," he said.

Now it was my turn to laugh. "Excuse me?"

"Picture it, Bobby. Your picture on the front of our magazine, maybe shirtless, cradling a football. A huge feature article on you. You'll be famous. You'll have guys writing you from all over the world, asking for dates."

I wanted to hang up on him, or curse him out, but I knew that wasn't the right thing to do. "Mr. Morley," I said. "I'm pretty sure I'm not ready for that."

His voice had an edge to it, cold, calculating. "Why not?" he asked.

"Are you serious? I'm seventeen years old, Mr. Morley. I'm still a—" I stopped myself, embarrassed to be talking to a stranger about my personal life. "I'm seventeen, okay. Isn't that enough?"

"I'd have to check with legal," he said. "When do you turn eighteen?"

I hung up on him, my stomach queasy. I looked at myself in the mirror. Bobby Framingham, cover boy. I thought of that, and then thought of Austin's reaction, and soon I was laughing. Right, good career move, I thought. What was next, *Playgirl*?

Dad has cancer. That night I fell into one of the deepest, darkest sleeps I'd ever slept. I felt my body slipping into it and then free-falling, falling through the bed. Usually that would wake me, but I was too tired.

I kept falling until I hit something that felt like a beanbag and my body splayed out on it. And it seemed like then I would be able to just rest, but then my head began to tremble like it was full of something and I didn't know how to get rid of it all.

I got this idea that if I could just dampen the thing stuck in my head, I could cry it out of my eyes, and I squeezed as hard as I could to make water, and as hard as I squeezed, my eyes stayed bone-dry. But I wouldn't stop pushing despite the dryness and then a syrupy drip started pouring down my cheeks and I kept waiting for it to end. But my head stayed full, like the syrup could drip down forever and I'd never be done with it.

When I next opened my eyes, it was just after 11 A.M. It was Friday, a school day, so I was three hours late to school and my mom hadn't woken me up. Then I remembered Dad.

I got up slowly and it felt like the inverse of Christmas, the opposite of when you want to run downstairs and see what's there, under the tree.

I went down to the kitchen and my mother was sitting at the table, across from my aunt Roberta. They were drinking coffee. Roberta was a very small woman, with dark graying hair and a huge smile.

It felt so weird, like my dad didn't live there anymore. What if he didn't get better?

As I walked into the room my aunt rushed over to me and enveloped me in a hug.

"The average person needs twenty hugs a day," she said. "Today, let's go with thirty for you, okay?"

I let her hug me. "We let you sleep in," my mom said. "You just seemed so out of it this morning."

"Where's Dad?" I asked, knowing the answer but not knowing what else to say.

Roberta sat back down. "He's off to Arizona," she said.

"How are you doing, honey?" my mother asked, sipping her coffee.

"I don't know," I said.

"I don't know is a valid answer," said Roberta, standing and giving me the second of thirty promised hugs. I stood there, taking the hug, feeling empty inside, wasted.

"So it's okay I missed school?" I asked.

My mother took a sip of coffee. "I couldn't bring myself to wake you this morning. You've been through a lot, sweetie."

I went back upstairs to rest some more and then showered. Everything seemed to take me twice as long as usual, which was weird.

At about one-thirty I told Mom and Aunt Roberta I was going out for a drive. My mother looked concerned.

"Where exactly are you going?" she asked.

"Rahim's," I said. I hadn't known for sure until I said it. He always went home on Fridays to rest before games. "I guess I'll go straight to the game after that."

My mother looked at my aunt and I realized my mom didn't want me to play. That wasn't an option for me.

Roberta looked back at her and something was communicated. My mother said nothing more about it. I gave them both quick kisses and went off to Rahim's house.

Rahim's car was in the driveway when I arrived. His mother came to the door and smiled her wide toothy smile when she saw it was me.

"The famous Bobby Framingham, to what do I owe this great fortune?" She opened the door and enveloped me in her soft arms. When she felt my weight she pulled back and looked at me. "Child, something is not right here. What's wrong, Bobby?"

I didn't speak, at least not right away. I stood in the doorway feeling like some other person, totally unable to talk, while Mrs. Bell's face got more and more illuminated with each passing second. Her eyes got real wide, and then her mouth, too. I wondered if she thought I was taking drugs or something.

"Standing in the doorway like you're not part of the family," she said, grabbing my hand hard and leading me into the living room, where Rahim was playing Xbox football. He looked up and quickly paused the game, springing to his feet to greet me. "Sweetheart, help me sit this boy down on the couch," she said to Rahim, who helped lead me to a seat. "Too much media? Someone looks a little overwhelmed." Mrs. Bell smiled, and I tried to smile back, but failed. "Child, talk to us!"

"My father has cancer," I said, and Rahim's face immediately registered regret.

"My Lord," Mrs. Bell said, and she came to me and held me tight. I stood there, limp in her arms. Rahim stood back a few steps. I was embarrassed. In a very short time I'd become a problem person, the kind of person I always hated, who needed everything to be about them. I was afraid to look up at Rahim, afraid that he could see how pathetic I had become.

"You up for a walk, B?" asked Rahim. "Fresh air would do you good."

I nodded, and without a word we headed outside. Rahim's subdivision is a lot newer than ours. Where we live the houses all look a little different from one another, but here they all looked alike. Carrie called them McMansions once. I didn't care, I liked them.

"I gotta get my mind on the game," I finally said, studying the ground as we walked.

"You don't have to do anything but take care of yourself," he said.

I turned to him. "How can you say that? There's gonna be media from across the country there. The team needs me. How can I turn my back?"

We stopped walking. Rahim stretched his arms up at the sky, and I looked up, and suddenly felt very small, there on the sidewalk of a suburban neighborhood in Durango, California. The sky was huge. *We're big guys, but not so big when you think about it.*

"You can't take care of everyone else's problems. You got issues. I say, deal with your shit before trying to take on all sorts of other people's shit."

"So you wouldn't be pissed if I didn't play?"

Rahim smiled at me and put his hand on my shoulder. "Doesn't matter, Bobby. Who cares what I think? You have every right to do the right thing for you."

I shook my head at him, resigned, and he understood, and we walked on. "You're probably right, but you know I'll be behind center tonight, don't you?"

"Yeah, I know," he said.

"How'd you get so smart?" I asked.

"My mom, mostly. She has a lot of answers. Lots of questions, too."

Rahim left his car at home and we drove to school together. We didn't talk. My mind kept pulling up images of my dad—in the stands watching me in the playoffs last year, swimming in the ocean with me when I was ten—and each one sent a shudder through me.

I felt totally unprepared.

If the only thing separating me from playing in front of a huge crowd was about two hours and my uniform, that maroon-and-gray jersey had better have some serious magic powers, I thought.

We parked, and as we got out of my car, we saw a group of people with picket signs standing near the entrance to the school. Rahim and I quickened our pace, curious to see what was up.

It was a group of weird-looking people holding up the signs. ROT IN HELL, BOBBY FRAMINGHAM, one read. FAGS GET AIDS, read another. A third one, huge black letters on red poster board, read GOD HATES BOBBY.

I felt nauseous, like a huge bubble was stuck in my chest. Their apparent leader, a short, squat older man with a very pink face, saw me and Rahim.

He recognized me immediately.

"Die, Faggot Die!" He began the chant, pointing at me. Soon all of them were pointing and chanting.

Rahim grabbed my arm to pull me away, but I had already lost it. I felt the acid in my chest start to bubble, and then like a volcano it exploded, and I threw up, at them. Rahim jumped away. The protesters recoiled in horror, as if I'd found their kryptonite. Once finished, I stood up, feeling better. I wiped my mouth with my hand, wiped it on my pants, and turned and walked away with Rahim.

"That's one way to get back at them," he said, and I shrugged, feeling like I'd woken up in a parallel universe, where nothing was the same as it used to be.

In the locker room, I sat by my locker and stared into space while Rahim told the story. Most of the guys had seen the signs, and had been pretty shocked by it all. Rocky said it was a church group from Irvine that is big in the pro-family movement, whatever that means. Apparently they once protested the funeral of a gay kid who got beaten to death in Los Angeles.

Dead. I couldn't get past what I had felt when they all were pointing at me. *They hate me. Me. They want me dead.*

The locker room was noisy as I started undressing, psych-up music and rowdy offensive linemen. I felt like I was watching it on TV. Rahim walked over and touched my shoulder. "You want to tell Coach about your dad?" he asked quietly.

"Should I?"

"It's up to you. I would," he said. I nodded, put my shirt back on, and walked into Coach's office. He was eating his pregame orange. When I entered, he looked up, distracted.

"What is it, Bobby?" he asked. His tone said: *The Answer Had Better Be Nothing.*

I took a deep breath. "My dad," I said, focusing on a crack in the wall behind and to the right of Coach.

Coach blinked quickly. "How's he doing?" He sucked some pulp out of an orange section.

I cleared my throat, feeling very mature and controlled. I wanted Coach to see that I was a team leader. "He's in Arizona getting radiation therapy," I said, as straightforward as possible.

Coach closed his eyes and sighed. "Oh, Bobby," he said, standing and quickly swallowing what was in his mouth.

"Yeah," I said, standing tall but totally numb inside. "He has lymphoma, I guess. They think he should be okay."

Coach ambled over and hugged me, and I tried to be as nonchalant as possible in receiving the hug. "How you holding up?"

"I'm fine," I said, swallowing hard.

He pulled back and looked at me. "You look terrible. You'll sit this one out, Bobby."

I felt an involuntary tug in my abdomen. "I have to do this," I said. My face felt like it was twitching and I wondered if I was just tired. "They're all here to see me."

"You're in no shape—"

"No!" I said, fending off another twitch. "I can do this."

Coach sighed and put his hand on my head and left it there. I stood still, feeling like a marionette awaiting a tug, something to make my arms move. "You're a strong guy, Bobby Framingham. Have to be, going through all you're going through. I think you're making a mistake here, though."

"I can do this," I stressed. My mouth was bone-dry.

"Well, get through this one game, and we'll talk later. Can you do that?"

I needed water. Water and a place to sit and be quiet. "No problem," I said.

"If anyone can do this, it's you. Keep your eye on the prize."

I nodded and stumbled out of his office, hoping I looked strong, but completely unsure of my ability to quarterback a team to victory in front of a huge crowd.

The stadium was jam-packed, even more than the usual homecoming crowd. There were TV cameras everywhere, and the first one was in my face as soon as we exited the locker room and hit the tunnel that leads to the field. A guy with a bushy mustache blinded me with a bright light in my face. "Sorry, poor lighting," he said.

I felt wobbly as we got to the end of the tunnel. Austin came up behind me and knocked me gently on the head with the back of his hand. "Rahim told me," he said. "Play the game and I'll catch you later." I nodded again. We ran out onto the field and were hit with a deafening cheer from the stands, louder than any cheer I'd ever heard, sort of like a thunderbolt that shook the ground beneath us. "Holy shit," Austin said as he left me, sprinting out onto the field. I followed, and as I began to run I heard the chanting.

It sounded like two chants, like a radio tuner in between two stations. I heard "Bob-bee, Bob-bee" loud and clear. But there was another, shorter one, too. It took me a few seconds to adjust, and realize they were saying "Fag! Fag! Fag!" in unison. I saw a commotion in the lower stands to my left. There was a fight. I tried to swallow it all down, push the feelings down below my stomach.

We circled on the field and did warm-up drills. Rahim ran over to me before we started and punched me lightly in the shoulder. "Tune it out, B, tune it out," he said. I looked to the sidelines as we did calisthenics, and watched as several news reporters stood in front of the cameras, microphones in hand, saying God knows what.

I wanted the game to be over. I wanted a blanket over my head. I wanted my mom.

"Cracks are showing, Bobby, toughen up!" said Rahim, next to me, as we bent over, touching our toes. I immediately bolted upright, and felt for the back of my uniform pants. Rahim saw this and started to laugh, really loud. "Not that crack, B!" and when I realized he meant emotionally, I started to laugh, too, and pretty soon I was feeling a bit looser. *This is what you live for, play your game.*

• • •

We led 10–3 going into the second quarter, despite my wandering mind and the fact that I was not all there. Certain plays were vivid, every sound, every sight, every smell, every feeling heightened as they filled my senses. Other times, it seemed like I was watching the play from above, totally disconnected.

I took the snap and saw the breakdown in our blocking and then felt the defender's shoulder pads as he hit me directly in the sternum. I felt the air pushed out of my mouth, my nose, my eyes. I was on the ground, gasping for air, and the defender who took me down got in my face.

"Fuckin' queer," he said, spewing his words into my face. I came away wet with his saliva.

I walked back to the huddle with my head buzzing. *Hey! Where are my teammates, my brothers who don't let other teams talk to me like that?*

The next play, I rolled left and found Somers for a nice gain, maybe fifteen yards. Just as I released the ball, I heard the hit before I felt it, a shot to the side, and once again, from the ground, I was greeted by a defender from Los Amigos in green and white.

He put out his hand as if to help me up. "Brave man, Framingham," he said. I stared at him, unsure if I should trust his hand. "What you did is really cool. God bless you."

I took his hand, nodded to him, and he helped me off the ground.

Up 17–10 and driving into their territory with time running down in the second quarter, I lost my footing on a running play and wildly tossed the ball back to Mendez. It didn't go anywhere near where he was, and the ball was loose in our backfield. The crowd roared. A lineman fell on top of me, and I struggled to free myself from him. I watched from the ground as Somers tried to recover it, but one of their linebackers scooped it up and went the distance for a touchdown. After the kick, the game was tied, and it was my fault.

I could hear boos from the crowd, and I tried to shake it off, but I couldn't. I just kept playing the bad toss over and over in my mind, and by halftime, I was a wreck.

"No harm, no harm," Coach told me at the half, grasping my shoulder.

That's when I noticed it. I couldn't feel his hand.

"Keep your head in the game, Bobby, you're doing good." But as he said it, I looked down at my hands and they were shaking. My hands were moving, vibrating, wildly out of my control. I hid them from view and didn't tell anyone.

I can control this. It's all in my head.

We got the ball to start the second half, and my hands wouldn't stop shaking. I saw my father's face when I looked at Austin in the huddle. I looked away. I fumbled the first snap, but luckily we recovered. In the huddle, I tried to apologize, but the words came out funny. My mouth had dried up. A paste had built up around my lips. I swallowed, seeking the wetness of saliva, but there wasn't any. "Messy," I said, when what I meant was, "I messed up." The guys looked at me funny. I finally got the words out to call for a long pass to Rahim.

I looked down at my fingers and told myself to get a grip. The hiked ball hit my jittery hands, and I knew there was trouble. My whole left arm was shaking as I dropped back. I saw Mendez's eyes as he was blocking for me and they said it all; I was more out of control than I could have ever believed. My throwing motion was fine, but my shaking arm undermined everything. I pulled back my arm and struggled to not hit myself in the face with the ball. I unloaded, shaky arm and all, and unleashed a pass about twenty yards shy of where I was aiming, and slightly to the left. It was a gift to the same linebacker who had just scored a touchdown prior to the end of the first half. He caught it and made a nice gain on the interception return before he was tackled.

My arm was gone.

I walked slowly to the sidelines, aware of the damage I had done, and the fact that I had no confidence that I could shake it off. Coach saw it in my eyes as I took my helmet off. He came over to me and put his hand back on the top of my head. I could feel the heat of his thumb as he lightly pushed down.

"We're going with Haskins," he said to me quietly. I looked up at him and tried to speak, but by now the whole world was shaking.

In my head, the phrase had come as *Are you sure? I can try harder, Coach.*

"T-t-try?" I said, stuttering.

He put his arm around me and guided me to the bench. I couldn't speak. Coach went over to Haskins and got him to warm up. I sat and hid my head in my hands, rubbed my temples gently with my thumb. I wished no one could see me from the stands, but there were television cameras everywhere.

So I hid my face. While I sat like that a funny thing happened to me. Suddenly it was like I was alone out there, in my own private space, with my head hidden in my hands. And my thoughts had a chance to gather and things calmed a little.

I pictured my arm flailing in the wind. *I can't even control my own body.* But instead of feeling horrified and embarrassed, I felt nothing. And then I pictured my father lying in a hospital bed, out of control as well, with all these tubes connected to him, and he had this yellow glow on him, like he was radiating. And I felt a jolt in my tear ducts and knew that I should be crying, but instead my mind was strangely calm.

And all I really wanted was to be alone, out of the football stadium, with my own thoughts.

As I heard the crazy noise swirling in the air around my head, I realized that I shouldn't have played, I shouldn't be there at all. I was full. *Okay*, I thought, *okay*. I let all the catcalls go. The screaming floated like a cloud over and around me.

"Yeah, boy-eee!" Rahim shouted across the locker room toward Austin and me. The game was over, we had won 31–17 after our defense took over. Haskins played well enough at quarterback for us to win.

I didn't see a minute of it.

In the locker room, I don't know if people were avoiding me or not, but everyone was excited. I pasted a smile on my face, gave Rahim a long-distance thumbs-up, and buttoned up my shirt.

They should celebrate. I just need to be alone.

My eyes not moving from the road in front of me, I drove fifteen miles to China Cove Beach after the game with my mind nearly blank. I parked in the empty parking lot.

The beach was deserted.

It was a moonless night, and as I took off my shoes and stepped onto the chilly sand, the only light was coming from the lampposts behind me in the lot and off in the distance to my right, Long Beach. The sand went from fully visible under my feet to wet and chilly grains that I could barely see as I continued to approach the water. I could hear the ocean hissing in front of me, but it looked black without the light of the moon.

I stood, facing the water and the crashing waves. In the pitch-black night, I could see the Long Beach lights and wondered what it would take to get away from all light.

I wanted pitch blackness so I could be truly alone, no interruption.

I flopped down onto the beach and took my shoes off, buried my feet in the sand I could feel but not see. I couldn't tell where the water began but figured it was about thirty feet away from the slightly distant hissing of waves.

What do I do now?

The night chill made me shiver as I tried to make sense of my life. What if my dad died? What if the radiation didn't work, and he didn't get better?

And what if football was over? What if Coach never let me play again? Who was I going to be if that was taken away from me? If my arm could just shake uncontrollably on the field, how could I say I was in control enough to be a college star?

I gasped and inhaled chilly sea air at the thought of how much my life had changed in the last couple of days.

As I pinched sand between my toes, I thought back to times my parents took me to the beach when I was a kid. I remembered how my dad would take me into the water. He'd make me stand in front of him and hold my elbows, and when a wave came, he'd wait until the very last second to lift me. Just as I could feel my heart jumping in my chest and the mist of the wave approaching me at eye level, he'd lift me high up, above the wave, and then bring me down gently into the water.

That was always my favorite game.

I dug my feet into the sand and lay back, looking up at the blank sky.

There wasn't a goddamn thing I could do to make my dad better. Or start the game over. Or change the fact that I was gay. Or anything.

Other than lie there.

Or what?

In the chilly night breeze, I slowly sat up and faced the ocean, totally taken with a crazy idea.

I have to go into the ocean.

To cleanse my mind. I just need to go.

Standing, I took my shoes in my hands and stepped forward into the water. Waves crashed and sizzled, exploding into white foam and licking at my ankles, ice cold penetrating the bones of the soles of my bare feet. Each wave sent a shock and a shiver up into my body as it passed, and again as it receded, forming puddles behind my heels. Goose pimples dotted my forearms.

A cold sweat beaded on my forehead and suddenly I couldn't swallow or catch my breath. A dull ache had formed in my throat.

Wave after wave crashed into me, soaking the bottom of my jeans and making them feel heavy.

It was colder than anything I'd ever felt.

I took off my football jacket and tossed it carelessly behind me. Underneath I wore a T-shirt, and despite the chill, I took that off as well, flinging it behind me. Now I was just in jeans and I felt my nipples hardening from the cold night air. I thought about how the denim would feel against my skin if I walked into the surf, how it would cling to my thighs and weigh me down when I most wanted to feel free.

This is real. I'm Bobby Framingham and the whole world knows I'm gay. My dad is in the hospital and I'm no longer a starting quarterback. This is who I am. My breathing quickened as the reality hit me.

The freezing air and water brought moisture to my face. Mucus dripped from my nose to my lips. My sinuses burned, and I felt the wetness in my eyes that had been so dry.

And the first tear fell.

My eyes flooded with them and I screamed as loud as I could scream.

I charged blindly into an oncoming wave, breaking it with my bare chest as best I could before it flung me back toward the shore, frigid salt water rolling over my head, mocking me.

I regained my balance, paused for a sliver of a moment as my body adjusted to the shock of the icy waters, and silently, shivering and convulsing, walked past that wave, out into the dark, mysterious ocean.

The chill of the water I still could barely see shocked and enveloped me, and I found myself out of control and thrashing against the approaching waves. But then I gained my footing and stood, the water waist-high, I imagined, though it was hard to tell. My body felt numb from the shocking freeze of the ocean, but the night air felt even colder. The water level rose and fell along my body, leaving my body warmer below and colder above, disorienting me.

I let out a hoot as I caught my breath.

I braced myself before another invisible wave could knock me down. I heard the swell seconds before it crashed into me and took the hit to my side, hearing the smacking sound and feeling my body fight the impact of the forceful current. The water flew off my body in all directions, hitting me in the face like frozen nails.

I screamed. Everything poured out of me as a wave smacked me in the chest and sent me toppling under the salt water and I felt like I had when the defender had tackled me and called me a fag, insulted and pounded together in a way that squeezed at my gut. Frigid liquid lodged into my nose and ears like ice cubes. I went under, trying to locate the bottom of the ocean with my feet. Frosty salt water flooded over my head and my thoughts garbled and all I could hear and feel was water rushing into my ears.

I looked up into total blackness, gasping for air and wiping the water from my eyes. I couldn't be sure my eyes were open until I touched my face and blinked, darkness and just a blur of lights to my right.

My heart was pounding in my brain; I could hear it louder and louder with each pulse. I looked toward the beach, my eyes at water level, and just before a wave crashed over my head, I saw it. A figure, standing on the beach, looking out at me.

As I emerged from the wave I heard my name. I recognized the voice, and I whimpered.

I let the ocean push me in to the shore, jumping to allow the wave to carry me and paddling along with it. When my chest hit sand, I jumped to my feet and eluded the next crashing wave behind me. When I reached Bryan, I collapsed on the sand, trying to catch my breath. Bryan took off his jacket and enveloped me in it. I couldn't feel the heat, couldn't feel anything except my brain, spinning still, and what felt like a layer of ice over my entire body. It stung like a hundred bees. My teeth would not stop chattering.

He hugged me through the jacket, and I allowed myself to go limp in his arms.

"You okay?" I heard him ask.

He dried me off as best as he could, wrapped me in his dry jacket, and while I still couldn't feel my body, the bee stings were getting lighter and lighter until they were just pinpricks and finally, just cold.

My jeans were sopping wet. In the darkness he took them off of me.

Bryan dried off my legs and in the dark I tried to clear my mind so I could say something that would make this all make sense. After the ocean, every feeling was heightened and shivers zipped up my spine. I looked up and I could see the outline of Bryan's face and wanted so much for him to understand what was going on in my brain without having to say it.

I couldn't tell.

Bryan took off his jeans and put them on me.

Once I was zippered up, I watched his silhouette as he stood there in a T-shirt and his briefs. He bent down and pulled me up, and we stood silently, looking out at the nearly invisible ocean.

"They hate me," I said finally. "I can't ever go back there."

Bryan put his arm around me and leaned in to me. "Yes, you can," he said. "And you're going to have to get used to some people not liking you."

"I hate this," I whispered, and the words, the world, seemed to fade in the wind.

Bryan paused and gripped my shoulder tighter. "I know. Me, too."

I looked out into the blackness, where the horizon was supposed to be.

"I feel like things will never be the same again. It feels like the end of the world."

Bryan faced me then, and stared into my eyes. His eyes were so peaceful, and he leaned in to me and closed his eyes, and then he put his lips on mine and we kissed. His lips were soft, the softest, most angelic thing I'd ever felt.

"It isn't," he said, and he took my hand and walked me toward the car.

Austin and I were up in my room, chomping through a box of Oreos. "Hey, look," Austin said, shaking his leg. "Looks like a weeklong vacation for me, too."

"You prick," I said, half smiling.

It was Thursday after school, or at least it was after school for Austin. I'd stayed home for my fourth straight day and still had one more to go.

After the homecoming game, both Dr. Blassingame and Coach Castle called my mother to check on me. When they told her about what had happened at the game with my arm, she sort of freaked. She took charge, and decided I was going to take a few days off from school to "slow things down," as she said. I didn't like it at first, especially because she was implying I'd sit out a game. But after talking to both Blassingame and Coach, I kind of realized it had been decided for me. I was off for a week and that was that.

A couple of days into it, I realized it wasn't a bad idea because I began to actually relax for the first time in a while.

"How's Haskins look?" I asked.

"How many times are you going to ask me that?" Austin answered. "He's awesome. He's the best quarterback we've ever had. Coach keeps saying that we're lucky that Bobby kid went crazy."

"Shut up," I said, a little pierced by his comment.

Austin punched me in the shoulder. "You're such a baby. I'm kidding, dude. We need you back for the playoffs, okay?"

"Okay," I said, a smile creeping over my face.

"Anyway, I'm glad you're getting your head shrunk," Austin said. "It was getting pretty big there for a while."

"Shut up," I said, but I was wondering if he was right. Maybe I was full of myself. Maybe the whole problem had been that I think too much about things and think my feelings are more important than they are. Maybe if I just chilled out, I'd realize—

"Dude, I was kidding," Austin said.

I snapped to attention and smiled at him. "I know," I said, defensive.

"Whatever," he said.

My mother knocked on the door and pushed it open a bit. "Have you gone through all of those cookies?" she asked.

Austin and I looked at the empty plate. "No," I said, smiling with chocolate crumbs in my teeth.

She smiled back. "You have a visitor," she said.

Austin jumped to his feet. I wiped my mouth and started to tell him to stick around, but he beat me to it.

"Big game tomorrow," he said, and he gave me sort of a half hug and bounded out of my room and down the stairs, waving to my mom as he passed her.

"I'm glad you two are still friends," my mom said, and I rolled my eyes because my mother should like write Hallmark cards or something.

I walked down the stairs and saw that the visitor was Coach Castle. He was sitting on our couch, drinking a glass of water. He was so big he made the couch look miniature. My mother followed me down the stairs, and when the three of us were standing there in the living room in awkward silence, my mother said, "Why don't you guys have lunch together today?"

Coach clasped me in an awkward hug. "We're going out," he said.

"Sure." And I followed him out the door.

I suggested Five and Diner, and he drove us there. We didn't say much in the car, and we were pretty quiet at first at the table. It wasn't like he was angry at me, more like it was awkward and neither of us knew where to begin.

I wanted my usual hash browns and root-beer float, but I didn't think Coach needed to see how poorly his quarterback ate. So I went with a big chicken salad instead. He ordered a burger.

"How are you, Bobby?" he asked, after we ordered.

"I'm actually pretty good," I said.

"You look good. You keeping in shape?"

I looked down at the table. "Not so great," I said. I saw the tide of anger rise in him, pure Coach Castle, ready to pounce on weakness, but then I saw him quickly change his impulse.

"It's good that you're taking care of business," he said.

"Yeah," I replied.

"How's your dad?"

"Okay," I said. I had talked to him every day and he always sounded pretty much like himself, only exhausted from the treatment. Apparently, the radiation strategy is to kill the cancer, and everything nearby, too. So you get healthy by feeling much worse at first. He was staying an extra two weeks now, which sucked, but he convinced me it was for the best. He said the doctors were very optimistic he would be cancer-free after that.

The conversation sort of went on like that until our food arrived and I wondered why we were there. But after a few bites of burger, he got to the point.

"I need to apologize," Coach said, looking directly into my eyes. "I should never have allowed you to go out there for the homecoming game."

I waved him off. "No, no. I wanted to. I—"

"I'm the coach," he said. "Not you. I'm responsible for looking out for your best interests, and I failed. I'm sorry."

I thought about that. I didn't know what to think. Maybe I'd ask Blassingame the next time I saw him.

"You're coming back Monday?"

"Yup."

"I need to know whether you want to play," he said, staring into my eyes.

"Of course . . ."

"No, not of course," he said, his tone more like that of the coach I knew and loved. "I'm asking you if you really want it, Bobby. Do you have that spark to play like you used to, or do you want to hang it up for the year? Haskins is doing just fine in your place."

I surprised myself with my vehemence. "No, Coach, that's my job. I want to play. I'll do anything."

He smiled, and I was relieved. It was like seeing an old friend again, after sitting across from a stranger for fifteen minutes or so. "Good. Because Haskins, I'm telling you, Bobby, it ain't gonna work in the playoffs. He'll beat a bad team tomorrow. Good teams will shut down the running lanes and we'll be in some deep shit."

I'd gotten the reports from Austin and Rahim. They told me practices weren't quite the same with Haskins back there. I laughed. "Good to feel needed," I said.

"Well, we do need you. So get your ass to the gym later today, and get your mind on the game. It's showtime for the Bulldogs."

It was the first time in a couple weeks that my heart skipped a beat in that inimitable way that only happens around football. I felt alive, and grateful to Coach for believing in me.

"Showtime!" I said, smiling too quickly after a bite of chicken. It slipped out of my mouth. I looked up at Coach and the laughter made it feel, for the moment, like nothing had changed from September. I knew it had, but I loved the feeling of being back in tight with Coach.

"I don't know, scared shitless?" I told Dr. Blassingame, when he asked me how I felt to be back at school.

He laughed. It was Monday and we were in his office at the start of the school day. It was time to return to the real world, and football, and I felt a little woozy, like you feel when you've had the flu and go back to school too soon.

"You'll be just fine," he said.

I was definitely feeling more comfortable with Blassingame these days. He had visited me at the house twice during the week and we had talked. It was cool, even though it was a little weird having a teacher invade the private space of your room.

"Do you think there will ever come a time when I'll be glad this happened?" I asked, picking up a stray rubber band from his desk.

Blassingame laughed. "I'm already glad."

I looked at him like he was crazy. "You're nuts." I stretched the rubber band and it snapped, biting me lightly on the fleshy area between my thumb and index finger.

"True as that is, you learned a lot through this adversity, Bobby."

I massaged my rubber-band sting. "So if I hadn't been gay, and Finch hadn't written that story, and my dad hadn't gotten sick, I wouldn't have grown?"

Blassingame shook his head. "You're one tough customer, aren't you?" he said. I shrugged and stretched the rubber band as wide as it would go, testing whether I could pull it apart. "It looks to me, my friend, like you're ready."

"We'll see," I said. And with a firm handshake, I was off to face the world of high school again.

At lunch I found out what happens when people feel like they know you better than they really do. Obviously word had gotten out about my breakdown, because complete strangers were coming up to me and confiding in me their secrets.

"I actually have two moms," said this guy with a Mohawk as we stood in the checkout line.

Carrie heard this one as she walked up. Her eyes were like saucers. I gave the Mohawk kid an understanding nod and we watched him put his tray down and pay the lady at the register.

"My sister's best friend had a nervous breakdown," this pimply-faced girl, probably a freshman, told me after I finished paying.

I nodded solemnly and waited for Carrie to pay for her lunch.

"Are you a confessional now?" Carrie asked.

"Apparently," I said.

"Cool," she said. "I'm having impure thoughts about the dishwasher guy."

That made me laugh, and I felt better.

• • •

"Glad to be back?" Bardello, our third-string quarterback, asked me as we started the first of five laps around the football field. I nodded. The day had gone well, but the locker room had been strange. I thought we had solved the "Bobby's gay" problem when we had all been laughing in the shower. But now I was back after missing a game and a week of practice, and there was this awkward silence, like they thought I was going to snap at any moment. I didn't hear one joke, and that's what I wanted to hear: Laughter. It would tell me that everything was fine again.

My legs felt tight, my hamstrings like creaky wires in need of oil. But after missing a week, I savored it all, especially how good the cool breeze felt on my skin.

"You think I could catch Haskins if I tried?" I asked Bardello. As usual, Haskins had sped off to a big lead, while Bardello and I did our usual jog.

He looked over at me and laughed. "Sure thing, Crazy," he said.

My one-week hiatus had gained me a new nickname. I sped off, leaving Bardello in my dust.

With Haskins at the helm, we'd beaten Westminster La Quinta 31–0, mostly on the strength of Mendez and our running game. Haskins had done well, but I was the starter again, and it felt good. Haskins was even pretty cool about it, telling me in the locker room before practice that it was good to have me back.

As I was rounding the final curve of the second lap, my pace felt good, my legs felt loose, and I was enjoying the slow burn in my chest. I was also slowly catching up on Haskins, who wasn't aware we were racing yet.

"Watch out, Haskins, I'm gonna pass you," I yelled, still a good fifteen yards behind him. Haskins looked back, keeping his pace effortless while searching for me with his eyes. I saw him laugh and turn back, picking up his pace a step.

"You keep dreaming, Crazy," he shouted.

"Crazy is coming to get you," I yelled, and I saw Coach just ahead of me, working with the linebackers on a drill near the thirty-yard line. He looked up as I said that and grinned.

I saw Austin running routes with the receivers. He glanced up at me and gave me the finger just as I whizzed past him on lap three. I laughed and felt a tingling in my chest.

Lap four was always the tough one, but it was especially hard today, after having missed a week of conditioning. I got within ten yards of Haskins as I hit the final lap. Bardello was a good half lap behind us. I had something to prove today. To hell with everyone telling me I was slow. I was whatever I chose to be, and at that moment I chose to be faster than Haskins. I pumped my legs harder and felt myself accelerate. I enjoyed the feeling of speed, whooshing through the wind and knowing that as this race picked up steam, the rest of the team had stopped to watch. I could feel their eyes on me, could feel them as I closed the gap between Haskins and me, could feel him begin to panic about losing out in a race to the slow and crazy gay guy who was about to take his job. *Who is this masked man who comes back from a weeklong hiatus stronger than ever, and faster, and—*

As I turned the third of four corners, my legs moving faster than my body usually moves, my head narrating the race, I lost the rhythm in my legs. Like a steady drumbeat and then the drummer misses the snare, there I was, my torso too far ahead of my lower body, and I knew it was inevitable. The stumbling began, and I heard the collective gasp of the players, who were just ahead, standing in the near end zone to my left. My left leg hit the turf of the track awkwardly and soon I was toppling, top-heavy, down onto the track, a huge one-man crash followed by a dramatic rollover. Trying to control the fall made it worse, and as I struggled to my feet again, I fell a second time. The gravel showered into my face as a dust cloud enveloped me.

For a few moments it was pure silence out there. Splayed out on the track, I felt like a freak, and then it began: the applause. I don't know who started it, but soon the entire team and coaching staff were clapping for my spectacular fall, and I flipped over onto my back, looking up at the blue sky until I burst out laughing, as hard as I'd laughed in a long time. Soon there were hoots and whistles and catcalls, and whether it was what they meant or not, I felt the love in my bones. I rose up, a huge smile on my face, and bowed. I finished my final lap, a slight burning where I'd scraped my left knee, but I didn't care. I was now trailing even Bardello, to a rising chant. "Crazy Legs! Crazy Legs!" they yelled in unison.

"C'mon, Bobby," Austin yelled. "Shake an arm . . . I mean a leg!"

I'm back in the game.

"Is this normal?" Carrie asked, using a tiny white toy shovel to fill her neon-green plastic pail with wet sand. "I get the feeling this is not at all normal behavior for high school seniors."

I looked up from where I was sitting, at the foot of our sand castle, and addressed the question to Bryan. "I don't know. Is it normal for us to be doing this now that we're almost out of high school?"

"Totally not normal. Not at all. Once you're in college, you can do this stuff, but face it, you two are freaks," he said, meticulously carving bricks into one of the towers.

"I thought that was possible," said Carrie, throwing a full pail high into the air and watching the sand fall out in clumps. The wind blew some of it onto the castle. She then twirled in circles like a four-year-old. "Weee!" she screamed. The group to our right, a bunch of middle-aged men with major beer guts, looked at her and frowned.

"Carrie," Bryan said, mock stern. "Do I need to put you in time-out?" I loved that they'd known each other for thirty minutes and were already acting like old friends.

Carrie stamped into the sand right in front of Bryan and crossed her arms tightly across her chest. "No fair!"

"Life isn't fair," Bryan said. "Now get to work. We're falling way behind. If we lose this contest, it'll be your fault, young lady."

"Life isn't fair," Carrie agreed. "I'm at the beach with two adorable *gay* guys." She said this really loud as well, and I blushed as the folks next to us looked over at us again. They didn't care. They went back to work and ignored our little area of dysfunction.

Bryan looked at me and offered me an exaggerated grin. I offered him a toothy grin back, and shrugged. "We are adorable, aren't we?" I asked him.

"Totally," Bryan responded. Carrie stuck her finger down her throat as if to vomit, and then coughed violently, because her finger had been covered in sand.

At Bryan's request, we'd entered into the annual Seal Beach sand-castle contest. I'd never even heard of it, but then again, I was a somewhat-normal human being. For Bryan, sand sculpture was like a religion.

We'd set up close to a concrete wall, which had seemed like a good idea at first—an actual wall to play off of, Bryan explained—but now that the other contestants had all claimed their spots, it was a bit of a struggle to step around groups to get to the prime wet sand. And without wet sand, our castle had nothing to stand on.

Literally.

The night before, I'd returned to the football field against Bolsa Grande, a team that had just one win. We'd won big, 54–7. I didn't play the best game ever, but I threw the ball well. Coach was happy with me, anyway.

It was playoff time. We'd won our league and were 9–1 overall.

On Monday we'd find out who we were playing first, but based on our record, we knew we'd be a high seed and get to play at home.

When Bryan had called and asked if I'd want to go to the contest, at first I wasn't sure, because it wasn't the kind of thing I'd normally do. I asked if I could bring Carrie along, and was glad when he didn't even hesitate in saying yes. Carrie thought it was a great idea.

"Where else can you build a sand castle and have people look at it?" she said enthusiastically, over the phone.

"Any beach," I said.

"True," she replied. "But where else can we do it this weekend where it's a contest and I can meet Bryan?"

"That's true," I admitted.

I looked around at our competition. We were building a castle, but others were working on sand elephants, cars, even a SpongeBob. Bryan had wanted to do something more creative, but I insisted on a castle when we began that morning. Ours was the only castle in the area. Even though it was mostly Bryan's work, I really wanted us to win.

Carrie came around to the front and took a careful look at our handiwork. Bryan had been the main architect and had done all of the intricate work, since Carrie and I proved to be deficient at sand-castle building in general. She was best at filling up buckets and either throwing them up in the air or pouring them out randomly. I was good at digging and hopeless at designing.

"I think this needs a veranda," Carrie said, observing Bryan's circular towers.

Bryan looked up at her, grimaced, and asked the appropriate question. "What the hell are you talking about?"

"I don't know. I'm not actually sure what a veranda is, but I'm sure this would be better with one," Carrie responded, quite sure of herself.

"It's a porch, silly girl," Bryan said.

Carrie put her hands on her hips and stomped for emphasis. "I'm a woman, damn it! I'm part of this sand-castle building team, and I'm a silly woman. In fact, after that chauvinistic comment, I'm considering changing that to *W-O-M*-Y-*N*, okay? Bobby, stick up for me!"

"You're a *W-O-M*-Y-*N*," I said, not looking up. "Stand up for yourself."

Carrie laughed, probably not having realized she was contradicting herself, as she often did. "Still, kick his butt. He hurt my feelings."

"I will if you want me to," I said quickly, driven by the urge to tackle Bryan.

"Don't you dare, Bobby," Bryan said, bracing himself as I leaped to my feet. He started to step backward, away from me. I smiled and decided to let him be. He tentatively sat down again, content to work on the castle.

Bryan was a great designer. Even with Carrie and me messing things up, the castle was awesome. He'd created two perfect circular towers, above a multilevel base with flawless squared-off walls. He had me digging, I realized, to keep me busy and out of his way, sort of like how Carrie's multiple personalities had kept her occupied.

Currently, she was carving elongated phalluses into the sand in the corner of our little lot. "Sand carrots," she said with a proud smile, presenting them to us. The fact that one had a scrotum at its base made it clear that this was no carrot. I raised an eyebrow at her. "If you thought it was something else . . ." she said. "That says a lot more about you than it does about me, Bobby Framingham." Bryan laughed.

The judges came around at about 1 P.M. By then, I had gotten excited about the fact that our castle was really good. We'd filled in the hole I'd dug, and demolished Carrie's carrots. It looked professional to me.

"We're actually going to win," I said. Bryan and Carrie just looked at each other and shrugged. Apparently I was the only one who was concerned about winning.

The judge, a fiftysomething man with a white ponytail and a really skinny build, was walking around with his pad, taking notes on each sculpture. I was trying to gauge his reactions.

What could I say? I loved winning.

"Shaundra is now a full-fledged prostitute," Carrie said to my back. Bryan laughed, not knowing the history of Carrie's neighbor and former best friend.

"No, she isn't," I said, my attention on the judge. He was smiling in front of SpongeBob, and had his hand on his chin.

"Well, all I know is that at her house there's a turnstile where a door should be, and grown men line up in front of it every morning," Carrie said. Again, Bryan laughed.

"Uh-huh, sure," I said, distracted.

"What are you doing, Bobby?" Bryan said.

"Waiting for the judge."

They both laughed. "Why?" Carrie asked. "Do you have a crush on him?"

I glanced back at them. "It's a contest, isn't it?"

Bryan stood up and came over to where I was standing. He dropped a kind hand on my shoulder and rubbed gently. "We're not gonna win, B," he said.

I looked at him. "But you did such a great job! You deserve—"

He smiled and interrupted me. "Yes, *we* did," he said. "But the more creative ones always win. SpongeBob will win, or that cruise ship."

I looked at our castle. "Why didn't you say so? We could have done something else."

"Oh, Bobby," Bryan said, mussing my hair. "We did it for fun, not to win."

I took a deep breath. What was it with me and winning? I looked over at Carrie, who seemed to be creating some new pornographic sand design, and looked back at Bryan, who was smiling and looking directly in my eyes.

I laughed. He laughed back, and I laughed some more and it felt really good.

Carrie stood when she saw us and her face lit up and she came over and tugged on my shirtsleeve. "I'm working on a new sand design. It's called *Sister Needs a Straight Man.* Wanna look?"

It was a faint outline in the sand, without a discernible shape.

"Very surreal," I said. "I love it."

We three looked at her outline and then Bryan laughed, so I did, too, and Carrie as well. And part of the world then opened up to me, because I heard myself laughing and it sounded strange and familiar all at once, like I had laughed before but maybe not like this. And it occurred to me for the first time: *It really doesn't matter. Life can be full of sand castle building and Bryan and Carrie and that's truly, purely good.*

Finch lived about a block away from Rahim, about a half mile closer to school than I did, in a subdivision where his family had lived as long as I'd known him. It was a Sunday morning in late November, and after a talk with Bryan, I decided meeting with Finch in person would be a good idea.

As I parked in front of his house, I remembered how, five weeks ago, Finch had come to my house, uninvited. I'd been watching football with my father, just minding my own business. He'd stolen time with my dad in order to dupe me, I realized. Blood surged into my temples, but I remembered my purpose, and realized that anger would solve nothing right now.

The Gozmans lived in a large white house, nicely manicured in the front. As I walked up the cobblestone steps to the front door, I saw that the hedges had been trimmed perfectly, and it made me wonder if Finch's parents had any idea of what he had done to me. Such an ordered family ought to know, I thought.

I knocked on the door, and Finch's mother answered.

"Hi, Mrs. Gozman," I said. "I don't know if you know who I am but—"

"Of course! Bobby Framingham! How have you been?" Finch's mother was a small woman who wore horn-rim glasses that made her look older than she was.

"I'm okay," I said. We stood there at the door, awkwardly. "Is Finch around?"

She offered me a tight-lipped smile. "I believe he's upstairs. I'll call him for you," she said. And then she disappeared, closing the door in my face.

A few minutes later Finch peered around the door at me. "What's up?" he said coldly.

"I want to talk to you," I said, my voice slightly trembling.

"We can talk from here," he said, keeping the door open just slightly and allowing me to see him through the sliver that remained open.

I sighed. "I'd rather talk to you face-to-face, Finch," I said.

"Do you promise not to hit me?" he asked. *What a dork. You commit the crime, be ready to do the time.*

"Yeah, I promise," I said begrudgingly.

Finch disappeared for a moment and finally opened the door, pulling his purple windbreaker over his head. Once his jacket was on, he spoke. "I just want you to know I did what I did knowing it would be good for you," he said.

"Right," I said. We stood at the front door, looking at each other.

"No really," he said, kicking the concrete. "I mean, obviously I wanted the story, but talking to you, you were so miserable. You needed to do it," he said.

"Whose choice was that?" I asked.

He said nothing.

"I want an apology," I said. "That's all I want. I want you to say you misled me, and that you're sorry. That's all."

"You jocks," he said, mumbling.

"Excuse me?" I said, turning and looking directly at him.

Finch shrugged. "You jocks have no idea what it's like to have a hard time."

"What are you talking about?" I asked, narrowing my eyes at him.

"Bobby, everyone likes you. You think being gay will stop people from liking you? I bet it didn't. I wrote that article, and for like a day, people came up to me and made me feel like I was something. Then it was over. It was like I didn't write it at all."

The laugh came from deep in my gut. "Poor Finch," I said. "That must be hard for you, not being popular."

"Fine. Make fun of me—"

"Really hard, not fitting in. Something a gay quarterback would have no knowledge about, right?"

He bowed his head and turned away. "No. I don't think you get it," he said. I couldn't see it, but I could hear the tears in his voice. "You're someone. I'm not."

I sighed. "Look at what you did to me. Should people like you? You screwed me over. I wasn't even close to ready and you decided it was time. How could you?"

"I did what I had to," he said. "Look. I'm sorry. Are we done here?"

"Almost," I said. "You really think Stanford will be impressed by that article?"

Now it was his turn to laugh. "I don't think that, I know that," he said.

“Best of luck,” I said. “From the bottom of my heart.”

He turned and slipped back behind the door, and I walked, victoriously, down the cobblestone steps back to my car.

I felt in my jacket pocket, found the stop button, and turned the digital recorder off.

I'd told Bryan I had the tape, and he could write the article. He refused.

"This is your story," he said. "You write it."

"You sure?" It was Sunday night and we were talking on the phone. I told him what Finch had said, and Bryan was enthusiastic that I had all the evidence I needed.

"I'm sure, the *Orange County Register* is sure. I told my editor on Friday what you wanted, and he told me all we needed was proof on tape. It's a go, Bobby."

"What if my writing sucks?" I said. "I mean, I'm a stupid jock, right?"

"Kinda doubt it," he said. "Just write the thing, we'll take it from there."

I got off the phone and sat down at my computer, staring at the blank screen. *I'm glad I'm out of the closet now, but it wasn't my choice,* I wrote, and then I erased that line completely. I had no idea where to start. Bryan had said to write my story, not to worry about length. Include everything, he said. Whatever I was comfortable sharing.

"Your story will help so many people," he had said. "I'm already proud of you and you haven't even written it yet."

I stared at the blank screen for minutes, until inspiration struck, and I slowly typed out a sentence:

I've never been very good outside the pocket.

I stared at the sentence on the screen. It was true, and I liked it. Then the second line came to me, and the story began to pour out of me.

I could hardly type fast enough to keep up with my racing thoughts. My fingers searched out the right letters and I pounded away. Putting it in words helped me feel better.

Even though it was late when I finished, I called my dad and read him the article. A few days earlier I had opened up and told him about what had happened with Finch.

"You just wrote that?" he asked.

"Yeah." I could hear the praise in his question and I felt like I was glowing, I was so happy.

He chuckled. "Can you send me a copy? I'd like to share it with some people here. It's great, Bobby. Really great."

I was waiting for the *but,* which never came.

"Really great," he repeated. "Your mother tells me you're dating someone."

"Whoa," I said.

"It's fine, Bobby. I'm glad. Is this a nice . . . boy?"

I laughed. "This is weird."

"Is it?"

"A little," I said. "How did Mom even know?"

"She said Carrie called for you and you were at practice and they talked."

"Yikes! Getting weirder," I said.

"I don't know, Bobby. Sounds like you're a little homophobic."

"No. It's just, this was all sort of my secret for a long time. I mean, being, you know, gay. And now it's just weird having my family talk about it. I'm not used to it."

"Well, you came out, didn't you? What did you expect?"

"I don't know," I said. "Can we talk about something else?"

"You okay?" my dad asked.

"I'm okay. I just, I think I'll need to get used to this, too."

"We all will. So is he nice? Does he play sports?"

"He plays gay flag football."

"Is that different than regular flag football?"

I laughed. "No, it's just played by gay people. There's a league in L.A."

"Ah," he said. "Does this gay flag-football player have a name?"

"Bryan," I said.

"Is he in school with you?"

"He's . . . a year older than me. A freshman at Irvine."

"Hmm. You sure you wouldn't do better with someone still in high school?"

"You'll like him," I said. "He's not going to call and play pranks on you."

My dad laughed. "I like him already. Time for me to get some sleep, kiddo."

"Love you, Dad," I said.

"Me too."

I went to sleep feeling as relaxed as I'd felt in ages.

It's kind of nice, having no secrets for once.

On the phone the next night, the editor sounded pretty excited about the whole thing. “Other than a few grammatical errors, I’m not changing a word,” he said. Knowing now what I’d been through, he couldn’t wait to tell the rest of the world.

“I’m straight,” he told me, “but your story really opened my eyes.”

I laughed to myself, wondering why he’d felt the need to tell me he wasn’t gay. He congratulated me for getting Finch on tape. Now there was no way we could be sued.

I went downstairs to tell my mother, who was reading a magazine in the den.

“Are you sure you want to go through this again?” she asked.

I smiled, as confident as I’d felt in a long time. It worked. I saw the worry fall away from her.

“Just read the article in the morning, would you?” I said. I kissed her on the cheek and headed off to bed.

That Tuesday morning, I ran downstairs to get the paper first thing. I tore through it looking for the sports section.

There I was, on the front page, a huge picture of me in my uniform, smiling. I couldn’t remember when that picture was taken. I’d never seen it before, but I liked it a lot.

“Perfect,” Bryan told me, over the phone when we talked that morning. “I knew you could do it. Congratulations.”

“I’m a little freaked.”

“It’s gonna be fine, Bobby.”

“Thanks for all your help,” I said. “I owe you a lot.”

“That’s true,” he said.

I laughed. “Shut up.” I was driving and talking, which is a bad thing to do, but I’d been dying to hear his reaction before school started.

“It’ll be a huge success, no question about it,” Bryan said.

"By the way, have you finished your personal essays yet for your applications?"

I had not.

"Just cut the thing out, and put it in the mail. No questions asked."

I hadn't thought of that. Sounded like a plan.

Another call buzzed in and I picked up. It was the *Orange County Register* editor. He sounded excited. "Looks good," he said. "We're getting lots of calls and the story is being picked up by the Associated Press."

"Wow."

"Also I just got a call from Finch Gozman's lawyer," he said.

"What?"

He continued. "He told me he'd see us in court. I asked him on what grounds? When I told him we had a tape of Finch admitting what he'd done, he said he'd sue us for unlawful recording of his client. I laughed at him. He realized they have no case, and he hung up on me."

I laughed. "That's awesome!" I said.

There was a lot of support at school. A bunch of people came up to me and told me what a dork Finch was. One guy I'd never talked to before, a junior with pink hair, came up to me in the cafeteria during lunch period.

"Bobby? Hi, I'm Reg? You don't know me?"

Everything he said was a question. I recognized him from *Hairspray*. He'd been in it with Carrie.

"Hi," I said.

He looked around surreptitiously. "I just wanted to say, that was very brave? What you did?"

"Thanks," I said, smiling at him. I wondered if this was some sort of come-on. I tended to be attracted to guys who had hair that's less pink, or any other neon color.

He leaned closer. His breath smelled of peanut butter. "One thing that people don't know about me? Is that I'm gay? You've given me the confidence . . . to maybe do the same?"

It hadn't occurred to me that this particular guy was not gay. But who was I to judge?

"That's great, Reg. Let me know how it goes," I said. I shook his hand and headed over to Carrie, who was sitting alone at a table near the Coke machine.

Before I got there, Todd Stanhope came up to me. I'm not a stalker, but if I was, he'd be my stalkee.

"Hey, Bobby," he said to me, as if we talked every day. We definitely didn't.

"Hey, Todd," I said, and we stood there, facing each other.

I was hoping I wouldn't crumble at the knees as we stood next to each other.

"Your article today was cool," he said, his eyes wandering around and finally making contact with mine. "I have a brother who's away at college. I'm gonna send it to him."

It was interesting to me that he didn't say "gay," but I knew what he meant. I also was thinking: *How old is he, and does he look like you?*

Instead I nodded and said, "Thanks, Todd. Are you cool with him?"

"No, not really," he said, laughing. "But maybe I'll try harder. If I do, it's because of your article."

I was half astounded, half disappointed. Here was the most beautiful guy I'd ever seen, and he was telling me my article had opened his mind. But on the other hand, if he wasn't cool with his gay brother, that meant he was straight. "Thanks," I said.

"You around this weekend?" he asked me, looking slightly beyond me.

"I think so," I said.

He waved to someone. "I'm having a party Saturday night," he said. "Bring whoever. That weird girl you hang with."

"Thanks!" I said. "Will do."

He pointed at me as his way of saying good-bye, and I watched him walk over to another friend.

"You cheating on Bryan already?" It was Carrie. She had walked up behind me and now her chin was on my back. She rested her nose on my left shoulder.

I continued watching Todd. "Nah. Todd has nothing on Bryan," I said.

She smirked at me. "Yeah, right," she said.

"He's eye candy," I said, and I blushed.

"You can do better," she said, ignoring my comment. "He's a complete idiot. He's in my math class."

"He speaks highly of you, too," I said, turning to her. "He told me to invite the hot, weird girl I hang with to his party."

"Awesome, he's hot. I'm so there," she said, and we laughed.

GAY QUARTERBACK COMES CLEAN

by BOBBY FRAMINGHAM

November 18, 2007

Special to the Orange County Register

I've never been very good outside the pocket.

As a quarterback, I've always preferred to know

where my protection is, then set my feet and throw. Anytime I have to scramble, I get nervous because throwing on the run isn't really a strength of mine.

Last month, I was forced out. Of the closet, in this case. A reporter for my high school paper found out I was gay and wrote the story without my permission. I'm not going to say anything more about him, other than what he did was wrong. He really didn't think about the repercussions, or what it meant for me.

I wasn't ready to have my family and teammates know. I was just starting to get comfortable, and then everyone knew. Talk about scrambling! I'm still learning to accept being gay for myself.

At the time I felt like he had stolen my dream. There's not exactly a fraternity of openly gay high school football players, let alone players at higher levels. It's not hard to figure out why. Being gay means you're supposed to be effeminate and someone like that isn't going to make it in sports.

I don't have a ton of role models as an openly gay football player, but I have good friends, and a great coach and teammates, and an awesome family, and everyone is doing their best to help me out, and I appreciate it a lot.

My dream has always been to make it as a pro. I don't know if I'm going to make it. I'm not sure if I have what it takes to begin with, and now there's this new obstacle. I've only been out for a month and it's already been a real challenge.

But so far I've been all right, and I plan to keep going. I'm going to try to face every challenge as it comes. No one gets to be a pro athlete by avoiding adversity. Gay or straight, you have to step up, work hard, and never take no for an answer.

So I'm out now. And I'm learning how to throw on the run, and I'm learning to accept who I am. And none of it is easy. But learning to scramble on the run is making me a better quarterback.

And I guess I should be thanking that reporter. Because even if it wasn't my idea, being honest about who I am has made me feel like a better person.

On a rainy, chilly Saturday at Durango High School, we opened the playoffs against Corona Del Mar. The Sea Kings were a good running team, Coach told us; if we couldn't stop the run, we'd lose.

"We gonna let them dictate this game?" he asked in the locker room before the kickoff.

"No!" we shouted.

"We hungry?"

"Hell yeah!" I looked around and smiled. We looked hungry. I saw a lot of serious faces, and it gave me some confidence when I needed it. My stomach felt way queasy.

The Sea Kings ran their way to a 7–0 lead. On our first possession, I ran onto the soggy field and got an ovation from our home crowd that warmed me. I could feel that they were on my side.

As we neared the fifty-yard line, Coach called a play-action pass where all our receivers flood the right side of the field. Rahim ran over before flanking out wide right.

"Lean on us, Bobby," he said, looking into my eyes. "You don't need to do this all yourself." I gave him the thumbs-up sign.

The grass felt soft and soggy beneath my feet. I looked down and saw that my cleats were already mud drenched, and tried to remember what Coach had said about running in mud. *Stay over your feet,* I remembered him saying.

Bolleran hiked the ball and I faked the handoff to Mendez before rolling left. There were puddles of water everywhere and I felt the splash on my socks as I scrambled. I looked downfield and their entire defense was on that side. I couldn't find an open maroon uniform anywhere.

In a split second, I sprinted forward and to the right.

In my quarterback career, I'd probably run past the line of scrimmage less than ten times. But as my strides got longer, I began to feel sure-footed and balanced. I saw the open field ahead. One linebacker had stayed home on that side and I saw his eyes, brilliant with fear. I galloped toward him and he held his ground. Tucking the ball close to my sternum, I juked right and sidestepped him to the left, my feet slipping in the mud.

He crumpled to the ground. I was now at their forty-yard line and from the corner of my left eye I saw a swarm of players from both teams dashing diagonally to cut me off. I saw two defenders gaining on me; Rahim was alongside one of them.

I cut back, stopping on a dime as I had never done before, and when the first defender did the same, Rahim delivered a blow to his chest, hammering him to the ground with a perfectly legal block.

I continued running, now inside the twenty, and I could hear the crowd screaming for me. The second defender closed in on me at around the fifteen, and I saw him lunge, diving for my ankles.

I hurdled him, avoiding his grab.

I'd never scored on a long run at any level, and crossing the goal line, I felt an exuberance deep in my chest, a floating feeling of being above things and looking down on the celebration. Touchdown. My teammates jumped me, and I gladly collapsed under them in the mud of the end zone.

"Yo, Crazy Legs! That's what I'm talking' 'bout!" yelled Haskins as I ran to the sideline. He gave me a high five and I felt elation in my bones.

We led 21–7 by the middle of the second quarter. We were backed up near our own end zone on a third down, needing just one yard for a new set of downs. Coach called a plunge up the middle by Mendez. It was a safe call, given that our line was having no trouble dominating theirs. As we approached the line of scrimmage, I noticed that the Sea Kings had stacked the line, hoping to stop the run.

With eight men on the line, they had just three to cover the backfield, and the only one to my right was directly on the line opposite Rahim. I knew he'd never be able to keep up with Rahim, and looking to that side, I realized we had a quick touchdown if I changed the play with an audible.

But was it too risky?

My head spun, thinking of all the lessons I'd learned, and I couldn't decide.

I handed off to Mendez who dove up the middle for three yards and a first down. It was a decent outcome, but Coach signaled for a time-out and waved me over.

"Aren't you Mr. Audible?" he said to me as I hurried to the sideline.

"Just trying to be smart, don't want to make any mistakes."

He sighed. "You're the quarterback. You see a weakness, exploit it. Okay?"

"Okay," I said.

"Hey, you did the safe thing, good thinking." I ran back onto the field, hoping for another chance to do the right thing.

Five plays later, they stacked the line again and this time I quickly called an audible. Rahim cruised past their defender, who seemed stunned that we were throwing. I lobbed the pass to Rahim, who ran it in painlessly for a forty-two-yard touchdown.

"Attaboy," Coach said when I got to the sideline and removed my helmet. He rubbed my head affectionately. "I think you're onto something."

In the locker room after the game, I was changing when I saw a bunch of guys, including Rahim and Austin, huddled in the opposite corner.

My shoulders tensed up just seeing it, because things were going so well. I knew it was self-centered, but I was afraid it was about me. It's not all about me, I know. But anyway, enough had happened recently that I guess it wasn't the weirdest thing to think.

As I dried my hair and buttoned my shirt, I kept peering over. About six of them were huddled together. Finally, I decided to go over and just see what was going on.

As I approached Rahim saw me and pulled back from the group. They'd been fussing with a large metal boom box, the one we use to play psych-up music before games.

"Hey, it's Bobby!" Rahim shouted, which was a little strange, because why wouldn't it be? And they all turned around and greeted me like they hadn't seen me in a year.

"Hey, Bobby!" Austin said, smirking.

"Hey," I said, suddenly very nervous.

"We have something for you," Dennis said.

"Uh," I said, wishing they'd stop freaking me out. Rahim turned back to the boom box, and seconds later I heard it.

The opening notes of a familiar tune.

I looked at Austin. He had this look on his face that I had never seen before, sort of like a bad boy who's just been caught doing something and is a little embarrassed.

And then the dancing started. And the singing, the horrible, terrible singing, of my teammates.

"Young man, there's no need to be down.
I said, young man, pick yourself off the ground . . ."

They had choreographed it, and with every line, there was some horrible hand movement, all of them almost in sync but not quite.

And I lost it. I fell on the ground in hysterics. It was the strangest, funniest thing I had ever seen.

My friends were serenading me with the Village People.

"It's fun to stay at the Y-M-C-A . . ." they shouted along with the music, spelling out the letters with their arms and bodies. I watched them from the locker-room floor, tears streaming down my eyes.

"Make it stop!" I screamed. "Help! Please! Stop!"

"We just wanted you to feel welcome in the locker room," Austin yelled above the music. And as the guys continued their awful, pathetic attempt at some sort of gay tribute to me, Austin smiled real wide and winked at me.

I could tell some of the guys were singing in support, and others were being a little nasty.

I chose to focus on the supportive part.

Todd's party was the night of our opening playoff win. I brought Carrie, but not Bryan. I thought that was maybe a little much, and Carrie thought that was way weak of me. It made me think of my dad, when he was asking about Bryan. That made it two of the people closest to me who seemed more okay with my gayness than I was. Weird.

Carrie got lost in the crowd in the living room, and I wound up, as usual, with the football team. In Todd's bedroom. I was trying to figure out how I could get my entire team out of there, and Todd in. Yeah, I know, Bryan wouldn't like that too much.

We were all celebrating the win and getting pretty stupid. I got teased a little about gay things, but that's just how we all are. If they didn't make fun of me, I'd be a little scared. Half of the guys were drunk. I was drinking soda.

"What kind of gay guy are you, not drinking?" asked Austin. "I thought at least gays drank a lot."

I just rolled my eyes at him.

Rahim was playing cards with Dennis on the other side of Todd's room, and I was hanging out with Austin, Colby, and an underclassman named Scooter, who plays on the line. Somers, Mendez, and Bolleran were all in the other room. They didn't hang out with me away from the field anymore.

"We need to teach you to talk like a straight guy," said Colby.

"Go for it," I said.

"Nice rack," Scooter said slowly. Austin and Colby laughed. Rahim and Dennis put down their cards and looked at us.

"Nice rack," I repeated, even slower, as if I'd never heard it.

"Nice can," Scooter said, moving on.

"Nice can," I replied, like I was learning how to pronounce the words.

"Now that one he's said before," Austin said. They all broke out laughing, so I did, too. It was basically harmless. Austin gave me a high five.

"Why am I hanging out with you losers?" asked Dennis, standing. "I need to get me some action."

I shielded my eyes. "Please warn me when you're gonna get naked," I said. "I don't want to start bleeding from my eyes."

Rahim laughed loudest, and Dennis swatted at him. "Shut up," Dennis said.

"Go scare some girls," Rahim said in return, smiling.

Dennis jogged out of the room, removing his shirt as he went. I groaned. After he was gone, we were all sort of quiet for a while. That's the thing I knew I'd miss about this team. They way we could all just hang together, the way we didn't need to always be talking.

"You think we're gonna see La Habra again?" Austin asked.

"They beat up on Laguna Hills today. Probably," Rahim answered.

"Good," I said. "I want to beat the best."

"True dat," said Austin. And we were all quiet again, imagining the glory of winning a title game.

At around 11 P.M., just about half an hour before I had to get us both home, Carrie came galloping into Todd's room. With her was Todd, who didn't seem to mind that we were strewn out all over his floor. Carrie and Todd was not a pairing I'd expected to see, ever. She had the manic smile on her face that she got when she was really excited.

"Bobby, you have to see this!" she shrieked. I stood up, but she motioned for me to stay seated. Then Carrie looked at Todd. "Ready? Okay, go!" Carrie said, and Todd, totally straight-faced, lay down on his bed.

"Unplug me!" he hissed. I started laughing. It was our old euthanasia skit.

"What, honey?" said Carrie, holding his hand.

"Unplug me!" he hissed, harder.

"No; no, honey, you're not ugly." I saw Todd's lips twitch, and then Carrie suppressed some sort of giggle, and finally the two of them broke out laughing like it was the funniest thing they'd ever done. I felt sort of silly, having been that guy that Todd was now, but I loved the glow in Carrie's face. Todd, it seemed, had a similar one. I smiled at her.

"Sister found . . ." I said.

"Shut up!" she shrieked at me.

"What the hell are you all talking about?" said Austin.

"It's some sort of gay thing," Colby said.

"Yeah, that's what it is," I said, punching him in the shoulder. "A gay thing. Moron."

"That's their car, pulling up," Coach said, looking through the blinds.

"Quick, everybody hide," yelled Carrie.

"Right, great idea. Scare the cancer patient to death," said Dennis.

Bryan scowled at his cousin. I didn't like the way Dennis had said it, but I had to admit, for once he was right.

The party had been my idea, actually. It was a Sunday morning, a day after another win for us, this time against Fullerton, to put us in the semifinals. My dad was coming home after five weeks and I knew he'd want to watch football on TV, so I made it a welcome-home brunch. Most of the football team came, and a lot of people from my dad's work. Bryan came, too, which made me sort of nervous. I knew it was wrong, but I couldn't help but feel weird in front of my teammates.

We didn't hide, and there wouldn't have been any point, anyway. There were dozens of cars parked along the curb near the house.

The key jiggled, and in walked my mother, leading my dad by the arm.

He was totally bald, which was kind of shocking, and his face was a bit red, but otherwise, he looked good. He pretended to be surprised, but it was clear he wasn't.

"Oh my God," he yelled, his face lighting up. "Look at all this!"

I ran to him and hugged him tight. "Dad!" I said.

He put his arms around me and squeezed.

This time it was me crying. Ever since missing that week of school, I'd learned a couple things about holding in emotions. I sobbed onto his shoulder and he held me tight. I didn't want to pull away.

He stroked my hair. "I know I look horrible, but I'm really good. Cancer-free," he said.

I just kept holding on and crying.

When I did pull away, I tried to avoid looking at my teammates. But I found Austin's face and saw he was wiping his eyes. I looked around and there wasn't a dry eye to be seen.

My father greeted his guests, getting hugs from his employees and my coach and shaking hands with some of my teammates.

"Where's the food?" he asked. "I'm starved."

"It's out back," I said, glad to hear it. We'd set up a buffet in the backyard with all his favorites.

Carrie, who had never met my dad in person before, grabbed him by the arm and led him out back like they were old friends.

"Now that you're not going to be my father-in-law, I feel like I can be honest about a few things," she said as they exited through the patio door to the backyard.

A lot of the team headed outside after them, leaving just a few stragglers. Bryan was one of them. He was sitting on a stool near the kitchen counter.

I walked over to him. "You ready?" I asked.

"Of course," he said.

We walked, slowly, over to my mother, who was tidying up, picking up some used plastic cups off the dining-room table.

How do you introduce your boyfriend to your mom? It was all so weird. I stopped walking, and figured Bryan would do the same, and I'd do some formal introduction.

Instead he just kept going.

"Can I help you with that?" he asked.

She looked up and smiled. "That would be lovely. Thanks."

"I'm Bryan," he said, sticking out his hand to shake hers.

"Call me Molly," she said. They walked into the kitchen together, and once again there I was, the one making everything harder than it was.

Later, after he had eaten and many of the guests had left, my father thanked me for organizing the party.

"I'm still a little tired. Hope you don't mind, but I'm going to just sit down and watch me some football," he said.

"Me, too," I said. "Can I join you?"

"Of course."

"Can I?" Bryan asked. I hadn't had a chance to introduce them yet. Bryan had stayed on cleanup patrol with my mother, who now absolutely adored him—finally, a son who cleaned—and I was hesitant to make a scene with the team around.

My father, who had flopped down on the couch, looked up. "You must be Bryan," he said, like it was the most normal thing in the world.

"I must be," Bryan said.

"You like football, Bryan?"

"San Diego Chargers, all the way," he said.

My father smiled. "Now that's what I like to hear. I keep telling Bobby, if he could just survey the field like Phillip Rivers, he'd be an even bigger prospect."

Bryan sat down next to my dad, intent on his every word, and I smiled, glad to know, if nothing else, that bald man was still the father I knew too well.

"It was awesome. That's two easy wins. And two to go," I told Dr. Blassingame as we sat in his office on a Thursday afternoon. It was December 4. After beating Corona Del Mar, 35–10, we knocked off Fullerton, 26–9, the following week. One more win the next day at Western would put us in the finals, and I was walking on air.

He stood up and smiled at me. "Things are really coming around for you, Bobby."

I nodded. "I guess so."

He turned around and reached for the bent golf club on his wall. "Remember when you were so angry about that initial article?" He unhinged it and put it on the desk in front of me.

"That seems like forever ago."

"Yet it was just six weeks ago. Bravo," he said. "Did I ever tell you the story about this club?"

"Nope."

He stared at it while he told me the story. "When I was in my thirties, I was a fairly good golfer, believe it or not. I loved golf, but I also had a temper. One day, I overshot the green on my second shot on a par four. I hit it into the woods, a good twenty yards past the green.

"I was furious, Bobby. You wouldn't know it to look at me now, but back then, when something didn't go my way on the golf course, the clubs sometimes felt the wrath. That day, when I couldn't find my ball in the woods, I got so furious that I wrapped my club around a tree."

I looked at it. It was pretty nicely bent. "Wow."

He touched it, and slowly pushed it over to me. "I want you to have this," he said.

"Dr. Blassingame—"

"No, no, let me explain," he said. "I've kept this around for many years, as something to help me remember an important lesson. I have a feeling you may know the lesson to which I am referring."

I shrugged. "Something about getting angry, I guess?"

"Well, yes, in general that's so," he said, nodding. "Specifically, it was the lesson about what happens when I try to control things I can't, such as past events."

"You get a bent five-iron," I said, nodding.

He laughed. "Precisely. And you've learned this lesson, Bobby. In order to remember it always, I'd like you to have this. It's time for me to pass it on."

I shook my head in disbelief, and touched the club. "Thanks a lot, Dr. B."

He smiled at me.

"Can I ask you something?"

"Of course, Bobby."

I looked directly into his eyes. "How do I know when to take control, and when to just let things go?"

"Now that, Bobby Framingham, is an intriguing question."

"So what's the answer?"

"If any of us knew, we'd all be just about perfect," he said.

"Well that sucks as an answer," I said, pulling at the club as if to straighten it. It wouldn't budge.

"I can tell you what I do. It's just me, but I can tell you my way of doing things."

"Okay," I said.

He leaned in as if telling me a secret. "I listen to my heart, Bobby. If I really want to know what to do in a certain situation, if I'm not sure if I should take control of something or let it go, I listen to my heart. I let my heart tell me what to do."

"Heavy . . ." I said.

He laughed. "Well, as I said, that's just me. Perhaps over time that will mean more to you."

I smiled at him. "I get what you're saying, I just . . . well, I get it."

He looked at me for a moment, and a smile poured over his bearded face.

"Yes, I really believe that you do," he said.

It had to be a rematch with La Habra. To get to the title game, we'd beaten Western, a great team that had knocked us out of the playoffs the previous year. It had been a real defensive struggle. I played well, but neither team could do much offensively. With less than a minute to go, Rocky split the uprights with a short field goal, and winning 16–13 felt better than some of the blowouts we'd had earlier in the year.

We were not surprised at all to see who we'd be playing next. We should have known, after that September classic—the one we'd won on Rahim's blocked kick—that we'd be seeing La Habra again in the playoffs. At the time, it would have been hard to imagine that the rematch would be the championship game.

I barely slept the night before the game. Instead, I talked on the phone with Bryan deep into the night.

"Wish I was there to calm you down," he said, his voice soft.

"You only think that," I said. "I'm not particularly good company right now. I don't even want to be with me."

"Well, I do," he said.

"Their defense is tough," I said. "I have to be just about perfect or we'll lose."

"It's a team sport, Bobby. Don't put it all on you."

"I'm not. Coach is," I said. Coach had told me that I needed to make good decisions in this game. Mendez, he told me, could have an off game and it wouldn't matter. It was up to what I did with the ball when chased out of the pocket, because, as he said, that would happen all day long with these guys.

"Will you be okay? I need to get some sleep," Bryan said.

"Yeah," I mumbled. "I'll be fine."

"I love you, Bobby."

He had never said that to me before. My thoughts flew and I couldn't breathe.

"Bobby?"

I had no words. He was kind and caring and handsome and I loved spending time with Bryan. And the new things. All great.

Maybe I do love him, but isn't it too fast? And on the phone? Should I say it back? Thoughts flooded through me and it took a while to speak.

"You too," I finally said, and I hated how lame that was.

He exhaled. "You too, what? There are two roads here, Bobby. Pick one."

"I'm sort of freaked out tonight, okay?" I swallowed hard. "Give me time."

He was silent for a moment. "Fair enough," he said. "I'll be there tomorrow."

I liked this angle better. "I wouldn't have it any other way," I said.

He laughed gently. “Good. Well, either way, I love you, Bobby. Sweet dreams.”

In the locker room before the game, I called the team together and gave a little pep talk. I hadn’t done it in a while, but it felt like the right thing to do.

“This is it, you guys,” I said. “I know one thing. I could never ask for a better bunch of teammates. You stuck with me through a lot of stuff this year. But I don’t want to go there. All I want to say is I wish we could always be teammates. Let’s go out the best way we know how, and win this thing!”

“Yeah!” I heard as the cheers began. “All the way! All the way!” The team began to chant and the energy in the room went through the ceiling.

“Whose house is it?” yelled Rahim.

“Our house!” screamed our underclassmen.

“Are you ready to conquer?” Rahim yelled.

“Hell yeah!”

“Lock and load!” Rahim shouted, pretending to aim a rifle.

“Open fire!”

We’re going to win the title game.

“Can you beat La Habra?” asked a television reporter as we ran onto the field. The championship game was being televised, which had our team pretty excited and me pretty nervous. Last time I’d played my way out of a televised game.

“Hope so,” I said, truly excited.

Another reporter got in front of me and shoved his microphone in my face. “How has it been, being the openly gay leader of this team?” the man asked.

I frowned. “After the game, please,” I said.

The La Habra crowd was trying to taunt me, but it wasn’t working. Somehow, the few calls of "faggot" that came from the stands were not affecting me at all.

The game started, and what was expected to be a defensive struggle was the opposite. Both teams drove down the field with little trouble. Our line held theirs in check for the most part, and though I was chased a bit, I kept on making good choices and finding the open man. I completed my first nine passes, two for touchdowns. At the half, it was 28–21 in our favor.

By late in the third quarter, both defensive lines looked worn out. Their star running back, Frank Ritzi, was approaching two hundred yards, and had scored twice. We had to settle for a couple of field goals, and at the start of the fourth quarter, they led, 35–34, and were about to get the ball again.

"We gotta slow them down, defense!" yelled Rahim on the sideline, before our defense took the field again. I looked at our guys. They looked exhausted.

On the first play from scrimmage, the Matadors went deep, going after Dennis, who was covering their flanker. I held my breath, worried that he wasn't energized enough to make a play.

The ball came down and I watched as the flanker in green and gold went up for the ball. Slightly after he jumped, up went Dennis. He outtimed and outjumped the receiver, and took it away from him. The flanker fell down, and Dennis sprang to life. He ran like I'd never seen him run before; holding on to the ball with two hands, he juked and pivoted around a couple Matadors before finding a path to the end zone. He had blockers ahead of him. I watched him zigzag past one last defender before diving into the end zone. We were leading once again.

Coach decided to go for two. If we made it, we'd be up by seven. He called for a play we'd only run a handful of times in practice. I'd bootleg to the left, with two running backs behind me like an option play. Austin would pretend to block ahead of me, and at the last moment he'd go out for a quick pass. An easy two points, I figured. I liked the call.

I took the hike and sprinted left. The Matadors shadowed me. If it were a true option, where I could either run or flip the ball back to a running back, we were dead. Just before I crossed the line of scrimmage, Austin snuck into the end zone. I tossed him a chest pass, afraid to give it away by raising my arm like I was throwing. My chest pass was weak, and sailed low on Austin. He came back for the ball and caught it at the two. He was tackled before he could stretch back to the end zone. We'd failed. Our lead was 40–35.

"Tough luck," Coach said as I trotted back to the sidelines. I nodded. It was my fault, but I knew we'd have another chance.

La Habra took its time with their next drive, giving us a heavy dose of Ritzi left, Ritzi right, and Ritzi up the middle. We couldn't stop their ground attack. They took a full eight minutes off the clock, and the drive ended with Ritzi heading off tackle left into the end zone for his third score. They tried for two as well to give themselves a three-point lead, but couldn't convert. They led 41–40, with six minutes remaining.

We huddled on the sidelines. "This is where we need to be smart about time management," Coach said, his arms around me on one side and Rahim on the other. "This is where we take our time heading down the field. Don't take it for granted, but take your time, guys."

We nodded. It was the right idea. If we scored too quickly, they'd get the ball back. This game would be won by whichever team scored last.

We started the drive at our twenty-five-yard line. We took our time and with a nice mix of running and passing we approached midfield with less than four minutes to go. Then, on a third-down play, I dropped back and found Austin on a little button-hook route. He expected to be hit immediately, and when he wasn't, he rambled down to the thirty-five. There were now just three minutes left.

I felt my chest expanding. If we just took care of business, we were going to win the title game. My breathing quickened.

We took the clock down to the two-minute warning with some nice runs to the outside. The Matadors fans were making more noise than I'd ever heard fans make, aside from that nightmare homecoming game. I pitched the ball back to Somers and he sped around the left side and had he not tripped at the twenty, he would have probably scored or gotten really close to the end zone.

"Way to go, Bobby! Somers!" Coach was screaming like I'd never heard before and I saw our guys on the sidelines jumping up and down. I looked and saw Rocky warming up to kick. The clock was ticking down to under a minute and a half. We were out of time-outs, and so were the Matadors.

We stalled on a run on first down, and on second down, Jessie Montoya, our fullback, dropped a pass. "No harm done," Rahim said as we huddled again. It was third-and-ten with thirty-nine seconds remaining. We were at their nineteen-yard line. Coach called in the play. It was a run up the middle, a safe call. Coach must have figured we'd run the clock down, pick up a few yards, and have the ball right in the center of the field. I called the play, we clapped in unison, and headed to the line.

I looked out at the defense, and was amazed. On third-and-long, it's a passing down, and I had expected they'd play their safeties deep to avoid getting beat by Rahim and Austin. Instead, their coach must have realized that we'd focus on running out the clock. Their linebackers braced to blitz the run. I gulped and tried to catch my breath. If we were stuffed, Rocky would have a tough kick for the game winner. I looked left, looked right. Rahim and I caught each other's eye in what must have lasted all of a millisecond, but it was enough. I called an audible.

"C-thirty-four!" I yelled. "C-thirty-four!" That told the team to shift into tier formation. Somers hustled from where he had been, wide left on the line of scrimmage, to behind Mendez in the backfield. It was the first time I'd ever changed into the tier. It also alerted Rahim and Austin that they would be my targets. The defense crept up closer to the line, figuring Somers would act as another blocker. *Bingo! We got 'em! I did it!* Bolleran hiked the ball into my hands and I faked the handoff to Mendez. The entire defense bought it. Their linebackers rushed through our line and one second after the fake, Mendez was blasted by two defenders at about the twenty-four-yard line.

I hurried back into my four-step drop and saw Rahim facing single coverage on a down-and-out. He ran forward and then made a razor-sharp cut to the sideline. I drilled him with a perfect spiral. He caught it at the fifteen and the defender fell in front of him, trying to knock down the pass. Rahim looked downfield and made the split-second decision to head for the end zone, knowing that he had just one man to beat, the free safety, who raced toward him from the middle of the field. Rahim pivoted, faking like he was heading toward the middle of the field. It was a smart move, because if the defender bought it, Rahim could head outside and step out of bounds if he wasn't going to score. But the defender didn't buy his fake. The guy forced Rahim inside, knowing there were linebackers to help him there. I could feel it in my heart, what Rahim was feeling. He lunged back outside, hoping to power his way through, but the defender held on. Rahim's a big guy. He wouldn't go down, but instead tried to carry the defender out of bounds with him at around the twelve-yard-line to stop the clock.

The whistle blew. He was still in bounds by inches.

A whistle means forward progress is stopped, the tackle is made. We were short of the first down, meaning it was now fourth down, and the clock was ticking, less than twenty seconds remaining. Coach called for the field goal. The offensive players not involved in the kick sprinted off the field, and Rocky and his holder sprinted on. I looked up at the clock. Eighteen, seventeen. We were going to be okay. He could make this kick.

"Spectacular," Coach said to me quietly as I got off the field. I smiled and was thinking about it when Rocky, running onto the field, slipped and fell. A collective gasp came from our sideline. The clock was down to ten seconds. He quickly hopped to his feet and got into position as quickly as he could. The ball was snapped with about four seconds to go. We all held our breath.

The ball was snapped, and I watched as Rocky strode gracefully toward the ball. On the final step, his left foot slipped, and his right one, as it came toward the ball, ever so slightly nicked the ground first. We watched from the sideline as the ball hung in the air and seemed to lose momentum, falling just short of the crossbar.

The crowd roared, and I watched in disbelief as the La Habra fans rushed the field and hoisted some of their players into the air. I watched as Frank Ritzi was carried around, pumping his fists wildly, and felt my chest shrivel. Had the kick been made, that would have been me.

After all I'd been through, didn't I deserve that?

I put my head in my hands and willed the world to stop. High school football was over for me, and we had lost. I felt like crying. A hand clamped onto my back.

"You did one helluva job, Framingham."

It was Coach. I stood up in front of him and looked up into his eyes, expecting to see the anger I felt in my chest reflected there. I did not see it. Instead I saw a glimmer in his eyes that looked to me a lot like pride.

It shocked me. I was certain he'd be angry, but he didn't look it.

"Thanks," I said tentatively. I searched for the right thing to say in the situation, but nothing came.

The crowd was deafening, but I could hear Coach clearly. "I will never forget this season, ever," he said. "I'm proud to have known you, Bobby Framingham."

I looked away, ashamed that I had missed the moment. This was the last game I'd play with Coach leading the way. I gulped back the emotion in my chest and hugged him tight. He hugged me back.

"Thanks, Coach," I said, looking directly into his eyes.

There was nothing strange at all as he smiled and spoke back to me. "God bless you, Bobby."

Rocky looked so deflated, standing alone on the sideline, his head hung low.

"Hey," I said.

He didn't look up. "Hey."

"You're gonna come back next year and you'll get another chance," I said, not sure that was true. We were a pretty good bunch of seniors. But still, what can you say to a kid after something like that?

"I ruined it for you," he said, with tears in his eyes. "I let everyone down."

Austin and Rahim walked over, their helmets in their hands.

"Don't think like that," I said. "We lost as a team, not because of you. If I made that two-point play, we win the game and none of this happens."

Rahim put his arm around Rocky. "Chin up, bro. It's okay."

"Yeah," said Austin. "It's all on Bobby." I looked up at him, shocked. "Kidding, dude. God, you're so sensitive."

At least that made Rocky laugh, and the whole bunch of us walked him to the locker room, where we were doing pretty well for a team that had just lost a title game.

"Do you wish you could have that two-point play back?" a reporter asked me as we stood in the parking lot after the game. A bunch of them ambushed me, and I gladly took the questions, knowing it might never happen again, depending on what happened with college.

I thought about it. "No," I said.

"Why not?"

"What's done is done," I said, picturing the five-iron Blassingame gave me. "We make that play, who's to say what would have happened after that? The game is over. We lost, but at least we played well, you know?"

The reporters were silent. Maybe what I'd said wasn't what they'd expected, I don't know. The same guy who had asked me before the game about being a gay quarterback spoke.

"So how was it, being openly gay and quarterbacking a team to the championship game?"

In the ensuing silence, I could feel the tension. First lines for newspaper stories across the area and even the country were being devised as I spoke.

"I don't know. Sort of like being an openly straight quarterback, but with a lot more media attention on me," I said.

And with that, I walked off, unsure that what I'd said made any sense at all, but still glad I'd said it.

"Whoever said 'turnabout is fair play'?" I asked Austin. We were in my front yard on Christmas day, having just returned from our annual Christmas breakfast at Coach's house. He'd presented us with league-championship pins to attach to our varsity letters.

"Dude, I don't even know what that means," he said.

I laughed. "I'm saying that we beat La Habra on a muffed kick, and then they did the same to us."

"Yo, kid, all's I know is if Rocky had some freakin' balance, I could say I was on a championship team in high school."

"Well, you can still say that," I said.

He just looked at me.

"I mean, don't say it to anyone who might actually check to see if it's the truth."

He laughed a little. "I'm surprised you aren't more pissed off," he said.

"Me too," I said. "I don't know."

A football rested under the tire that hung from the oak tree. I jogged over and grabbed the ball and tossed it to Austin.

"I'll miss this," I said.

"Shut the hell up," he said. "You'll do this the rest of your life."

I threw the ball hard at his midsection. He caught it. I'd meant I would miss doing this with him. We'd probably never play football on the same team again.

"By the way, it's not a bad picture of you." He tossed the ball back to me. I knew he was talking about the cover of *Out & About* magazine's December 28 issue. After my article came out, another guy called who was much nicer, and this time I agreed to do it. "Thank God they convinced you to put a shirt on."

"Screw you, they wanted me naked," I said. "It was my modesty—"

"Yeah, dude, you're way modest," Austin said. "Still, it's cool."

"Yeah, I mean, how many gay guys can claim to have almost led their team to a title for one of California's three hundred and thirty zillion divisions?"

"I don't know," said Austin. "Five? Six?"

"That's probably true," I said, and we laughed together.

Austin caught a pass and tried to dunk the ball like it was a basketball, over a branch that's about ten feet high. No good. "So where do you think you'll be next year?"

"I have no idea," I said. "Stanford probably won't recruit me."

"Yeah, I saw they'd already recruited a quarterback. Biggs from Los Alamitos."

I hadn't known that. I felt my stomach fall a bit. "Oh well."

"I'm hoping for Fresno State," Austin told me as he chased the ball.

"That would be awesome," I said. "Probably Colorado State for me, but I still have a few I hope to hear from."

"Cool, we'll stay in touch," he said, and I nodded.

Austin tried to sit in the tire, but it wouldn't hold his weight. It buckled under him, and he skipped away from it. "So the tier formation. Turned out okay, huh?"

"Yeah," I said. "Better than I thought. Remember how we hated it?"

"You, mostly."

"Yeah, right," I said.

We sat on the grass, which was cold but dry. "How's Rhonda?"

He sighed. "Shit if I know." *Austin still* went *through girls like I* went *through pizza.*

"Oh well," I said, pulling out a tuft of grass and throwing it onto Austin's lap.

"Plus, I'm done with all that running around," he said.

"Get out."

"No, really," he said. "It's stupid." He took the grass off his lap and sprinkled it onto my head.

"Okay," I said, wondering where my friend Austin was and who they'd replaced him with.

"How about Bryan?"

I wiped the dirt and grass off my head. "How'd you know his name?"

He screwed up his face at me. "What am I, an idiot? I saw him at the party. Plus, people talk," he said.

"He's good." I smiled.

"What's he like?"

"He's nice. I mean, he does weird stuff, but he's cool."

"What's weird, and do I want to know this?" he asked.

"Weird like refinishing old furniture."

"Yeah. I don't know anything about that," he said. "I guess that's like if I'm dating a girl and she likes to go shopping."

"Just about exactly," I said, smiling at him.

Bryan is coming over later for Christmas dinner. It's a little weird, because my parents clearly like him more than they like me. He knows exactly how to listen to all my dad's stories and ask good questions, and he laughs at my mom's jokes. It's a little annoying, tell you the truth.

I'm not sure what any of this means yet. What does it mean that I've just been through the worst months of my life, lost the title game, and feel so happy I could almost burst? I'll probably wake up out of this soon and everything will be back to normal. Bobby the gay football star will be gone, and Bobby the regular guy will be back, and it'll be like putting on a well-worn sweater. I'm pretty sure that's what will happen, because life isn't like this. We don't get to live a life where the good is so purely good that you can taste it, like the sweetness of an orange.

But until that time, I guess I'll enjoy this make-believe, fairy-tale life. Because it feels better, you know? Better than anything has ever felt.